# "Captain! I am going aboard that ship!"

Norden declare[illegible] be aboard?"

"We could [illegible]e," warned Conek.

Norden wa[illegible] cautious. "Captain, if you se[illegible] off a destruction charge, we won't live to complain."

Conek knew when to give in. With Cge at his side, he led the way onto the unknown vessel...

"Where are we now?" Conek asked the droid.

"Cge does not know." His blinking panel showed his agitation. "Cge should know. Cge does not remember."

Conek stopped. He caught Cge's arm and turned him around. "Okay, Bud. What's the trouble?"

"Cge's programming storages over-heat." One small metallic hand reached up, touching his top cylinder.

Conek stood up. "Just what I always needed. A droid with a headache."

"What's the matter?" Andro asked.

"I thought Cge could warn us of trouble," Conek replied. "Now it seems we're on our own. If it's a war ship, we get out, and *fast*!"

# LEE McKEONE

POPULAR LIBRARY

An Imprint of Warner Books, Inc.
A Warner Communications Company

POPULAR LIBRARY EDITION



Cover illustration by James Warhola

Popular Library books are published by
Warner Books, Inc.
666 Fifth Avenue
New York, N.Y. 10103

A Warner Communications Company

Printed in the United States of America

First Printing: February, 1988

10 9 8 7 6 5 4 3 2 1

# CHAPTER One

"Damn!"

Conek Hayden dashed into the shadow of a sand dune on the desert planet of Beldorph. He could still see the pulsing entry glow of a fast ship.

His mind clicked into an assessment of the heavy, narrow layer of atmosphere surrounding Beldorph and the size of the fireball just above the horizon. Years of keeping a cautious eye out for patrols, pirates, and other contrabanders had taught Conek to estimate an entry accurately. The incoming vessel hit the protective outer layer at close to hyperspeed. Its ability to withstand the impact testified to either an advanced shielding or some new type of armor plating.

A Vladmn patrol, he decided as he ran. He cursed himself for not knowing about their new innovation. How was the crew protected? he wondered. Maybe they suffered the rough ride knowing that the reward for apprehending a suspected contrabander with a cargo of evidence would be worthwhile. His cargo had been picked up, but he'd pay hell explaining his presence, and they'd keep watching the planet, so he'd lose his hidey-hole.

He scuttled around a dune, knocking sand about in an effort to cover his tracks. He rounded the second dune, heading away from the cave in semicircles as he stayed within the valleys. He felt as if he were on an old-fashioned merry-go-round—without a horse. Merry hadn't come along, either.

Staying in the shadows made a lot of sense; they'd provide as much protection from the ship's sensors as they would from a laser beam. He had little hope of escaping and tried not to think what might happen if he did. Dressed only in a light, loose-fitting plasticized suit with neither shelter nor water, he'd dehydrate in the heat of the day and freeze at night.

*Cheer up,* he told himself, remembering he'd scorned the full space helmet and wore a filtered mask separating the oxygen from the toxins in the air. *Your filter will give out, and the air will kill you first.*

If he got out of this mess, he'd get a good-guy license and turn honest.

After skirting the next dune he slowed, stopped, and raised his distance glasses. The intensity of the glow dimmed. The drag of the heavy atmosphere slowed the ship; still it came at him as if homed in on his heartbeat. The straightness of its course and the lack of any braking thrusters assured him no patrol came after him. There was too much recycled villainy around; a Vladmn patrol wouldn't risk a ship and crew on only one smuggler. The sudden arrival came in on a suicide mission.

The ship drew close enough for Conek to make out the shape; he stared. The long, black, sharp-nosed tube could be a ship out of lost centuries when the lack of shielding limited the design. It came still closer, and he saw the ragged tears piercing the hull. A ghoster—sailing through space for who knew how long. The old relic came to its grave but still fought for the right to fly. The closer it came, the higher it appeared, and for a mili-unit Conek thought it might still bypass the small planet. He rooted for the gallant old vessel, wanting to shout his encouragement. Hope faded as the nose lowered. Then bursts of fire showed red in the atmosphere as a series of braking thrusters fired.

*Another theory shot all to hell!* he thought as he dived for cover. With still functioning engines it was not ancient, so it had to be an alien vessel, possibly off a world just entering their space age. *But I haven't guessed right about it yet.*

He missed seeing the ship hit, but the first shock, and then the second, told him she came down in one piece. Aided by her line of trajectory, the braking thrusters, and the soft, sandy surface of Beldorph, she skipped like a stone on the water. The sounds of roaring engines and plowed sand seemed to continue in his ears after he knew the vessel had stopped. It was probably buried beyond locating.

Conek rolled over and lay still, saved by his quick wit, his superhuman reflexes, and by the fact that the ship didn't give a damn about him. But he gave it a considerable portion of his mind.

The tears in the sides of the hull probably meant death for any life-forms aboard. If the vessel was a ghoster, he could claim it for salvage. Once he'd flagged it, any honest salvager would respect his claim. Most ghosters were looted in space, but there was always a chance . . . and alien technology brought big money from the government and private research institutes.

Maybe his good-guy license was closer than he thought.

He needed two more ships. Added to the two he already owned, they would give the Hayden Freighting Company enough weight to keep a full schedule of legitimate trade.

And he had all the contacts. For the last part of his father Tobard's life, and during all of Conek's career, a legal cover was a necessity. When Tobard Hayden wrecked his old freighter, trying to escape a Vladmn patrol, they were out of business. Unable to buy another ship, they went pirating at a spaceport in the Osalt Federation, Vladmn's territorial enemy.

Most freighters of Vladmn could depend on a certain anonymity among the thousands of nondescript ships plying the busy ports. But the Haydens returned with vessels that stood out like boulders on a dusty plain.

Tobard's vessel dwarfed every freighter in Vladmn. Conek's choice was nearly a kilometer in length.

Conek and Tobard returned with their stolen ships to find themselves heroes, a confining honor for contrabanders.

Tobard swore and complained about the difficulty of smuggling when half a galaxy trailed behind waving flags.

Conek's two vessels hauled as much freight as any five Vladmn "teacups," as he called the smaller vessels, but the big boys who ran industry worked by blind, block-form policy. They didn't talk to freight companies with less than four registered vessels. He could probably steal two more from the Osalt if his luck held, but he wanted a thick financial buffer to cover repairs and the hiring of pilots.

And if the ghoster carried any valuable technology, he knew where he was getting his stake. He already had part of it salted away, the proceeds from ripping off three other ships from Osalta and selling them to his main client, Dursig.

He rose and plodded through the soft sand on the way back to the "cave," a shielded structure created out of fused sand. From the outside it appeared to be just another dune. Who built it or why remained a mystery, but it was a perfect depot for off-loading smuggled cargo.

Conek's whistle of relief came out as a blur-rp through the filter. The ghoster passed within thirty meters of the cave and plowed a deep gorge in the sand. His cargo, picked up during the night, was safely away, but if the shelter had been destroyed, Conek would not have lasted the day in the Beldorph heat.

The sand, displaced by the ship's landing, piled up knee-high against the door. Not much to shovel away, he decided, and he'd leave clearing the door for later. He wanted to see the ship, and the heat of Beldorph's day was increasing rapidly.

He started down the canyon recently created between the sand dunes, then decided he was about as bright as a black hole. What if somehow the beings on the ship were still alive? Coming down that hard could give the creatures one hell of a headache—if they considered heads standard equipment. They might not want visitors. Walking between the dunes took him longer, but the less direct route might save his life. Being the first in Vladmn to experience the business end of some foreign weapon wasn't high on his list of priorities.

He'd walked nearly half a kilometer when he came across a split carton, thrown through one of the rents in the hull. Hoping he'd found something of value, Conek knelt and pulled out the carefully packed tubes—some straight, several curved, a number of them elbowed. They shared a commonality of each having a reduction on one end, a do-it-yourself framework for insanity. Useless junk, at least in Vladmn. He stacked up an armful, carried them around the dune, and dropped them in the gully left by the ship. He kicked enough sand to cover them, knowing the wind would soon fill the trough.

He moved on, keeping an eye out for scattered cargo. While he had hoped, he hadn't really expected there to be cargo aboard. Salvage laws didn't take greed into account. He could flag the ship as his, but any cargo spread around Beldorph belonged to anyone who picked it up.

A kilometer farther on, he spotted another carton, gleaming an obscene bright blue against the gray sands of the landscape, just lying there for anyone to see. He trudged over to it.

The sun was high in the sky now, and as he bent over the square alloy carton, sweat dripped from his forehead. His searching time was running out. The temperature would soon rise from "bake" to "char," and he had to get back to the protection of his hidey-hole in the sand-dune cave. In addition to worrying about the heat, he kept an eye out for windstorms. On Beldorph they were vicious.

The catch was ingeniously designed but easy to open. He swore as he stared down at what appeared to him to be large bowls. Either ships and fuel were plentiful enough on the alien territory to ship domestics, or the cargo served purposes he couldn't imagine. Maybe they ate plastic. To him it was useless junk.

He carried the lightweight carton over to the gouged ship's trail and tossed it in. He watched it roll down the slope and realized the ghoster's track had shallowed. Less than a kilometer farther on, it disappeared completely. Had the vessel buried itself or bounced up into the air again?

He searched the sky. On the horizon he could see the telltale grayness of blown sand, signaling one of the frequent Beldorph windstorms. His walking-around time had run out. If the ship dug in, he might be standing almost on top of it, and further searching would be futile. If it skipped up in the air again, who could tell how far it would go?

Without a clear trail he'd be lost in the repetitions of the dunes before he'd traveled three kilometers. Not his idea of a lovely day, not when the temperature could reach 200°F. And the coming storm could scour away his suit and flesh. Beldorph was no place to walk for exercise.

Disgusted, he crossed the deep track and started back toward the cave. He'd only found two cartons thrown from the ship. If there were more on the other side, he wanted to check them out. No matter how alien the technology, he couldn't believe it used interstellar ships to carry restaurant supplies and worm mazes.

His strength drained away with the heat. The short gusts of wind, announcing the approaching storm, tried to knock him off his feet every time he climbed a dune to search for lost cargo.

Near the cave he found the third carton, smaller than the others and more substantially constructed. He picked it up, considered the light weight, and almost tossed it aside. Impatient with the discomfort of the heat, he was disgusted with the ghoster and any technology it might have. Apparently a cheap plastic society, he decided. Still, he should check the contents of this one last carton. He swore again as he lifted out what appeared to be some shoddy attempt at sculpture.

The bulbous, bright orange top paled in color as it curved in to form a stem. As it widened out to create a base, the pastel coloring gave way to pure white. Pretty, but not worth a damn!

"Of all the cheap junk!" he yelled at nothing in particular, and threw the trash against the side of a dune.

The dune disappeared.

So did the next twenty.

Maybe more were gone, but the dust from the coming storm prevented him from seeing farther.

Conek stood completely still and stared down a glass-lined, semicircular valley disappearing into the distance.

A whole hell of a lot of nothing was where part of the surface of Beldorph should have been.

He backed up several paces, then sidled back toward the thing on the edge of the rearranged landscape. He picked it up carefully, very carefully, making sure he kept the elongated end of the bulb turned away from him until he knew he didn't have a hand on the nonvisible trigger. The business end was nonvisible too.

Great idea for a weapon, he thought. Somebody takes it away from you and there's a fifty-fifty chance he'll blow a hole in himself. And with the power of that baby, he'd get the next five thousand people behind him.

Conek gingerly ran his hands around what he took to be the back of the gizmo. His thumbs neared the base. He couldn't spot the trigger by sight or feel, but a soft white light sprang from the front, and another line of dunes marched into oblivion.

Time to put baby to bed, he decided, and matched idea with action. Encased, the thing must be relatively harmless, since it had taken the fall from the ship without blowing the case apart.

He closed the cover, picked up the box, careful to remember which way the violent end pointed, and crossed the vessel's deep track to reach his shelter.

His first priority was to get out of the storm. He didn't worry about the evidence of his having shot off the weapon. The blowing sand hid long holes from any view from above, and by the time the storm blew itself out, the gouges in the surface would be filled in, along with the track of the ghoster. Nor would losing the ship's track matter; he could find it by sensor.

Outside the fused-sand cave, Conek put the carton aside and bent from the waist, throwing the sand between his legs as he freed the door.

He eyed the old curlicued letters cut in the metal door. Some long-dead spacer had used a blaster on it; the resulting molten slag had dripped and hardened, leaving a sloppy mess. And the message didn't make sense. Years before, he copied the words and checked out the old language. No evidence indicated a voice-code lock had ever been installed on the door, so why would the message be, "Open sez 'a who?"

Inside, he flipped on his area light, carried the carton back to the far end of the huge cavelike structure, and sat heavily on an old packing case—Vladmn-style and familiar. After a short rest he stripped off his suit, took a towel from the flight bag he'd brought with him, and dried the sweat from his body. He turned the suit inside out, gave it a quick whisk with the towel, and spread it on the floor, letting the dryness of Beldorph take care of the rest of the moisture.

He couldn't leave it off long or he'd start to dehydrate, but the cave was cool, and the lower temperature would refresh him. He changed the filter in his mask and took several swallows of water. After he dressed again, he spread out the grav-bed, a metallic sheet carrying the impulses from a fist-sized generator. He lay down, turning off his light.

He needed to sleep, and if he couldn't, well, he thought better in the dark. What would he do with that crazy alien cannon? If he kept it, he could rid himself of enemies in a hurry, he thought. But he couldn't use it. Turning people, ships, and—by the power of the thing—even towns into instant nothing just might start gossip.

If he was too dangerous, he'd have three galaxies down on him, and who knew when the gizmo would run out of zappola? He'd stick to a blaster like the Good Lord intended.

If he sold it to the Vladmn government, the proceeds would set him up in business—he could give up the wrong-side-running and take his downtime where the beautiful people played. But if he ever went back to smuggling, the patrols could wipe out his occupation. They'd do the same thing to a lot of pretty decent characters who didn't see life in Vladmn triplicate.

Keeping it would be a headache. To protect his own life, as well as his customers', he was stuck with the patriotic bit, not letting the Osalt get it. Some of his smuggling cohorts would be just as dangerous.

And if he didn't sell it to Vladmn, where could he keep it? It wouldn't fit in his pocket, he didn't want it on his ship, and he couldn't see leaving it in the cave.

No one knew about the cave except Lesson, the pilot of his second ship, Dursig, his client, whose supplies were unloaded here for the humanoid to pick up, and himself. They owned the only receivers able to pick up the homing signal for locating the cave. Once every three standard months, he met with Dursig, the leader of the Gordotl, to discuss business. Lesson brought him in, left him with the cargo, and came back after the Gordotl departed. Because of some quirk in the Gordotl thinking, they arrived, loaded or unloaded, and took off in darkness. Conek thought his clients were nuts with all their taboos, but he was well paid to stay in the cave for two Beldorph days. When they arrived, they blew the sand away with the force of the ship's thrusters, and covered it up when they left. Usually the piled sand hid the door, trapping him inside but protecting him. A storm had uncovered the entrance during the previous night.

Conek had been outside, assessing the possibility of the cave being found, when the alien ship came down. At least he used the storm and his vulnerability as his excuse to take a walk.

These visits to the cave gave him his primary reason for wanting to get his badge of honesty. Sneaking around to meet clients, and doing business on the sly was boring as hell. He wanted to do business over drinks and a good meal like the rest of the world.

Yeah, he could take his alien weapon with him if he wanted to argue about the check.

Just what in the hell *could* he do with that thing?

# CHAPTER Two

The dust from the vessel's landing hung like a dry fog in the windless morning. With his visuals ineffective in the grainy mist, the android turned his sensors to help him in the search. He fell through the split in the control cabin wall when the ship hit the ground. He rolled and tumbled, losing two of his extremities, his right utilitarian and his left loco motive. The rest of his unit held together, but when he tried to move, his computer rattled. He forced power through his circuits—small implosions and fusings smoked and crackled. Then he received an output again.

He could input, but could he trust what he received? Readouts raced through his circuits without command, conflicting with one another. They lacked the solid authority of computation. He wanted to find the ship, and perhaps the masters could repair him; but no, they had given no commands for many rechargings of his storage batteries.

Homing in on the closest of his missing parts, he rolled over on his back. By using the remaining arm and foot, he pushed himself across the sand, working steadily until he reached his disconnected leg. He picked it up and raised it to his sensor. How was he to take it with him? He tried holding it and pushing with his foot, but he needed his single, attached utilitarian to move himself along.

Tie it to himself with his charge and computer cables. He could not trace the source of the command. It lacked computation. Could he trust it? Did he have a choice?

His cables were not meant for the attachment of physical appurtenances. He kept trying, but by the time he could get a cable unrolled, the leg would fall off his rounded module, the cables recoiled by automatic command when he dropped them to catch the leg. He was suffering the mechanical equivalent of being out of breath when, on the sixth try, he succeeded in fastening the leg so he could carry it with him.

*I am not programmed for this*. The idea sneaked through the confusion. He made a positive effort. *I am programmed for . . .for*—Something jammed with a loud crackle. With so much damage his efforts to trace his trouble were ineffective. *I am programmed for . . .for*—Stuck again. A vague discomfort came over him, something other than the loss of his limbs and the jangled circuits. He was unable to recall even the general nature of his original purpose. He knew that this place of grainy dust was not meant to be familiar. The emptiness created a new sensation—more than discomfort, though he knew no word or thought for personal fear.

To drive the feeling away, he concentrated on reaching his disconnected arm. He struggled with the cables until he had both dismembered parts secure enough so he wouldn't lose them. Then he probed the area.

Nothing existed but the sand and the trail of the ship. He scooted along on his back, slowly following the vessel's track, the only course with any promise.

Every few meters he paused and probed the area. After more than a dozen tries his computer clicked with news. An entrance! Almost a meter wide and two meters high, his experience told him it only served droids. He scooted closer and turned so he could see it. An alien writing was sloppily burned into the metal by the handle.

His computer sang out *shelter* and *safety*. Safety? The

word should not be a part of his output. His programmers deliberately omitted self-survival. Only the masters must survive. He had no master. They had all left him alone. He had been alone for a long time.

To reach the handle he was forced to brace himself against the shelter and stand on his one locomotive. When the door swung open, he tumbled in, rolling on the sandy floor. Behind him, the door swung shut, cutting out the light and heat of the strange planet.

Automatically he switched from primary visual to probes, reading the proximity of objects and recording his surroundings. The space seemed a part of the land from outside, but when he examined the cavern, he saw that it was fused sand. He met the resistance of heavy shielding. The area reminded him of the storage holds on the ship, crowded with crates and barrels. These were aging crates—old far beyond his ability to measure time. Some held equally ancient machinery, while others were empty.

He detected the mustiness of aging cartons, but the prevailing atmosphere was fresh, dusty like the winds blowing on the dunes. Someone—something—had used the shelter recently.

Perhaps a master.

Then he wouldn't be alone.

A master could repair him. Moving slowly, he drew himself into a corner and stood, relieved to be still. The unfamiliar action of propelling himself on his back drew severely on his stored energy.

Unwanted output bothered him. What if no master came? The questions of where he was, how to repair himself, and what to do for energy when his storages were empty crept into focus. He shut them off, refusing to face the answers. And why did these ideas come to him unbidden? Worry conflicted with logic, and his programming called for . . . for—logic, he reminded his computer. When he was repaired, he hoped those worries would be corrected. They bothered him.

Sounds! His audio sensors flashed a warning. He probed the dense stack of containers at the far end of the cavern. From behind them came a life-form with a bright light. He switched back to primary, but beyond the brilliance he could see nothing. His damaged circuits were running wild. His readout said *Flee! Get away!* But no commands reached his transistorized extremities.

His circuits slowed, then raced again, as the blinding glare stopped and the mechanism illuminated the immediate area. He saw what discovered him.

*An android!* His visual sensors reported. *A carbon-based life-form,* his probes contradicted. *An android,* he decided. The probes were still shouting *life-form,* but his discoverer's shape resembled his own, though twice his height. Suddenly it turned toward the door. A blast of heat and light came in as it probed outside. He called to it in his language when he thought it would leave him. He wanted its companionship.

Shutting the door, it returned and, with a strange agility, sat on the floor, probing him. Then it rubbed the ends of its utilitarian members together and clapped them; the sharp sound echoed through the cavern.

*Communication!* He sought the end of his disconnected arm and struck his two holding mechanisms together. At his movement, the life-form clapped its members again. He repeated the action, his circuits going wild. Master or droid, he had at least found a companion. He was no longer alone. By imitation he could learn its ways. He reached out to it, unbalanced himself, and started to fall.

When the door to the cave opened, Conek Hayden knew his time had come. His blaster wouldn't stop anything tough enough to live through both the prior damage and the wreck of the ship, and by the time he unboxed the alien weapon, the intruder would reach him. He heard a scraping movement. Then silence. Something waited or searched for him. The thought of a strange and alien being touching him in the dark drove him to take the offensive.

The last thing he expected was a little android—and damaged, at that. He stood staring at it, not quite ready to accept it after his mental picture of horror and doom.

Feeling ridiculous holding the blaster, he holstered it and flipped his illuminator from high beam to area light. The little character seemed harmless enough, but he wondered if anything, possibly something more lethal, might have followed it. He went to the door and heard the droid whistle as he left it. A quick check outside convinced him nothing else threatened him, so he sat down two paces from the robot, observing it.

*Droid* was really the term for it, he decided. Centuries before, people had forgotten that the word meant anthropoid-shaped. This one more closely resembled a human frame than anything he'd seen. It would never pass for human, of course. The body was blue-gray metal and was hardly more than a collection of cylinders fitted together with ball joints, but the tubes corresponded to head, body, upper arm and forearm, thigh and calf. In size and shape it resembled a small, stocky five-year-old human child.

Its creators had made no attempt to give it a human face. A rectangular, smoky gray sensor panel crossed the top of the head module, and behind it a blinking light pulsed rhythmically. A similar rectangular break beneath it was apparently a speaker or an audio sensor; Conek couldn't tell which. At the moment he wasn't into too much experimentation.

Despite the beating it must have taken the metal was unscarred; some fantastic alloy. The little mechanical must consider itself repairable, otherwise why would it be clasping its disconnected limbs?

He'd never owned a droid. Talking machines weren't good risks in his business, but if he could fix it, there might be a profit in the effort. It would be a curiosity, a conversation piece for those with more money than sense. Never one to turn his back on an opportunity, he inspected it carefully, staying back a bit until he knew more about it.

He noticed the hands—they *were* hands. Metallic, certainly, and with only four digits, but made with a palm of sorts and jointed fingers, even a thumb.

He smiled and rubbed his palms together. Raising his original estimate of its market value, he clapped his hands in anticipation of the sale. The droid tried to imitate him. He tried again. Yes, it repeated the action. He started to clap a third time, then stopped abruptly.

*I'll be damned if I'll sit here playing patty-pat with a machine,* he thought.

The droid's sensor panel flashed as it pushed itself away from the wall. It whistled a discordant tune again as it stood, reaching toward him with its one hand. When it started to fall, Conek scrambled forward and caught it, surprised at its lack of weight, hardly more than a myriagram.

While he held it he heard, through the closed door, the faint but unmistakable sound of engines—a teacup freighter. He put the android on the floor and prepared to up-end an old crate over it. He hesitated a fraction of a mili-unit. The sudden, speedy blinks of the sensor panel cried *panic*. Their dimming said *disappointment*.

He shook his head. *Stupid! Robots don't have feelings!*

Then he forgot the android as the roar of the engines increased. Drawing his blaster, he hurried to the door and opened it a crack.

The roar of powerful engines sounded close overhead. He saw the nose of the ship coming in over the false dune from behind him. It moved slowly, and not twenty meters above his head. As it passed, he watched until he could see the rounding of the engine pods coming into sight. Grinning, he slammed the door. They were coming from the wrong direction to spot the entrance, and they were low enough that their passing windstream would blow tons of sand against the door, hiding it. The sounds faded too quickly for distance to be muffling them. He tried the door, but the weight against it held it shut. He was trapped inside, but effectively hidden from the searchers.

He stood, legs apart, arms akimbo, staring at the wall as if he could see through it, wondering who searched Beldorph's surface. The ship was a fast freighter, not a patrol. What did the pilot hope to find? Him? His deposit point? He made a mental note to take some time off and visit some of the drinking spots patronized by his occupational cronies. The inevitable gossip would tell him who might be on his trail.

The contrabanding fraternity boasted a number of

members who'd cheerfully burn him down to get his client. Some of his smuggling competitors originally shared the Gordotl trade, but they ruined themselves with robber prices.

But now he could only wait. Lesson would pick him up in six standard hours. The time would pass more quickly if he slept.

He reached over to turn down his area light, then hesitated. He knelt, raised the end of the wooden box, and looked beneath. The android lay on his back, his loose parts still attached by the cable. He lay still, his faceplate dimly glowing with a slow, pulsing flicker. Shut down, getting some rest, Conek thought. He shifted his balance slightly and took the weight of the upended box in his left hand.

The poor little character had had a rough ride. Conek was reaching out, ready to put his hand on the metallic shoulder when he caught himself. He hastily lowered the crate, turned down the light, and flopped on the mattress. You don't pet robots, even if they are small and broken, he told himself.

He was losing his mind! This planet drove him crazy! Too much being alone and stationary messed up his head. Strange, he thought, because he liked being alone on a ship. If he could explore the ghoster while he waited for Lesson —*that's* what the freighter had been after!

The searching vessel was looking for the ghoster. The pilot probably had seen the ship come down and hoped to scrounge around in the wreck for salable junk. That made more sense than to think they were after *him*.

But Conek wanted any cargo from the ghoster for himself. The weapon and the little droid proved that not everything aboard was junk. He could do without more sculptured armament, but if there were more droids. . . . He considered the profit he could make from the little droid; his mind went into its calculation mode, turning him into a rich man.

His imagination soared above the realistic and headed for the absurd before he brought it to a halt. Big expectations brought big disappointments, he warned himself.

Turn his thoughts elsewhere. On Beldorph, he usually went to sleep thinking about the cave, his litany to wear away the time. He lay, staring up at the ceiling, wondering where the builders had hidden the homing device. He periodically searched the walls of fused sand without success. He wanted to find out how the ancient mechanism could continue to send its impulses halfway across the galaxy and yet not be picked up by modern sensors.

He had been prowling in a ghoster in space when he'd found the receivers for the cave's signal beacon. What would he find on the ship he'd seen come down on Beldorph? More plastic worm mazes, more little droids? Anything valuable enough to turn a little money put him closer to his good-guy license. With a legal shipping company, he'd be free to go all the right places, meet the women he wanted, live the good life.

Yeah, if the ship carried anything of value.

But if it held more of those damn weapons, he was heading for trouble.

# CHAPTER Three

An insistent noise woke Conek. He sat up, checked the galactic chronometer on his wrist, and realized he had slept seven standard hours. He recognized the sound as Osalt thrusters. Lesson had arrived to pick him up. The sound of the engines grew louder as their backwash cleared the sand over the door. He hurriedly changed the filter in his mask.

He rolled his mattress and was just fitting the carrying strap over his shoulder when he noticed the gun's carton and remembered the droid. With so much to carry on board, he decided to use an old crate. Otherwise he needed four hands.

He waited in the darkness by the door until the sound of the thrusters softened to a dull roar. The Beldorph night was bright beyond the shadow of the ship, but where she hovered, posied on her powerful tractor beams, she cut out the light of the moons.

Lesson let down the grav-rev beam on the front hold and raised the disk with Conek and the crate aboard. Conek put the box and its contents down in the dim cargo area and started for the air lock to the living space. The flicker of the droid's panel illuminated the dimness as it slowed. Conek's footsteps dragged with it.

Oh, hell, did the damn droid think he brought it out of the cave just to leave it in a storage hold? Conek told himself he didn't have time to lay out red carpets for unexpected passengers. The flickers changed to slow blinks. Swearing at himself for being ridiculous, he rushed back, picked up the little droid, and plopped him down on a reclined seat in the lounge on his way to the bridge.

But he couldn't leave the weapon just sitting around in the hold, either. If they hit a rough spot, it might shoot the tail off the ship—if he'd pointed the business end in that direction. True, it hadn't discharged during the rough landing, but perhaps he'd taken off the safety. He went back, took the carton into the stateroom he used when he traveled on *Anubis*, and stowed it in the locker-style closet. Conek entered the small control area to find Lesson watching him.

Alstansig L. Lesson, as his pilot's papers listed him, was an aging pilot who, at thirty, had made himself a legend in all three galaxies of Vladmn. By the age of forty, he'd pickled his reputation in every run-down bar from Agnar-Alpha to Conseg. A small, dry stick of a man at fifty, his drinking blackballed him from every freighting company. He was ignored or laughed at by the rogue freighter owners. He'd liberated more spirits than an exorcist.

Conek had given him a job in return for helping him regain *Anubis* after the pirate Gerdozd killed Tobard and took the ship. Conek and Lesson had been together for years. The old pilot often reminded his captain that he didn't really work for him. He just flew *Anubis* and drew his pay.

Lesson turned back to the controls as Conek fastened himself in the copilot's seat.

"What did you bring aboard?"

"Prepackaged Morse code," Conek replied as Lesson raised ship. "And something pretty weird. Maybe our fortune, maybe big trouble."

"You want to translate?"

Conek told Lesson about the ghoster, finding the weapon and how the droid found him. Then he returned to the subject of the gun. ". . . And about as handy as a portable hell. Problem is, you can't even tell which end shoots."

Conek pointed at the track of the ghoster, still slightly visible, though the windstorm had partially filled it with sand. "Head straight along that course, and keep the sensors on high. I want to find that ship."

But two hours later, they were still looking.

"Probably wasn't a ghoster at all—they repaired whatever brought them down and took off again," Lesson said.

Conek didn't believe it, but he was too pressed for time to engage in long treasure hunts. He needed to get back to Agnar-Alpha and his own ship.

"Go out on the other side of the planet," he instructed Lesson. "Another ship followed it down, I think. Maybe we can throw them off the scent."

To please Conek, Lesson raised *Anubis* in a long orbital curve, taking them nearly a quarter of the way around Beldorph. They crossed the terminator line and were in daylight when Lesson abruptly slowed his ascent. Flipping on the distance viewer, he aimed it to port and down.

"Trouble—two freighters having at it."

"Dursig?" Conek leaned over, thinking his customer might have returned, but from his angle the screen was a blur.

"No, both teacups. Hey—it's Icor! It's his old CD-51."

Conek snorted. "That's all we need—to get into one of his fights. That old rocket-rider would get half the galaxy killed trying to keep him out of—Hey! What the hell are you doing?" he shouted as Lesson swung the ship back into ascent and away from the battle.

Lesson brought the ship around. Then Conek remembered the android. He didn't see any reason to let it get more damaged, and he raced back to the lounge, buckling the safety harness over the little robot. Conek could feel the sensor panel tracking him like a pair of sad eyes as he rushed back to the copilot's seat.

Lesson grunted. "You ready now, or shall I make an appointment? Maybe we can come back later."

"Just see if you can fly this tub," Conek returned as he checked the charges in the blasters.

Lesson frowned at the distance screen. "So Slug's come out of hiding."

"Slug?" Conek rechecked his aim. "There's a medal due me for this." He let go a tight-beam distance shot. Despite the illegal boosters on the weapons, the target was still out of range.

Jon Slugarth was the type of human the rest of the race wanted to disclaim. He was the pot even a kettle of cutthroats called black.

Conek fired again, hoping to draw off the newer, faster ship. Icor's old CD-51 yawed dangerously, one of its starboard engines out. Then the second starboard thruster sent up a plume of black smoke. With all power on the port side, the CD-51 spiraled down toward the surface.

A hopeless, helpless rage filled Conek, and infected Lesson as well. The pilot dived straight for Slug's trim, fast freighter, anticipating its every evasive turn. With gravity aiding *Anubis,* she closed fast. Conek opened up all six forward blasters, keeping a tight deadly pattern. He struck the smaller vessel twice.

Less than a kilometer from the surface, the Vladmn freighter suddenly went to gray. Dropping into time-comp and out of sight, Slug's ship disappeared with a shudder, taking the tops of the closest dunes with her.

"The yellow coward." Lesson snorted as he fought to bring *Anubis* out of her dive.

Conek secured his weapons and leaned back, satisfied with the result. While Lesson concentrated on his flying, he noted the strain on the other ship as it warped while too close to the surface.

"He probably did himself more damage than we could have," he observed. "He was too fast for us."

Lesson swung the big freighter around, staying close to the surface. They scanned the dunes, searching for the wreck. Neither expected to be of any aid to old Icor, but by silent consent they had to try.

"Ya-hoo!" Lesson shouted. "I don't believe it!"

Above them and to port, both starboard engines out and one ablaze, the CD-51 turned on its side, starboard thrusters down. It seemed perfectly balanced as it neared the ground.

"That old devil can do anything!" Conek muttered, fascinated by a flying skill that continually overrode the expected and aimed at the impossible. "If he can land it, he's outdone himself."

"If he can fly it, he can land it," Lesson said quietly. "It's up to us to put out the fire." He opened up on his thrusters, taking *Anubis* ahead as they watched the rear visual screens.

"There he goes—he's doing it!" Conek shouted. Through the small scopes they watched as the old ship righted itself and slid down the side of a large dune.

"And here *we* go," Lesson said as he swung *Anubis* around, moving just beyond the flaming ship. The eight retros roared as they held the huge freighter stationary. The thrust of the main burners covered the back of the damaged vessel with sand, smothering the fire.

Lesson landed far enough away to keep *Anubis* safe in case of an explosion. Grabbing masks and portable foamers, they dashed across the sand. They pushed through the air lock of the old vessel, following the sound of a hissing foamer to the aft compartment. With three portable foamers in operation, they sealed off the passage to the engines in centi-units. The fire died for want of oxygen. Conek lowered his gear and slapped his old friend Icor on the back.

"Icor, you're the damnedest rocket rider in all three—"

Conek stared as the figure turned. The suit and the stance were Icor's, but the face inside the helmet stopped him cold. The gray eyes meeting Conek's were set in a heart-shaped face. He gazed on a pert nose and the most appetizing lips he'd ever seen. Auburn hair framed her eyes and mouth with swirls of color. She was very young, but she filled the old space suit in all the right places. The pink lips curved in a smile.

"Thanks for your help, Captain Hayden, but I'm not dead. Did you mean to bury me?"

Conek blinked and smiled back. "Don't worry, honey,

Icor will understand." He glanced at Lesson, who stood staring. "Hey, buddy, find out where Icor gets his crew."

Her expression hardened. "Captain, *I* am Icor now."

Lesson stepped closer. "Gella! Conek, Cap, you remember Icor's daughter. Girl, you've really done some—uh, growing. Where's your pa?"

She dropped her eyes. "Buried on Siddah-II. He refused to give up a cargo to Slug's hired pirates."

Conek turned away, remembering the times the old smuggler advised him and kept him out of trouble. A friend of Tobard's, Icor was the only contrabander to assist Conek when he was green in the trade. Icor's temper and love of danger caused as many problems as he solved. His age and his daring flying won him the title of the original rocket-rider. He was centuries behind the first hot pilot in space, but he carried the title because no one could remember a time when he didn't outfly every Vladmn pilot and terrify flight controllers. Thinking of Icor's fantastic skills brought Conek's head up with a jerk.

"Then who landed this ship?"

"Captain, I'm the only one here," Gella said, meeting his eyes with a challenge in hers.

Lesson, shouldering hs firefighting gear, gave a low whistle. "You meant it when you said you were Icor."

She shrugged. "With his teaching, what else could I do?"

Lesson nodded solemnly. Conek busied himself with the belt on his suit, thinking her comment fitted Icor's skills.

"But why was Slug after you?" Lesson asked.

"He wasn't. I did the chasing."

Conek smothered an oath. "With this old crate? That's the craziest—"

Gella turned on him, eyes blazing. "*Starfire* is twice the ship your flying warehouses are! She can take any freighter —anytime, anywhere!"

"Well, you sure proved it with Slug, didn't you?" Conek retorted, indicating the damage with a swing of his hand.

"That slimy glob came in on me when I went after the other one." She wiped her hands on her suit and gazed at the mess in the aft compartment.

"Oh-ho!" Conek leaned against the wall, his disbelief plain. "So there was another one."

"Believe what you like!" She tossed her head. "If they didn't shoot off the galley, I'll get something to cool us down." She certainly knew how to stop a conversation.

Conek followed Gella down the passage, watching the seductive swing barely hidden by her angry stride. Was this really Icor's dirty-faced kid? he wondered. Three standard years ago, the last time he saw her, she was covered with grime, crawling around a dismantled thruster. He remembered telling Lesson she was the result of the love affair between Icor and his ship. "Check. I bet under the grease you'll find wrenches for hands," he joked. He shook his head. *Three years?*

Using the wind from *Anubis*'s thrusters, Lesson blew away the sand from *Starfire*'s engines. At a lesser speed, he passed air across the damaged engines until they cooled enough for emergency repairs. In an old work suit, Gella reverted to the grimy sprite Conek remembered. All three wore full suits and helmets in order to communicate. The soot, grease, and sand clung to their face masks but not their skin—still, the effect was the same.

Two glancing shots had caused the damage. Both port thrusters could be repaired with enough spare parts. The fires had melted some jury-rigged wiring. Depleting the emergency supplies from both ships, they were only able to complete a makeshift job of repairing the outer starboard thruster.

Conek slammed the hatch, securely bolting it down. "We'll just have to make do with one starboard engine," he said.

"We?" Gella wiped her faceplate on the cleanest of the greasy cloths. She put on as much dirt as she took off.

"We," Conek repeated. "That patch job is pretty sketchy. If it gives you trouble, you can't handle it alone and I'm getting *you* off this planet. If you want a war, have it somewhere else."

"Sorry, I didn't know Beldorph was now under private ownership," she snapped. "Thank you for your help, but I can get where I'm going alone." She gathered her tools, stuffing them in her kit with the hasty neatness of experience. Conek saw that her slim hands bore no resemblance to wrenches.

"You could, but you won't without me."

She slammed her toolbox closed. "And where am I going with you that I wouldn't go on my own?"

Conek took her toolbox, jerking it from her hand. "To Siddah-I." He turned to Lesson, who was just picking up their equipment. "Follow us."

Conek boarded the old CD-51 with Gella following close behind. Her expression fluctuated between anger and disbelief.

"Just what are you doing? This is *my* ship! You helped me and I thank you. If I can ever do the same, I will, but you can't come on here—"

"I can and I will," Conek said as he shucked the rest of his suit. He headed for the bridge. "How old are you? You're not old enough to have the registration in your name. Kid, if you want to keep this ship, your only chance is Vandort." Conek took the pilot's seat, checking over the controls.

"No, I won't go back to Siddah-I." She jerked off her helmet as she followed him. Her voice, unmasked by the filter, combined a womanly depth and childlike stubbornness.

"Girl, you don't have any choice. Vandort was your father's partner and, what, your mother's brother? He's your relative, anyway. You can't run around by yourself. You can't get a legitimate haul on your own ship until you're old enough to have a pilot's license and sign up with a captain. You don't stand a chance in a place like Siddah-II without Icor."

She flopped down in the copilot's seat. Her pout should have been childish; instead, it was seductive. Her long hair fanned out over her shoulders, catching the sun through the view ports. Conek gripped the controls tighter. She was Icor's daughter, he reminded himself, and he owed the old rocket rider.

"I can get work when I'm ready," she mumbled.

Conek fired the number-two port thruster, and she jerked around, glaring at him. "Easy! This isn't one of your Osalt tubs!"

Conek swore at himself. He'd used the effort it took to rev his own ships. The thrusters of the old CD-51 screamed under the unnecessary force.

Embarrassed, he frowned. "Okay, you take it up, but I'll comp it. Don't get funny with me or I'll jerk it out from under you." He pointed to the override controls on the pilot's side of the panel. Then he sat back, watching as she babied the old engines into obedience.

Gella delicately worked the controls. Conek admired her skill as she lifted off so smoothly, he hardly knew they'd left the ground. After they were in a gentle ascent she relaxed a bit, but he could see the tightness around her mouth.

"What did you mean, you could get work when you were ready?"

"I'm not ready. Slug killed Icor."

"And you're out for a vendetta? It won't work, kid."

"Oh?" She glanced at him and pointed below and to starboard. In the distance, the spiral of smoke on the dead planet could only mean a crash. Conek recognized the ship he'd seen over the smuggler's cave, one of Slug's old vessels.

"Okay, so kick me in the shins. I apologize for the cracks and not believing you. I'll even admit you're one hell of a pilot, but it still won't work."

"*You* did it." She eased back on the controls and gazed at Conek. Her eyes were both sad and challenging. "Icor used to talk about it. To him, your getting Gerdozd proved how much you loved your father—a sort of monument to Tobard. I wasn't the son he wanted, but I'll get his revenge for him. You can delay me by taking me to Vandort, but you won't stop me."

"Look, what I did—what you're *trying* to do—it's not the same thing."

"Why? Because I'm a female?"

No, baby, because you're a certain *type* of female. Shooting at a ship is one thing . . . boring a hole through somebody takes traits you haven't got . . . not a plus for anybody's character.

"No, the circumstances are different. I was older—"

"By only a year."

"I was bigger—"

"Size doesn't count with a blaster."

"I'd flown my own ship for three years—"

"*Icor* taught me. I can outfly you anytime."

In frustration Conek slammed his hand on the control panel. "But you can't outthink me. You can't now, and if you live to be a hundred, you won't, either. Did Icor ever tell you about me when I first came to live with Tobard? I was ten. My mother died in the plagues of Colsar. Tobard spent four years trying to find me. A kid alone lives rough in a place where an epidemic has practically destroyed society. I did *anything* to stay alive—like Slug does. You have to live it to understand."

"I've been around."

"You've been around with Icor! He was a hot pilot, and he thought of himself as the big bad man, but, baby, he was limited."

"Limited?" Gella's eyes flashed. "By what?"

"A certain decency," Conek snapped back. "That's the difference. Slug doesn't have any, and neither did Gerdozd. Tobard did—if he'd understood what they lacked, he'd still be alive, and so would Icor."

Conek searched for a way to explain. "It isn't the ability to fight, it's how dirty you'll get—and something else. I didn't go after Gerdozd just for killing my father. He had my ship and, I thought at the time, my name as a man until I got it back. And Lesson helped me. If Slug had killed Tobard, I'm not sure I would have tried to get the ship back. He has a bigger operation. Even for Tobard and Icor together, I'd do some long thinking before I went after Slug."

"Well, don't think about it," Gella said with a sudden nonchalance, as if the subject no longer interested her. "If you wanted Slug, all you'd have to do is turn around. He's after *you*."

With effort Conek kept a straight face. She really was young if she thought he could be drawn with such a transparent ploy. He punched the time-comp and sat back, watching the blackness of space turn to gray.

The time-comp system was automatic. Five standard hours later it would call them back to take over the conventional flying over Siddah-I. He stood and stretched. He walked back to the small living, sleeping, and eating area, and took one of the two shabby loungers. He barely concealed his disbelief.

"What makes you think Slug is after me?"

She shrugged and went to the galley. "Hungry?" she asked. Without waiting for an answer she took two prepackaged meals and popped them into the heating cabinet.

"Years ago I heard Icor say that Slug lost out to you on the Gordotl businccss. I suppose that's why. You know Slug dropped out of sight for a while over some trouble in Galaxy Beta—I never heard what. . . ."

Conck sat watching her as she leaned back against the counter. Her hands were palms down on its edge, her elbows slightly behind her, needlessly and unconsciously accentuating her figure. Innocence hung about her as if she were unaware of everything except the explanation passing right over Conek's head. As Icor's friend, he decided he should give her a warning about her posture—just as soon as he tired of the view. He tensed as he realized what she was saying.

"Thorin-Gamma, Agnar-Alpha, MD-439, Siddah-I, Rensig, Liston, back to Agnar-Alpha, and then Beldorph. On Thorin-Gamma, Rensig, and the second time on Agnar-Alpha, I came in close, but I couldn't fire on him over a crowded area."

"He was on *my* trail?" Conek bellowed. Her list of planets was his recent itinerary.

She nodded. "We've been in one line for the past ten days. He had to be homing in on you, just like I fastened onto him."

"Oh, shit! There I was, cruising along like—oh, shit!"

"That way, and wash your hands." Gella motioned aft. "We'll eat in five minutes."

While Conek scrubbed his hands he thought about Gella's information. He cursed himself all the time for never once back-checking his trail. The problem was his double life, he decided. So much of what he picked up for the Gordotl was too legitimate. He'd nearly forgotten he was a smuggler and had grown careless.

On Thorin-Gamma and on Rensig, he made legitimate purchases and deliveries as part of his cover. On Agnar-Alpha, his home berth, he kept hangar space for each of his freighters, an accepted practice in legal shipping. The other planets, contraband markets all, were as well-known to Slug as to himself. They were after the deposit point of Beldorph and probably followed *Anubis* too. Since neither Dursig nor Lesson detected them, they must have hung back a good distance. He dried his hands and went back to the galley.

"How far back did Slug stay when we'd come out of time?"

"Pretty far; I'm not sure. I didn't see you until we reached Rensig. I knew he was chasing somebody, though. Now it's my turn—I can't undo the food wrappers like this." She held up her grease-stained hands.

By the time she returned, Conek had removed the prepackaged meals and set them out. His stare as she took her seat was far from friendly.

"If you're spacing me, I'll break your neck," he growled.

Gella's eyes widened, her fork poised over her dish. "Spacing you? Why should I?"

"To get me involved in your battle with Slug."

"It would be a good idea, both of us after him. Too bad we lost him."

"He wouldn't be hard to find."

"Conek, you must have been really *busy!* Slug's back, but he's in hiding; I heard he is still in big trouble with the Vladmn patrols. He pops out, does his bit, and disappears again. I only found him by chance; otherwise, I wouldn't have spent so long on his tail." She took another bite and gazed at Conek thoughtfully.

"What is he after? You know, I never did ask you what you were doing on Beldorph."

"Minding my own business."

# CHAPTER Four

"Wasted effort," Lesson said as *Anubis* lifted through the atmosphere of Siddah-I after leaving Gella with her uncle.

Below them the trade center stood out whitely against the darkness of the swampy area around it. Warehouses and distribution centers lined orderly rows of landing pads, taking all the premium ground. Off to the sides, on barely habitable land, the living areas were spaced randomly, as if the buildings had been tossed from freighters. Siddah-I stood at the crossing of numerous routes serving thousands of inhabited worlds. With very little dry ground, no resources, and a bad climate, nothing recommended the water planet except its location. But the usable land was listed among the most expensive in the three galaxies.

"Wasted effort," Lesson repeated when Conek remained silent. "Been easier to take the girl back to Agnar-Alpha. We could have fixed her ship there."

"She can fix it as well as we can," Conek replied curtly. "She belongs with her uncle, and working on the engines will keep her out of trouble for a while."

Conek refused to admit the whole truth, even to Lesson. Gella had grown from a spindly, grimy kid into a beautiful woman. She offered too much temptation to be the daughter of an old friend. He felt the responsibility of old debts to Icor.

"Once her ship is fixed, watch out," Lesson replied. "Vandort is a mouse compared to her. If *Starfire* was in good running order, she'd stay just long enough for us to hit time-comp—which is now."

Conek watched Lesson as he reluctantly made preparations to comp. The old pilot hated to give up control of the ship. Distances requiring years of travel at warp speeds were cut to days and even hours in time-comp. But Lesson still distrusted it, even though the system had proved itself fifty years before he was born.

The alien technology came from a ghoster whose origins were still unknown. Vladmn computers could duplicate the time-warp system, but their explanation was in a mathematical form still beyond the scope of the current mathematicians. Numerous pseudo-intellects spouted theories over steepled fingers, but they failed to come up with a satisfactory explanation.

Outside the sky ports, the view changed from black, sprinkled with mutlicolored points of light, to the pale grayness of timing. They were now invisible to any friend or foe but also isolated from any communication.

Lesson stood up and stretched. "Now how about our new hand? Can he wrestle grub?"

From his father Conek had caught Earth Fever, as the study of the ancient planet was labeled. Tobard liked the ancient cultures. Conek was more catholic in his tastes. Lesson, who had caught it from Conek, stuck to the old Westerns. On the long, solitary voyages they both succumbed to the new fashion and read books. Society was going through one of its phases, considering holo-films the refuge of mental sloth.

Conek paused as he rose. "I believe you meant *rustle*."

"I thought *rustle* meant *steal*."

"Yeah"—Conek frowned thoughtfully—"but if I have a

choice, I'd rather have it stolen. Knowing someone fought my dinner all over the floor would take my appetite."

Lesson nodded in solemn agreement as he preceded Conek into the lounge.

Tobard stole *Anubis* on her maiden voyage. Both he and Lesson were fastidious in their care of the ship, and her lounge still glistened with newness. Osalt freighters were always decorated with muraled landscapes on the walls. The green floor flowed from scenic walls, unmarked. The eight reclinable loungers stood in four groupings, each pair with a small table between them. Only the safety harnesses, tucked in the side pockets of the seats, reminded the occupant he was aboard a spacecraft. Down the passage beyond the galley, the six passenger compartments provided the reason for the size and opulence of the lounge. In Vladmn, freighters seldom carried passengers, so two cabins had been converted into bins for fragile cargo.

Conek stopped, staring down at the android. Lesson had left it undisturbed. As Conek entered, it turned its head to watch him, the panel lights speeding up.

"I left it alone," Lesson said. "I didn't know what you wanted done with it, and I wasn't sure it was friendly."

"We'll have a pal if we can put it back together," Conek replied, deciding to give it a try. He knew little about droids, but a good mechanic would ask questions. Until he knew what the ghoster carried, the fewer who knew the droid was alien, the better. For most casual encounters he could pass it off as Osalt, but it wouldn't pass a close inspection. Neither Vladmn nor Osalt possessed the technology to produce the light, strong alloy of the droid's casing.

"Get me the small toolbox," Conek said to Lesson. "I'll monkey with him while you 'wrestle' the grub."

Lesson growled a reply Conek missed as he watched the droid. Every time he spoke, the sensor panel flickered.

"Is speech new to you?" Conek asked. "If it is, you'd better get used to it. Around here tongues get a good workout. We're not much on whistling."

"Whistling?" Lesson asked.

"Yeah." Conek didn't elaborate.

"Exactly what you needed, a musical listener for all your gab," Lesson said as he returned. He handed the small tool chest to Conek and stood gazing down at the droid.

"Since when did you go mute?" Conek asked his pilot.

Using a small, high-powered vacuum, Conek meticulously cleaned the sand and dust from the disconnected arm. While he worked, he told Lesson what Gella had said about Slug being on his trail. He still didn't believe it, but he warned the pilot in case the girl wasn't trying to space him.

Finishing with the arm, he started cleaning the leg. He gave the attached foot a whisk, and the droid extended his wheels, turning the pediment for a more thorough job. The android twisted and stretched as Conek continued up the leg and over the rest of the body. Unexpected panels opened so he could reach the interior. The inner areas were sand-free, but Conek noticed the motes of dust and some corrosion. Long time, no service.

The droid had been silent since leaving the cave, but now he gave out a discordant tune—almost an appreciative sigh. Conek chuckled. Everyone, everything, liked a massage. Maybe he'd treat himself to a massage cabinet installed on his ship with his profits from selling the droid.

When Conek finished cleaning the arm, Lesson examined its construction. He bent over, inspecting the shoulder.

"Never seen anything like this," he muttered. "Won't be anything to put back together. Funny, though, snap-on ball joint, inner framing, expect it was patterned after a human frame." For a couple of minutes he worked the fingers, considering the humanlike hand, and then rose, going to get a box of assorted wires and cables. The pilot took out supplies, and the droid turned his head to watch. Suddenly a panel slid open in the robot's lower main cylinder, exposing a variety of spare parts, including several coils of wire.

"Handy." Conek peered in, turning his attention from the cleaning. "No second-rate parts for you, eh, fella?" By the time he replaced the vacuum, Lesson had pulled out the coiled, insulated wire and compared it to the broken ends protruding from the arm.

"What are you going to do with it, assuming we get it fixed?" Lesson asked.

Conek frowned over the difficulty of cutting through the tough insulation. "Sell it when I don't need it anymore."

"Need it for what?"

"Exploring my ghoster."

"Hey, hey," Lesson grunted. "Better leave it alone. Might have a destruct mechanism. The first three aboard that ship with the time-comp were blasted right out of their hides."

"But I'm keeping the robot! He's my safety, and those jokers found the *time-comp*. A big discovery and we're set for life."

"Yeah, one false step and you've set yourself three galaxies away too. I don't like it. Besides, you shouldn't be in the open on Beldorph."

"No choice." Conek pointed a finger at the old pilot to emphasize his point. "I've got to check out that ship. How would you like to face Slug if he found it and discovered one of those guns?"

"Not my favorite fantasy, but you shouldn't be on Beldorph. Dursig pays pretty good, doesn't he? You want to risk his business?"

"Maybe just the opposite—hand me a splicer—I could put in a legal claim on the ghoster and use it for cover. Then any patrol spotting us would be our escort to opportunity."

"Still don't like it. Ties you to the place—funny lettering on this arm. I've never seen anything like it."

Conek held out his hand for the arm, inspecting the markings. "Well, you didn't expect to read 'ghoster', did you? If you squint, it could be c-g-e." He leaned over the droid, pointing it out. "How's that for a name, fella? Let's see, could be Ciggy—no, sounds silly. If we didn't pronounce the *c*, it could be Gee, that's a little better, okay?"

"Ka-a-ay."

Both men stared at the droid in surprise at the soft, highly pitched, metallic voice.

"Well, so much for the silent partner," Lesson said.

Conek wondered if it understood or just found a sound it

could imitate. Perhaps it just liked noise. "Ka-ay?" he repeated, pointing to the lettering again.

"Ka-a-ay."

"Ka-ay," Conek mused. "Hard *c*, silent *g*, and an *a* sounding *e* from the old medical language. There is a precedent." He shrugged. "Cge it is, then."

"Ka-ay," Lesson repeated slowly. "Out of c-g-e you get a sound like Kay?"

"Trust me, I just created a precedent." Conek grinned.

Lesson soon finished reattaching the right arm. He moved it experimentally, working the joints. He pointed his right forefinger at the droid, the thumb held up and the other fingers clinched. "Kew-w-w." When the robot failed to respond, Lesson repeated both the sound and the gesture.

Cge blinked his panels and mimicked the pilot in sound and action. "Ke-w-w."

"Well, my end works," Lesson said. He handed the droid the extra wiring and watched. It used both hands as it repacked the parts compartment. "Now I'm going to wrestle some grub, and knowing you, you need some too."

"I guess so," Conek replied without really hearing Lesson. He finished with the leg and repacked the toolbox, shoving it aside. Then he picked up Cge and stood him on his feet, squatting while he made sure the little droid was balanced.

"Make tracks," he told it.

The metal head swiveled until the idly flickering lights turned on Conek.

"Look! Walk!" Still squatting, Conek took a couple of awkward steps, motioning the android forward.

After three rapid blinks of his panel, Cge retracted his wheels, leaned forward, bent his leg joints, and duck-walked over.

"A clown!" Conek shouted as he jerked upright. He grabbed the toolbox and strode off down the corridor. "Just what we needed! Another damn clown!"

"Huh?" Lesson stuck his head out of the galley. His guffaw and the hum of wheels on the plasti-steel floor caused Conek to turn.

"Clown-n, clown-n." Still bent forward in a half squat, Cge rolled rapidly after him.

While Lesson slept, Conek sat in the lounge going over the list of supplies the Gordotl had ordered. He entered the items in his pocket computer and cross-referenced them against the location of vendors and warehouses. Hopscotching an Osalt freighter back and forth across three galaxies chewed a big hole in his profits. He planned his shopping for Dursig to coincide with other shipments.

The old books and holo-films showed smuggling and black-market activities, as some were called, to be full of dash and danger. Conek wondered if the world had changed, or if the writers had left out the boring details. Playing catch with blaster beams was no picnic—and no deep concern, either. He stayed just far enough outside the law to cause him to avoid most of the places he wanted to go. He was safe on the smuggler's protected worlds, but the bars were shabby and the food worse.

While he worked, he watched Cge. Lacking a means of communication, the droid adjusted to his new surroundings by imitation. Four new words had been added to his vocabulary: *Lesson*; *ConekHayden*; *damn*; and *no,* with a vigorous shake of the head.

Before he went to lie down, Lesson suggested the droid suffered from problems in its computer, or was a good con man. The little robot kept its design function a secret. It gave no appearance of having a purpose other than playing games.

But Lesson's training could be the reason for the droid's attitude. The old pilot followed up his initial Western-style finger-pointing gunshots with a long game in pistol-packing warfare. Conek had watched the shoot-outs as Lesson and Cge crouched behind the loungers, shooting imaginary bullets at each other. The captain wondered if his pilot wasn't using the excuse of the droid's childlike appearance to relive the stories he read on long space flights.

Cge climbed up on the seat of the next lounger, walked back and forth, and tried to sit. He bent as far as his body would allow and fell backward, resting on the back of his top module and heels. Conek laughed and reached over, reclining the lounger to fit. The droid sat back, his head turned toward Conek, panel glowing with satisfaction.

Unlike Vladmn androids, Cge's gray sensor panel flashed and glowed at different speeds, as if expressing feelings. The little character ought to bring a good price. He'd grow on a sentimental being pretty fast.

Some sucker would think the droid possessed some sensitivity, Conek decided, and if a machine could be spoiled, Cge would be. His owners would be catering to *him*. Conek remembered lowering the recliner for the droid, then excused his act as practical. He should get the machine used to Vladmn ways, shouldn't he?

He went back to the Gordotls' list. One request bothered him. Weapons. He keyed in the code for Siddah-II and let the computer put a stop on the planet into his schedule. Tsaral, the smuggling king, was his source for sensitive cargo.

Three years before, he would have known who wanted to unload a hijacked shipment of arms, but once he'd begun hauling for Dursig, he lost touch with much of the "in" gossip in the trade. Ninety-eight percent of the cargo he "smuggled" to the Gordotl were everyday supplies for a sparsely settled agricultural planet. Four years before, legitimate shipping lines had supplied the small colonies.

Then Vladmn found out about thereil. The high-density gems were to the new technology what diamonds had been on old Earth. The new metals required even harder surfaces to cut them. Thereil was the answer. The Amal, the intergalactic mining conglomerate, wanted to mine it. The Gordotl had not objected, but the Amal weren't satisfied with permission; they took over planets. When the Gordotl wouldn't give up their homes, the Amal scared off the legitimate freighting companies and tried to run the big four-armed, four-legged humanoids off their planet.

The Gordotl responded by catapulting themselves into a technological advance and doing their own mining. Conek supplied them by way of Beldorph. He was welcome to come onto their planet, but their weird and inflexible sense of honor wouldn't allow them to accept contraband there. He'd never understood their convoluted reasoning, but he didn't care where he off-loaded.

Now the Gordotl faced a different and equally serious problem. According to Dursig, they were being attacked by Osalt. They wanted weapons to fight back. Conek didn't believe in the Osalt theory; he thought the Amal staged the assaults, but if he wanted to keep his lucrative business, he'd better find some guns.

Maybe he should lend Dursig his new weapon, he thought, joking with himself. Using that thingamabob to destroy a few attackers would be like throwing a planet at a mosquito.

"Clown-n, clown-n, clown-n."

Conek came out of his thoughts to see Cge in his half squat, rolling back and forth by his feet, making a childish bid for attention. When he looked up, the android rolled over, brushing Conek's knee with his cold metal body.

Conek reached out and put his hand on the shoulder of the droid's main cylinder. "Yeah, you are one crazy robot—now go play somewhere else," he said, giving Cge a gentle shove.

The droid went back into his half squat and, still in reverse, circled the loungers at top speed. A toy! Conek thought. That's all he is, a damn toy.

Then his mind went back to Dursig. Hours later he was still thinking about the Gordotl when Lesson came into the lounge carrying two steaming cups of fiene. The pilot's face was puffy from sleep.

"Any problems?" Lesson asked as he handed Conek a cup. He settled back in a lounger, watching the vapor rise from the hot liquid.

"With the ship, or will anything do?" Conek asked.

"What's up?"

Conek told him about the Osalt raid on Gordotl.

"Hmmph! Sounds like the end of our deliveries. Mighty strange, though—wouldn't think the Osalt could get so far into our territory without being sighted. Ain't reasonable.

The more I think about it, the less I believe it." Lesson drained his cup and went to the bridge.

Suddenly he let out a stream of shouted obscenities. Conek jumped to his feet and followed the swearing.

Cge stood in the copilot's seat, one cable fastened into the ship's computer and another connected to the main electrical outlet.

Lesson started for the android, but Conek caught his arm and nearly jerked him off his feet. The droid might not be well insulated by human standards. If not, the old pilot could be burned down to the size of a computer chip.

"Don't touch him!" Conek yelled. He'd freed his pilot's arm but grabbed it a second time as Lesson started forward again.

Before he could explain, Lesson turned on him, the pilot's rage at the droid redirected. "You bring a spy aboard, one who could put us both behind bars for life—"

Conek stared at his pilot, wondering if he'd lost his mind. Did Lesson think aliens from another galaxy came all that way and destroyed a ship in order to learn the secret of Dursig's automatic cultivators? It made about as much sense as his traveling the same distance for the alien's mixing bowls.

Slug or Vladmn might try using a spy, but the droid was alien. Conek opened his mouth to reason with his pilot, but Lesson was too angry.

"And you want to turn him loose to do his damnedest. Well, do it on your *own* ship, but not on *mine*!"

Stung by the old pilot's words, Conek's own anger flared. "On whose ship?" he asked with deadly quiet.

Before Lesson could answer, Cge jerked his cables free. He retracted them with a snap, slamming his panels. Scrambling to the floor, he tilted backward to glare up at Lesson as he wheeled past, his sensor panel flashing.

"Cge is no spy!" he piped as he wheeled into the lounge.

The android passed Lesson and Conek, who stood staring at each other, facing the worst disagreement in their long relationship. Neither dropped his gaze. Lesson broke the silence.

"We're coming out of comp. Want to land *your* ship, *Captain*?" He made both Conek's ownership and his official rating into an insult.

"You're the pilot, earn your pay," Conek replied, turning back to the lounge. He stood glaring down at the android, trying to fit the blame for the fight on the little metallic shoulders. No go. One explanation would smooth the ruffled feelings, but the ship was Conek's, and so was the droid. He refused to make the first move.

He strapped himself and Cge in the loungers just as they dropped back out of time. From the bridge he could hear Port giving Lesson hell for timing it so close to the crowded air lanes. For years the old pilot's tight flying had kept a battle going between himself and Port. Valdmn would have grounded Lesson years ago, but their pride in the captured enemy freighters protected him.

"If you want me out of the way, give me clearance," Lesson bellowed.

"You've got it!" Port shouted back. With Lesson, the controllers had long ago given up the standard landing jargon. It left no room for the vitriolic feelings on both sides.

Moments later the ship lurched as it settled on the pad outside the hangar.

Without a word Conek rose, released Cge from his seat, and strode into the air lock. He pulled the silent droid behind him.

"I'm taking her over for refueling!" the old pilot shouted just as the lock closed behind Conek and the droid.

Conek didn't believe him, but Lesson announced his intention too late for Conek to do anything about it.

With Slug back and on their tails, Lesson could get into trouble if he wasn't careful. And *caution* was a word that left his vocabulary the minute he got mad.

# CHAPTER Five

Pausing within the open door of the hangar, Conek watched *Anubis* lift.

Off to some bar to drown his sulking, Conek thought. Lesson would be gone for days. Then he'd come back, landing as if he carried a payload of eggs and holding his head, or Conek would have to buy him out of some jail.

At least, if he had to go get the pilot, Conek could travel in his own ship. He looked up to see the gigantic *Bucephalus* gleaming in the soft light entering the door of the hangar. She wouldn't get much of a rest if he worked for two for the next several days.

*I ought to fire the old rocket-rider!* The threat eased his anger, but he'd never carry it out. Except for the old pilot, *Anubis* would still be in the hands of his father's killer. Instead of praise for avenging Tobard's death, Conek would have earned scorn as the crazy kid who'd gotten himself killed in a foolish attempt. He still considered it the luckiest night of his life when he crouched in an alley, hoping to ambush a stranger on his trail. Instead he found himself face-to-face with Lesson, who offered to help him get his ship back in return for being allowed to fly her. Lesson had kept *his* part of the bargain.

"Cge is no spy," repeated the android for the third time as they crossed the wide hangar space.

Conek's mind was on Lesson, but if he kept ignoring the droid, the little rolling recorder would never shut up.

"So you can speak the language, after all."

"After *all*?" A musical tone to the droid's speech gave it a curious emphasis. Aloud he explored the words Conek used. "After—subsequently later in time . . . later in *all* time?" He was bending backward so he could see Conek. "After the computer coded me for the communication of Conek-AlexanderHayden—carbon-based life-form and not an android—I could speak the language."

Not an android. Conek gave Cge another hard look. This little character needed to learn what was what. But he wasn't explaining the facts of life to an android. No way.

"You were using the computer to learn Vladmn Standard?"

"Affirmative. It is appropriate. I should learn to speak with my master," Cge said, pronouncing a satisfied judgment on his actions.

Conek wondered if Vladmn standard was the only language Cge would need, since he planned to sell the droid. He left his thoughts unspoken, remembering Cge's distress when he tried to convince Conek he wasn't a spy. Between Gella and Lesson, Conek had faced enough emotions for one day. Robots were incapable of feelings, but it seemed no one had told Cge. The droid remained tilted backward, waiting for Conek's answer.

"It's fine," he replied, patting the metal shoulder.

Ahead of them, *Bucephalus* stood in the dim light of the huge, abandoned government hangar, the only place on Agnar-Alpha large enough to hold her. When he and Tobard had pirated their two ships from the enemy, Conek had chosen her and never had regretted his decision. With so many other ships to choose from, his father was disgusted with the battered hulk his son wanted. But Tobard named her. From his studies of ancient earth he added Alexander as Conek's middle name and insisted that nothing but *Bucephalus* would do for a steed of Alexander, or Lex, as he had called his son.

The Osalt, because of the great distance between their galaxies, built to a scale dwarfing the largest freighters in Vladmn. Even in Osalt, *Bucephalus* was a Goliath. Vladmn considered her a monster, and when she settled to land in a port for the first time, people scurried away like ants while the local Port went berserk, wondering if she'd crush the three nearest vessels.

As they walked beneath her bulk, echoes of their footsteps traveled through the fifteen massive hatches, open for inspection and yawning like black caverns into her belly. Her upper ridge carried the weight of five gravity-reversal beams. Vladmn freighter pilots called her a flying warehouse, and she was larger than most of the storage buildings at which she picked up shipments.

Unlike Vladmn freighters, she originally served a triple purpose. With ten staterooms, she was designed to carry twenty passengers in comfort. The Osalt Federation was rumored to be lawless. She proved the stories by being built with enough armament to classify as a battleship. Conek and Tobard had masked her gun ports and switches, making sure Vladmn never knew how well they were protected.

Her time-comp system was Vladmn-made. In that particular field Vladmn was far superior to its enemy.

And she was no longer a battered hulk. Her spotless, painted hull gleamed in the dim light of the hangar.

With a firm hand on the droid's arm, Conek activated the remote for the forward grav-beam and rode into the air lock. He was already anticipating being home.

In his enthusiasm of first ownership, Conek redecorated. The lounge boasted luxurious brown carpeting, upholstered loungers in browns and blues, and a scattering of wall sculptures on soft beige bulkheads, a pleasing and sturdy decor.

Conek liked being back aboard *his* ship, but his contentment turned to anger when he entered the lounge. Three people had boarded in his absence. He recognized Major Andro Avvin, local Chief of Port. Conek stopped just inside the air lock; Andro jumped up and rushed forward. The major was a small, slender man, young for his rank, with a thin, sensitive, almost pretty face. He normally spoke in a soft, cultured voice. But the moment he opened his mouth, Conek's attention heightened.

"Captain, love, forgive our intrusion, but you must meet your guests—"

Conek stiffened with anger. Andro saw it and assumed an air of injured innocence.

"Now, dear, don't be a bear, be nice, and you'll see I simply couldn't leave the Quinta standing outside in an open hangar!"

What the hell *is* this? Conek nodded in reply. His gaze scanned the two people still seated and moved back to the major. The major was making a production of the surprise visit. Conek wondered whether Andro's act was meant to draw Conek's attention from his guests or vice versa.

Behind the pursed lips and batting eyelashes was the administrator of the largest and most efficient port service in the three galaxies. For several years Conek watched the little major mince around the port, using his affected mannerisms as a cover for a sharp mind. The veneer proved successful in catching people off-guard. Andro used any slips by the unwary with ruthless efficiency. Conek had twice benefited from Andro's particular talents; once he'd found it extremely uncomfortable to run afoul of Major Avvin.

Though Conek's acquaintance with the major was slight, he might have expected Andro to know all five of the Quinta, the top administrators of the Vladmn government. But why would an important official be aboard his ship?

So this was it, Conek thought. On Beldorph he'd felt restless, as if something had been left undone, as if some slip were waiting to catch him up. He'd been worried about the exposed door to the cave, but the problem was waiting for him here. At least here was the result—he didn't know yet what put the powers of Vladmn on his trail.

Andro chattered away. "And so, let me introduce you to Quinta Bentian." The spindliness of the humanoid's body appeared incapable of holding up the huge, misshapen bald head. "And Quinta Norden." Conek smiled down at the tiny human woman, a dark poised beauty.

Two Quinta! Conek stepped back. There was no need for him to act impressed; he was.

"Quinta, I'm honored," he said, flashing his best "charming" smile. If they were devastated, they hid it well. "Sorry I was out. Perhaps I can make up for it with some refreshments, though the fare aboard a freighter is probably a poor substitute—" He'd act as if nothing were wrong, and maybe he would get out of this mess yet.

Andro interrupted by throwing up his hands and laughing. "I warned you, he's never at a loss."

"We haven't time for social visits, Captain." Quinta Norden shifted on the lounger. Despite the elevated shoes, her feet barely reached the floor. She inspected Conek as if he were some specimen she was preparing to put in laboratory stasis.

By comparison, Bentian's cool stare was friendly. "Sit down, Captain. You're more interested in why we're here."

"It did cross my mind," Conek admitted.

The humanoid kept his eyes on Conek as with one thin hand he indicated a lounger, pointedly waiting until Conek took a seat before he continued.

Conek wanted to refuse and stay by the air lock, hoping for a chance to escape. He still had no idea what brought out their suspicions, and if he could get away, they could keep them.

Why in the hell were they chasing a smuggler, anyway? They should have better things to do. Maybe they got their kicks out of playing detective. If he did get out of this, he'd complain about wasting taxpayers' money.

He'd been too damn smart. In keeping with his good-guy cover, he had his maintenance and inspection work done on Agnar-Alpha, showing a look-how-clean-I-am face to the government. Somehow he'd messed up. If he could just get out, he might free his ship later. No chance if they locked him up.

"Captain, we're waiting. You'll do yourself a favor by cooperating," Norden prodded.

Hell, yes. He could be good and serve a hundred and nine years instead of a hundred and ten. He'd have to play the innocent through to the last. With a sigh he directed the droid toward the passage that led to the staterooms and galley, and took the seat Bentian indicated. The whole place was probably crawling with their men, anyway. As he moved, the major slipped out of sight. He'd made a mistake in not keeping an eye on Andro.

"Captain, I'll come straight to the point. Did Dursig meet you?"

"Who?" Conek turned suitably blank, but now he understood why he was facing the heavyweight officials. When he took on Dursig's job, he'd stepped into the middle of a political issue. The problem was worse than he'd expected. If the Quinta decided he'd trespassed into a sensitive political area, he'd be thrown in jail—no trial, no anything. One of the forgotten people.

Where was that damn major? Was Andro behind him?

He sat back, hoping to give the impression of relaxation while he tried to think of a way to escape gracefully. Lacking grace, he'd settle for alive as a satisfactory substitute.

"I asked you, Captain, if you delivered the last shipment to the Gordotl?"

"Gordotl . . ." Conek frowned thoughtfully. He refused to be tricked. "I've seen the name," he mused. "It must be on one of my charts."

"I think I can help you, Captain," Quinta Norden said quietly.

The glance Conek threw her lingered involuntarily on her dark eyes. He didn't care for the smug turn of her lips, attractive as they might be. Her voice mocked him.

"On your last trip you were trying to find Alcor thresher parts, a problem since the company disbanded thirty years ago. You don't think the Congrove agent found them without the aid of the central computers, do you?"

Bentian leaned forward, his yellowish skin gleaming in the soft lights from the bulkheads.

"Who in Vladmn would have the power to use the trigalactic information bank for something as mundane as spare parts for farming equipment?"

Norden smiled coldly. "You have an excellent face for stratagems and games of chance, Captain. You might have convinced me if I didn't know the truth. Save your bluffs until you have a chance of succeeding."

Bentian laughed, a tremendous noise from so thin a chest. "Now, Captain, did Dursig meet you?"

Conek knew when to accept the facts. If they knew the brand names of his cargo, they weren't bluffing, either. He suppressed a shiver at the thought of steel bars. He wanted to bolt, risking an encounter with any guards they might have outside the ship, but where was Andro? Probably behind him, blaster ready. He decided to wait until he could get the major in view.

"He picked up the shipment," Conek replied with deliberate resignation.

Both Norden and Bentian seemed to relax. Was the completed delivery the noose around his neck, or were they really concerned about Dursig? Were they trying to trick him? If he jumped up, turning as he moved, could he catch the major off-guard and disarm him? Not a sound came from behind him. Andro was probably braced and ready, not letting his attention waver for a second.

That reminded him of the weapon he'd found on Beldorph and left on Anubis. *Oh, crap! I was so mad at Lesson, I forgot it!*

He decided he'd better keep his mouth shut. They didn't need his help to hang him.

"Did he mention any trouble?" Bentian asked.

"Trouble?" Conek was playing it dumb for the rest of this trip.

"We're wasting time," Norden said sharply. "I didn't believe in this idea from the beginning, and after meeting this man—a smuggler, a thief, a murderer—"

"Hey, wait a minute!" Conek, leaning forward, was ready to deny the last two, but that would be almost admitting the first. Well, he'd done that by admitting to Dursig's shipment, but he didn't have to hit them over the head with it.

"The Quinta may be right," Bentian said softly. "We can prove you're a smuggler—I'm sure you know the penalty."

In answer, Conek leaned back, physically denying the threat, until he was pressed against the seat back.

"Are you looking forward to prison, Captain?" Norden asked, her voice almost a purr. "Incarceration and possibly mind-wipe?"

He didn't much care for the last part—not that he was exactly in love with the first threat, either.

"Or perhaps you'd like to make restitution in a way you'd find more profitable?" Bentian asked.

The conversation was taking an interesting turn.

"I'm going to repeat this one more time," Norden said. "I'm against using this . . . this criminal"—she and Bentian exchanged long looks—"but go ahead if you're sure."

Bentian leaned forward and hit him with a request, and it nearly knocked him off his seat with surprise.

"We need you to carry arms to the Gordotl. The Vladmn government will supply them, but it must seem as if we're not involved. You'll find it profitable, even at your rates."

He'd expected to be locked up for smuggling, and they'd come to hire him!

"If there's any assault in force, they'll need a lot," warned Conek. "And how can you be sure it's not the Amal?" Well, why deny he knew about the trouble if they were going to foot the bills?

"We can't be sure, of course," Andro said, and Conek turned his head, staring at the major. He'd entered the lounge from the passage, carrying a tray of refreshments. Surprise and relief turned to anger in Conek. He didn't need any real enemies; his mind could make up enough without reality helping.

"But the Amal are also asking questions," the major continued. "You understand, with the political situation as it is, we can't openly send support to Gordotl unless they request troops, so you're our best alternative."

"And we have a problem," Bentian said. "Between your regular deliveries and the arms shipments, you'll be spending nearly half your time on Beldorph. That will inevitably bring suspicion."

"Perhaps not," Norden mused. "The patrols in the area have reported an old vessel going down on Beldorph." She saw Bentian's inquiring expression. "We track derelicts to be sure they don't hit populated planets—but, Captain, if you were to register a salvage claim on the old ship—"

"I'd have a reason to be on Beldorph," Conek said, finishing for her. Should he laugh or swear? His carefully laid cover was no cover at all. He idly wondered if they also had a homing receiver for the cave, but he was carrying imagination too far.

They were congratulating him and themselves on their good luck when Bentian caught sight of Cge, who was watching them from the passage that led to the galley.

"Did you find the little android on the ship?" Bentian asked.

Conek nodded, glancing at Cge, who peered at the group from the entrance to the passage.

Bentian watched him with interest. "Do you plan to sell him?"

Before Conek could reply, Cge's panels flashed in alarm. He rolled rapidly across the lounge to stand by Conek's knees, tilted slightly backward to center his panel on the captain. One cold metal hand pressed Conek's knee.

"I could offer you a good price," Bentian persisted.

Bentian was one of the jaded rich Conek had envisioned when he repaired the robot. He readjusted his price—all profit, less a bonus for Lesson because he'd helped put the android back together. His freighting company was closer than ever.

Damn! Why did Cge keep looking at him as if he were father-creator or something. The stupid thing would be better off with Bentian. Better off? It's a machine! *You don't think about the welfare of a machine, you sell it and that's that! Don't be a fool!*

The red sensor panels flickered at agitated speeds; the cold little hand rested on his left knee, giving him a soft, insistent pressure. Somehow he couldn't take his eyes away from Cge's panel. The frog in his throat made speech difficult. He readjusted the price again, cursing himself as he did.

"Five hundred thousand cranas," he muttered.

"Five hundred at most," Andro corrected him. "The Quinta wants to buy a robot, not a planet!"

"Five hundred thousand," Conek repeated stubbornly, still staring down at Cge.

Bentian laughed. "It's obvious, Major, the captain isn't selling."

Bentian had relaxed, but Conek was still wary of Norden. she was tense, watching him as if he'd kill someone while lifting a glass. To her he was a criminal, and if he made one wrong step, he'd have one powerful enemy.

# CHAPTER Six

When the air lock clanged shut, putting an end to the argument with Conek, Lesson was surprised and hurt. He had expected Conek to make some comment; one word should have led to another, and their anger would have been forgotten. But the boy just took his little walking-talking machine and left. *So he'd rather play with that new toy.* "Well, great! If that's the way he wants it, it's just fine with me!"

Lesson sped up through the atmosphere, hardly hearing Port squawk. When he tired of the griping, he flipped off the switch.

Below him, Agnar-Alpha fell away like a nightmare receding from consciousness. The sun, just above the horizon, threw long, jagged shadows from half-demolished buildings. They crept across a thousand-square-kilometer network of broken walls. The gleaming wreckage showed the wealth and pride of not only a thriving port—a financial and industrial center—but also the seat of the tri-galactic government.

Periodically meteorite storms pounded the planet, the first

star-stone blazed a trail and the others following in its wake. Beyond the city, a few intrepid farmers still planted crops. They tilled their fields with droid-manned equipment programmed to flee the storms and take cover in man-made caves.

Only the fast-growing crops and the spaceport remained above-ground on Agnar-Alpha. The hangars had been topped with fantastically tall, steeply pitched roofs that rose in concave curves to a sharp ridge. From the air they resembled sword blades.

The city had burrowed deep below the surface. People, business, industry, education centers, parks, grass, trees, lakes, and many of its wild animals all went below. Some came uninvited. A kilometer below the surface, backyard farmers complained of small, tree-climbing rodents destroying the fruit on their carefully nurtured trees.

How people could live below ground was a mystery to Lesson. He needed room, the space of the universe . . . and at the moment he wanted to quench his thirst.

Once he reached Siddah-II, he would have a drink at the Starflower, some conversation, then another drink.

*Hell, when did I ever have two drinks? Ten or a dozen, but two? It's not worth getting off the ship for two.* He needed a good drunk. He'd wake up wishing he'd died and not sure he hadn't, but why not? He'd been working his butt off! And for what? To turn his ship into an education center for a damn robot? And a power factory? The mechanical had been recharging himself.

He punched time-comp and noticed the ship behind him. It grayed too. Then everything faded from the screens as *Anubis* swooped into the oblivion of warped time.

"Come on over, buddy, and I'll buy you a drink. It might be the last one I buy anybody if that damn robot spy learned anything."

Reason was overcoming his blinding anger. Why worry? The droid found nothing incriminating in the storage registers. Lesson erased what he didn't want known. After thinking about it he decided to see exactly what the android was after. The printout would be proof to show Conek.

He punched the keys: "List all commands received by circuit connection."

As the answers clattered out, he read: "Commands by circuitry: three. Entered in Endovarian mathematics. . . ."

*First command: What is a ConekHayden?*

*Second command: List communication code of ConekHayden—answer incomplete.*

*Third command: Give meaning of word,* spy*—connection broken.*

*The following answers were given—*

Lesson shut off the transmission. He sat glaring out into the grayness. Okay, so the damn droid wasn't a spy. Endovarian math. So it was a refugee off the old ghoster. But Conek accepted the thing like a long-lost friend, yanking him—Lesson—back when it got in the computer. As if he —Lesson—were the stranger, after all the years they'd been together.

Lesson jumped up and stormed out of the bridge, stomped around the lounge for a couple of minutes, then went into the galley. He jerked open the cold box and stared inside. Nothing tempted his appetite; he slammed the panel shut. He seldom carried passengers, but since the Osalt built all their freighters to be multipurposed, he still had staterooms. A check told him what he already knew. They were still immaculate from the last time he was bored and wanted something to do on a long comp.

Putting on a breather mask, he went aft. There were always loose cargo straps lying about, shelving for special cargo to be taken down before the next shipment was loaded.

Oh-ho, what's this? He stared at the old wooden crate holding Conek's pack and grav-mattress. He shook his head, wondering why Conek had neglected to stow his gear. He took Conek's pack forward and opened the door to the locker in the captain's stateroom. He stared down at the bright blue allow shipping case and remembered what Conek had said.

The weapon in it was worth a fortune.

*A fortune!* His mind raced. Everything he'd ever dreamed of: women; booze anytime he wanted it; no ending up in a gutter sick, hungry, and broke. He'd have his own ship and the right to jettison any damn robot who got into his computers. Nobody could give him orders, either.

He still seethed at the way Conek acted when he wanted that stupid hunk of metal out of the control area. The kid owned the ship, sure, but Lesson had helped him get it back after Gerdozd had killed Tobard. Now Conek expected Lesson to play servant, maybe, to his computerized pile of tin.

Conek could have the robot and the damn ship too. With as much money as Conek expected the thing to bring, Lesson could buy his own vessel—hell, he could buy a whole fleet of ships. It served Conek right, and what could he do about it? Conek had found it as a result of smuggling, so who could he complain to?

There you are, Captain, all nice and neat, Lesson thought as he put the pack down by the carton. Not that the kid would ever see it again, he thought.

But exactly how did he go about selling a weapon he didn't understand and hadn't seen? He should open the case, find out what he had. And blow the hell out of the side of the ship? No, he'd leave it where it was until he could land on some deserted planet and experiment with it.

He took a deep breath, feeling the need to relax, to make plans. But the alarm sounded; the ship was coming out of time. He hurried to the control room. He thought of passing by the smuggler's bar but decided to stop, after all. With the certainty of all the liquor he wanted for a lifetime, his good drunk could wait. He needed to hear all the local rumors. Before any of his great dreams worked out, he'd have to sell the gun.

*Hmmph! So he took me up on it,* Lesson thought as he came out of time and saw the ship behind him appearing out of its envelope. The vessel was a DU-14 with two extra engine pods. He'd even followed from Agnar-Alpha. Not that he'd actually made the invitation, unless the communication switch had been left open. Didn't look like it.

Well, anybody can come to Siddah-II, he reasoned, and started down into the atmosphere. The other ship hung back but still followed him. Acting on a sudden impulse, he raised the nose and started up. As he cleared the atmosphere he kicked in the hyperspeed. The converted job stayed right on his tail.

"That sidewinder *is* following me," he shouted, and punched the time-comp for Agnar-Alpha. Behind him, the other ship grayed as he did.

He wondered why anyone would tail him. He could understand a Vladmn patrol, or if he were carrying some special cargo—the weapon! His mind jerked. But how could they know about it?

Maybe they didn't. Maybe they were just after anything they could get. Well, they weren't putting a grubby finger on the kid's gun. He'd see 'em in hell first!

Then he laughed out loud, thinking how quickly he'd given up a fortune—beautiful women and a ship of his own.

"Easy come, easy go," he muttered, and patted the top of the control panel. "And who'd want another ship when they can fly you, baby?"

When he came out of time over Agnar-Alpha, Port yelled at him for timing it too close.

New shift, he decided. Behind him, the converted light freighter came out of time.

Let's see what you can do with this, buddy. He requested clearance for the fueling pad and taxied in under the protective, tunnellike hangar. Once in, he waited his turn, since the only exit was through the refueling station. Behind him, two teacups from the Galux-Trav Shipping Company drew into line. Another three vessels were behind him when he went down to the clerk's office to sign his chit. He scanned the area, couldn't find the converted job, but he didn't expect it. Whoever they were, they wouldn't risk being caught in the tunnel when he took off. He could outdistance them with a full load of fuel.

He left the station and set Port to screaming as he made a low, strictly illegal hop to the hangar. With his shadow hanging somewhere above, expecting him to lift off right away, he and Conek would have time to make a plan.

The landing gear had just touched the pad when he flipped the activator to open the giant doors. They had only swung back a few meters when he swore and threw the switch in reverse. Old *Bucephalus* was gone. He was on his own.

He looked up and spotted light freighters coming down on either side of him. The converted job moved in on the left. To his right, he recognized Jon Slugarth's craft.

# CHAPTER Seven

Years ago Lesson had lost count of the times he cursed the distance between the abandoned government hangars and the rest of the spaceport. He habitually added to his list of complaints when he had difficulty getting a port taxi. But for the first time his safety, possibly his life, was endangered by the lack of law enforcement officials close-by.

To starboard and just a little ahead of him, the converted light freighter landed while Slug came down to port. They positioned their ships so he couldn't take off without risking his own life as well as theirs.

Just what the hell do they think they can do? he wondered, but in answer several things came to mind. With the right kind of torches they could burn through a hatch. He could be there to blast them when they came through the air lock, but they would have thought of that. Of course, he could call Port for help, probably get a reward for Slug, too, but one word from Slug and he'd lose the kid's play toy, and probably his life, when the other contrabanders caught up with him. Whatever he did would be up to him and *Anubis*.

"We can take 'em, baby." He patted the control panel. "We need maneuvering room—let's rocket."

Jamming full power to the main and emergency braking thrusters and planning hard, he shot backward, up. *Anubis* yawed as her blunt rear end met the resistance of the atmosphere.

"Lesson! What are you doing?" came the hysterical scream from Port.

He glanced at his rear screens and saw the tower directly in his path.

"Scratching an itch," he replied laconically as he yawed to starboard.

Port garbled a shrill command as Lesson comped into the grayness of oblivion, his destination a point in the vacuum of space. The thrusters screamed; every metal brace groaned as if it were in pain; decks, ceilings, and bulkheads vibrated. Even in the light atmosphere of Agnar-Alpha, few ships could stand such a strain.

"Sorry, old girl, but we've got a pressing date with a war," he said as the ship came to terms with his demands.

"We've got one surprise, baby. Then we'll have to fight for the rest of it." Ten light-years in space, he suddenly threw them out of time, coming back to conventional speeds with a lurch and more growling from the engines. Slewing a hundred and eighty degrees, he faced the Vladmn freighters when they came out of time. Homed in on *Anubis,* they popped back into conventional flight with the same suddenness. Their pilots were caught off-guard by the sudden exit from time and by the sight of the monster freighter bearing down on them. Against the blackness of deep space, *Anubis*'s gray-white bulk rapidly filled their view ports. In the clarity of vacuum, every detail stood out with surrealistic boldness. Gun ports on the Osalt freighter gaped open.

Lesson opened up with all ten forward guns. He completely missed the converted freighter, but three scores against Slug's ships gave it a sound rocking. He passed between them to let go with the rear guns. With no time to aim, he expected only to keep the confusion going.

With the port forward and braking thrusters fighting each other, he turned again while they swung on him. Slug swiveled as if he were on a stick. The converted job, caught by *Anubis*'s rear guns, spewed pieces of debris from its starboard side. The damaged ship dissolved to gray. Lesson concentrated on Slug, sweeping a wide pattern. He might not reach a vital spot, but he'd hit something.

"Come get your reward, you son of a spavined mule!" Lesson shouted.

His three blaster bursts jarred the pirate's ship as he flashed past. Lesson turned slightly to port, pouring on the rear fire before he swung around again. A jar and a looseness in the controls warned him that *Anubis* had been hit. He bore down on Slug for the third time. The small ship grayed into nothing.

"Coward!" Lesson yelled into the void of space."Yellerback! Front? Stomach? Oh, hell, where's that book?"

But he had no time for reading. *Anubis* slipped under him, the steering lost in the damage. The computer jangled a fire alarm. He punched in a brief time-comp, enough to kill the fire or find out if he couldn't handle it and, if he could, decide what to do next.

A quick glance at the computer reading confirmed what he thought. A blast from Slug had ruptured the hull, cutting the planing linkage. With a flip of a switch he secured the access to the rear hold and blew the air lock. Instantly the fire died in the vacuum.

He felt drained by the time he had checked the rest of the computer output. In the galley he opened a container of reconstituted mealyon juice and drank it automatically while he analyzed his problems, the original one, his fight with Conek, forgotten. The pirates trailing his every move was past history. Once they comped out, they were no longer able to home in on him. They could pick him up again on Agnar-Alpha. If he stayed away from his home port, they needed more than their share of luck to find him. But Slug knew he'd hit the Osalt ship. He knew Lesson would have to go down for repairs.

*They'll check all the obvious places, and I'm limited.*

The biggest trouble with the Osalt freighters was the lack of spare parts when something went wrong. He needed a place where he could have parts machine-tooled.

He had to protect the kid's what's-it at the same time.

# CHAPTER Eight

"Be Lex's good girl and let's ta-a-ake it up." Since Tobard's death, Conek no longer used the diminutive of his middle name except when he talked to *Bucephalus*. With her, it still seemed to fit. He leaned back and winked at Cge, who stood in the copilot's seat where a newly rigged harness strapped the little android in place.

Below the rising freighter, the loading crew appeared to grow smaller. Conek knew they watched until *Bucephalus* disappeared in the clouds.

He had arrived early to pick up his shipment. By experience, he knew he would have difficulties getting a full cargo on board. Unless the loading foreman knew the Osalt freighter, the request for three times the usual loaders was either scoffed at or ignored. Fainthearted loaders sometimes took off when the monster freighter came down, causing irritating delays.

He smiled as he thought of the foreman below, who called a halt to the loading when *Bucephalus* held just over a quarter of its weight capacity. Used to people thinking in terms of Vladmn ships, Conek was patient but firm, and while he checked and tallied the increasing weight, the foreman stood back, shaking his head. The man was convinced they would have to take most of the load back into storage.

Conek gazed through the view ports, admiring the density and makeup of the cloud cover surrounding Arrin. Long-distance spying was practically impossible. The planet was a perfect place for a pickup of contraband. Timing in and out under the clouds, he would have to sit down on another ship to be discovered. *Bucephalus* plowed through the mist until the atmosphere thinned. Conek slipped the ship into time-comp.

"Great is the power of the Quinta," Conek muttered as the gray closed in on the view ports. "We're off on another exciting bookkeeping run."

"So many containers must hold a great number of books," Cge replied.

"Yeah," Conek agreed without enthusiasm.

He was stupid, he decided. Good money, no trouble, what else could he ask for? Getting chased and shot at was no fun. He was safe from the Vladmn patrols since he had filed the claim on the ghoster. Now he had a legitimate reason to be on Beldorph. Later he'd drop back and make sure Dursig picked up the shipment. And every delivery increased his bankroll.

Before long, he'd be enjoying downtime on—He reached in the pocket of his flight suit and pulled out the small cheap holo-cube, a resort agency giveaway. The name *Mauvenier* glittered above the scenes of gambling tables, fine restaurants, and fabulous aquatic scenery where robospheres carried beautiful women—and men—beneath the surface for tours.

His only real problem was Lesson. Conek had checked some of his haunts, but no one had heard anything about his pilot, and the old drunk had never stayed away this long before.

He wouldn't be any good until he sobers up, anyway, Conek thought, trying to force his irritation to cover his worry.

He set the time-comp to pop back into conventional flight mili-units from Arrin and stayed at the controls until he emerged into deep space again. Scanning a full three hundred and sixty degrees, Conek made certain he was not being followed. He'd made a habit of checking his back trail since Gella had told him about Slug.

When they were back in comp again, heading straight for Beldorph, Conek stood up, reaching over to unfasten Cge's seat belt. The android could have done it himself, but he always seemed unwilling, wanting Conek to do it for him.

"Too bad you're so short," Conek said as he lifted the robot to the floor. "It would be handy if you could take over the galley chores."

"It is bad to be short," Cge said as he followed Conek into the lounge, across it, and down the passage to the galley.

"No, I didn't say that. I said you're too short to cook."

"You would cook me?"

"Oh, forget it!" Conek reached for a cup and pushed the button to fill it with a hot fiene brew.

"It is erased," Cge replied. He rolled to the doorway, leaned forward, and looked out into the hall. "Only you will have cafina?"

"Just me!" Conek snapped, and plunked the cup on the counter, sloshing liquid on the polished surface. *Why in the hell didn't I sell him to Bentian?* he wondered. At first he enjoyed watching the droid try to imitate him and Lesson, but the mechanical mimic didn't know when to quit. Now he wanted to drink—and eat too, maybe. Squatting, leaning back against the counter, he grabbed Cge's arm and pulled him around so that they were eye to sensor panel.

"You and I are going to get something straight."

"Straight?" Cge's panel blinked slowly.

"Straight," Conek repeated. "Now you"— he jabbed his finger at Cge's main body cylinder—"are an android. I"—he thumped his chest with a fist—"am a human. If you want to scoot around playing games and being a clown, that's up to you. It's pretty damn silly, but I don't guess there's any law against it. I'm not sure about this business of you having your own bed. I don't think droids are made for lying down. . . . " Conek patiently went through a long list of what he considered Cge's misunderstandings of the differences between life-forms and machinery. ". . . And while I don't charge my batteries because I don't have any, you don't eat or drink."

Cge stood with slowly blinking panels, absorbing what Conek had said. He nodded, his entire body moving in the affirmative motion. "Androids do not drink fiene. Humans do—they drank before."

"Who?" Conek asked, puzzled by Cge's reply.

"They." Cge pointed toward the passage.

Conek raised his eyes as his hand went for his blaster. Major Andro Avvin and Quinta Norden stepped into the doorway. Conek froze, caught between his defensive reflexes and his recognition of the intruders; for a moment his mind seemed to shut off.

"Educating your little companion?" Smirking, Andro strolled into the galley. His eyes danced in anticipation of Conek's reaction.

Conek straightened slowly, trying to keep his face blank, but he could feel his fury snapping in his eyes. His contract called for the delivery of arms, nothing else. While he considered the advantages of ejecting both his passengers through an air lock, he tried to keep his anger under control.

"I haven't kept up with the latest laws. Tell me, Quinta, is stowing away legal now?"

Norden read Conek's controlled anger; her eyes turned, speculating, as she gave it her own meaning. "Are you in a position to report us, Captain?"

Conek shook his head. "Shame on you, Quinta—consorting with undesirables, picking up their bad habits. In case you don't know the vernacular, that's called blackmail."

Andro knelt before the droid. "Cge, you need to educate your captain in thoughtfulness. While they play their wit games, I'm dying of thirst. Where *is* the fiene?"

Cge rolled up to a panel concealing the disposable cups. He then gave Andro step-by-step instructions on how to get both the cup and the fiene. While the major patiently allowed the droid to offer advice and admonitions, Conek led Norden into the lounge and offered her a seat.

Before sitting, she gave it a cursory but deprecating glance, as if it might be contaminated. For a guest—and a nonpaying passenger, at that—she certainly cared little for her host and captain.

She was a knockout, he decided. He'd enjoy having her aboard if she could be pleasant and if she wasn't a Quinta, determined to put him behind bars at the first excuse. He didn't like her half-smile; it seemed as if she were reading his mind.

"You're not too happy to see us, Captain."

"On the contrary, Quinta. Surprise is the prevailing emotion. Traveling with you will be more interesting than spending all my time with Cge."

She laughed. "You're angry and want to know why I'm here."

"That's strange? You're not my usual type of passenger."

She tucked her feet under her, and clasping the arms of the lounger for balance, she leaned forward.

"Captain, I must see Tratha Dursig. Bentian should have come, but he couldn't slip away for a few cycles without raising curiosity. Your ship is the only way I can reach the Gordotl without attracting the Amal's attention." She paused, assessing the expression on his face. Her eyes narrowed. "You *weren't* going to Beldorph—"

"Stow it!" Conek snapped. "Go read the input on the time-comp. The next planet you see will be dry, sandy, and the second cousin to hell!"

"So, I'm sorry," Norden answered crisply. Her apology was as abject as a volcano was humble. "I won't go into the political reasoning, but suffice it to say that we're aware the Gordotl feel Vladmn has ignored their problems—"

"How can you say that?" Conek's sarcasm leaked out with every spilled word, but damn it, he liked Dursig, the tratha, leader of the Gordotl. "Why should they expect the Vladmn government to protect their rights, just because they pay for it in taxes?"

She matched his resentment glare for glare. "Captain there

is a little more to running a tri-galactic government than you apparently understand."

"Forgive me, Quinta. Obviously it's not doing the job people think they elected you for."

For a moment he thought she'd point her finger and strike him down with the lightning of Vladmn power, but with a force of will strong enough to push the ship through space, she shook her feelings away.

"You know the laws of Vladmn—you use them to your advantage often enough. We have no planetary jurisdiction unless Dursig allows it."

"He won't."

"The thereil is too vital to risk."

"No more so today than two years ago," Conek argued. He was a fool, fighting for a chance to lose his best customer, but in the three years he'd worked with Dursig, he'd learned to care about those big four-legged, four-armed humanoids. And caring was dangerous in his business.

"Two years ago Gordotl wasn't being raided. Since the Amal denies having anything to do with it, we can step in without publicly flaunting them," Norden's smile was sly. "They can't fight us openly, either. You could lose your trade if we can open the shipping lines back to Gordotl."

Conek shrugged. "I'd have to lower my markup a bit, but then I wouldn't have to worry about getting shot at." And he could wave good-bye to Beldorph. He hated that planet.

"Well, Captain, I'm offering Dursig the protection of our ground forces. That's the reason for my trip."

"And is the major the strong-arm of the Vladmn defenses protecting the Gordotl?" Conek suppressed a laugh as he thought of the small, effeminate Andro among the big, stolid humanoids.

"Captain, Andro is perfectly capable," she snapped.

"Of what?" Conek returned curtly, irritated at her tendency to take sudden offense. But battling on any other subject was better than any further discussion of her purpose.

"Why, at being a nephew, dear."

Andro chose that moment to walk in, carrying a tray with three cups. His gaze moved between Conek and Norden, and he chose to ignore the tension. "You of all people should know the Gordotl's stone-age attitude about women. They'd think it highly improper for a single woman to travel without the protection of a male family member." He handed a cup to Conek and one to Norden. Both reached automatically, still eyeing each other like two dogs circling for a fight. Andro's laughter trilled, falsetto-high.

"After all, I am a man, dear, or hadn't you noticed?"

The effect on Norden was electric. Conek sat back and concentrated on keeping his brows lowered as she lectured Andro, threatening him with being deep-spaced at the hands of the captain. Andro sat meekly under her censure, only answering with facial expressions. When she threatened him with an uncertain fate at the hands of the Gordotl, he appeared so interested that she started a fresh spate of warnings. Conek hurriedly left the lounge before he lost control and laughed.

Not that he felt much like it. He'd wanted to unload his cargo, do some concentrated searching for the ghoster, flag it, and be on his way to find Lesson. He hadn't heard a word from his pilot since the old guy took off in a huff. And that damn weapon was on *Anubis*. He wanted to get rid of it. Where? Anywhere, just so it was safe.

Years before, he had removed the furnishings from the stateroom next to the galley and set up a small workshop. He'd taken refuge in the work area and was tinkering with a sensor when Andro slipped in and shut the door.

"Whew!" Andro rolled his eyes to the ceiling and flipped a limp-wristed hand in an affected motion, wiping sweat from his brow. "You *owe* me one, dearie."

"Thanks," Conek said, turning back to the sensor. "For nothing. You brought her aboard."

"Me?" Andro sounded incredulous. "*I* don't bring *her* anywhere—she makes her own decisions. I just don't want to get deep-spaced over her suspicions. You're up to something—she knows it and I do, too, but getting thrown out of an air lock in the great black beyond isn't my way of solving the problem."

Conek turned to glance at the man behind him. The effeminate pose had disappeared. Instead, Conek caught the steely glint of speculation in Andro's eyes.

During the Beldorph night they unloaded the arms at the smuggler's cave.

Finding the ghoster wasn't so easy. Conek wore away a standard day on a fruitless search. He circled and criss-crossed, checking both visually and by sensor, but found nothing.

Norden's suspicion grew with every hour. She was ready to call in the patrols when Conek lost all patience.

"If you think you can do better, get up here and try!" he yelled at her. He hadn't expected her to take him up on it, but he found himself teaching her to handle the big Osalt ship. He was surprised to find she was a good pilot and learned quickly.

All during the trip the major tried to relieve the tension with relentless chatter, but Cge brought the only sense of normalcy. His untiring search for someone to entertain with his childish games was their safety valve. The "kew-w's" the sounds of his mock battles sounded up and down the corridor and from behind the loungers as he shot it out with anyone who took the time to join him in his play.

After two days he located the ghoster. Because of the alien alloy, the sensors were unable to pick it up from a distance of more than five kilometers.

Using the braking thrusters, Conek created a crater in the sand, exposing a tear and a blasted hatch in the ship's hull. With *Bucephalus* squatting over the hole like a huge bird on a nest of eggs, Conek attached a flexible corridor from his ship to the hatch and went back into the lounge. Over the objections of both Andro and Norden, he decided to allow himself the luxury of a drink and a rest before exploring. He wanted to talk them out of boarding if possible.

In the lounger across from him, Norden curled, her knees under her. She was luscious in a pale blue work suit. The significance of her clothing, her preparation to assist in checking out the ship, bothered Conek. He would have been happier if she looked great in something else.

"I'm taking Cge with me when I board," he said. "If there's anything to see and it's safe, I'll come back for you."

Andro's bottom lip came out in a pout. "I want to see it." He saw Conek's frown and blushed slightly. Both the capable administrator and the effeminate pose dissolved. He sounded like a kid deprived of an outing.

"Dammit, I'm usually stuck behind a desk, and I've never been on a ghoster," he said gruffly.

Conek laughed. "Good God! They're no different from any other ship, except they're usually empty and nothing works. I just put a claim in for cover. Some salvager probably looted it in space. They usually do."

He couldn't afford to have the Quinta snooping in case there had been more than one weapon on board.

He'd check out the ship, report everything he saw as a potential danger. By the time he'd finished, Norden would think it was worth her life to touch the hull. He hoped Dursig showed up soon. After seeing the Gordotl, she'd lose interest and want to return to Agnar-Alpha.

But as usual, he figured without Norden.

"We can tell if salvagers looted it," she said. "Cge, did anyone board the ship before the crash?"

Cge gave his full-body nod. "Affirmative. We were boarded before we left"—he whistled tentatively, his panel slowly flickering in what Conek called his thoughtful attitude—"Skooler, as I compute it in Vladmn Standard."

"Skooler? Never mind—I mean, did anyone board while you were in space? After your people were dead?"

Cge stood in the center of the lounge, rolling back and forth in a small area while his panel slowed again. "Dead—without life—no longer a life-form—" His panel flashed, resumed its normal blinking speed, and he stopped rolling. "After the masters were dead, nothing came aboard the ship. And the masters did not move about the ship. Cge was alone—all alone." Cge's panel dimmed, then brightened again. "After a long time, twenty-five charges of my storage batteries, it crashed."

Norden suddenly leaned forward until Conek thought she would fall out of the chair. "Are you in need of a charge?"

"No. Only a quarter of my storage capacity is empty."

"A quarter..." Conek calculated aloud. "He charged on *Anubis*, not fully. That was thirty days ago—between a hundred and twenty and a hundred and eighty standard days to a charge—eight to twelve standard *years*! And appeared, like it popped out of warp."

"Captain!" Norden's voice carried all the authority of her position. "I am *going* aboard that ship! Vladmn discovered the time-comp on an alien ship. Who knows what might be aboard?"

No fair. He'd used that argument on Lesson. Now she used it on him.

"We could stumble over a destruct device."

Norden wasn't in a mood to be cautious. "Captain, if you set off a destruction charge, I promise we won't complain. But it's not likely unless it's a warship. Cge, what kind of ship is it?"

Cge whirled around to face Conek, his panel slowing again.

"Did it carry freight like us? Was it full of people, or a warship?"

Cge answered slowly. "I was not programmed to know, I think. It carried many containers—not many masters. They left me alone."

"Cargo—a freighter," Norden said crisply as she rose. "If you're worried about your claim, Captain, Vladmn will honor it. We'll want a chance to examine everything."

"Well..." Conek objected. His plans didn't include unloading and carting around alien junk.

Norden's eyes narrowed in suspicion. "Just what did you plan to do with it?"

Conek thought of telling her the truth. He expected to leave most of the cargo on the ship, after he checked for any more of those damn weapons. Multicolored mixing bowls turned him off. She knew how to send his temper up like an extensible antennae. Vaguely he saw Andro shift from a relaxed position into a theatrical pose.

"Oh, just think, dearie." Andro's voice rose an octave. "You could be rich and famous. May I say I knew you?"

Conek held back his smile as Norden rounded on her nephew, rising to the bait again. Conek decided Andro shouldn't take all the blame.

"That depends on how *well* you say you knew me." Norden's head swiveled from Andro's direction to his.

The major threw a glance at his aunt and raised his eyebrows. "My dear, you show the ignorance of a one-sided education."

"Andro, behave," she shouted at him. "Sorry, Captain, but I do need him."

Conek could feel her effort to bring the conversation back to what he intended to do with the cargo, but Andro had successfully turned the subject and was determined to prevent another argument.

"Oh, yes, I'm needed." He stood and stretched lazily. "So protect me, because *I'm* boarding that ship."

Conck knew when to give in. With Cge at his side, he led the way. They brought lights, but their illuminators were unnecessary. Some energy source continued to feed the glowing panels along the walls. The sand, blown in through the blasted hatch, made rough going for Cge, so Conek carried him past it. When he put the droid down again, Cge stuck close to his side. Cge's blinking panel showed his agitation.

"Where are we now?" Conek asked him.

"Cge does not know." The panels blinked faster. "Cge should know. Cge does not remember."

Conek stopped, squatting in the corridor. He caught Cge's arm and turned him around. "Okay, bud, what's the trouble?"

"Cge's programming storages overheat," the droid answered softly. "Cge cannot get an output on what he wants to know." One small metallic hand reached up, touching the access panel at the back of his top cylinder.

Conek stood up, gazing up the passage. "Just what I always needed. A droid with a headache."

"What's the matter?" Andro, who had stopped to inspect one of the illuminating panels, came running up.

"I thought Cge could warn us of trouble," Conek replied.

"It seems he can't, so we're on our own. If it's a warship, we get out, and *fast*."

Conek grew more cautious by the minute. He had expected openings off the passage, and he felt turned around. Remembering the angle of the ship's descent, he thought they uncovered a hatch on the side, but the length of the passage had confused him. They approached an intersection of corridors and stopped, staring first one way and then the other.

"Are my eyes deceiving me," Norden asked, "or is this thing more than three kilometers long?"

Andro moved closer to Conek, Norden, and Cge, so they all stood in a huddle. Andro looked around. "A pretty fair estimate." He was almost whispering.

Conek shook his head hard, not really believing the evidence of his eyes. "I saw it come down, but without any frame of reference I had no idea it was so *big*."

# CHAPTER Nine

"Which way, lovies?" Andro stared toward the front of the Skooler vessel, pointedly indicating his preference.

Conek shook his head, vetoing Andro's choice.

"To the rear. If its a warship, we get off in a hurry—then you can send in your own people, Quinta. I'm curious, not stupid."

And he meant it. He wanted to keep the knowledge of those weapons to himself, but he wasn't greedy enough to die for them or it.

But the ghoster seemed to be a freighter. Down the center, passage hatches opened into huge storage holds; the first three were still airtight. When Conek dislodged the locking bolts, the big doors slammed open. The force of the condensed atmosphere within nearly knocked them off their feet.

Inside, a few of the crates were tumbled around, but most were undisturbed by the beating the ship had taken. Conek tapped gently against one of the cartons. They were interlocked. Restraining cables, two of which had broken, added more protection.

"They planned for some rough landings," Norden commented.

"Well, love, they got one," Andro replied.

Conek looked for cartons similar to the one that had contained the weapon he'd found. He checked the markings. "Cge, is that a packing list?"

The droid's sensor panel followed the direction of Conek's finger, his panels flickering rapidly. "I do not think I was programmed to know."

"Well, read it and tell us what it says," Norden ordered.

"Read?" Cge bent backward, blinking up at her.

"Certainly you can read!" Norden snapped. "Droid programming always includes—"

"Cge malfunctions!" The droid gave a squeal as a crackle of shorting circuits came from his top cylinder. His sensor panel went dark.

"What happened?" Norden knelt by Andro, staring at the darkened panel.

"I'd say you caused him to draw on bad circuits." Andro suggested.

Cge's panel lit up again, and he turned his head from one to the other of the humans bent over him.

"Cge malfunctioned." He sounded surprised.

"Then don't try to read, just—"

"Stop it!" Conek said, interrupting the Quinta. "I don't want his insides blasted apart—then he's not worth a milicrana." The last he added to foil the memory of how worried he'd been when Cge malfunctioned. Well, he had a right to look after his property, didn't he? That droid was worth a fistful of money.

"Cge, you go back aboard *Bucephalus*."

"Cge wants to stay with ConekHayden," the android objected. He put a period to his desire by suddenly retracting his wheels. The metal hemispheres of his feet hit the deck and rang like dull bells.

Conek frowned down at the droid, whose panels were flashing fast enough to bring on another blowout. "Okay, but dammit, don't *think*!"

In the fourth compartment the outer shell had been ripped. The crates had tumbled about, and judging by the amount of cargo in the other holds, a quarter of the contents had passed through the gap. Four large containers blocked the hole, and the rest were crowded around them like water against a dam.

Andro had just walked the length of the hold when he suddenly pulled his blaster and jumped back. He stood staring toward the hull of the ship. Conek drew his weapon and moved closer.

His path between the jumbled cartons brought him around a tall stack of cargo and within touching distance of a huge droid. The almost human shape, the black, unadorned metal surface, and the mindlessness behind the panel sent adrenaline trilling through his muscles.

He struggled to remember a robot was a tool, not a monster. His hand seemed reluctant to holster his blaster.

"It's harmless, but it *is* a big one." He stared up at the two-meter-tall droid. One arm and one leg were trapped behind a carton. Part of its body formed part of the dam at the tear. Apparently it had been in the same place since the initial rupture.

"A ship-repair and loading droid—his energy storage is empty." Cge had rolled up behind Conek and gazed at the huge robot calmly.

"I told you not to think," Conek snapped. He compared the two droids, their similarities and differences. Cge, small and less human-shaped in his short, barrellike construction, held no feeling of menace. Then his panel was constantly flickering, almost equivalent to human expression.

"I do not *always* malfunction." Cge turned and rolled swiftly toward the passage, leaving behind him an impression of injured dignity.

"He seems normal again," Andro remarked.

Conek watched Cge roll away, then he turned back, assessing the huge robot thoughtfully. As they explored, they saw others, all inactive, their storages empty. Without bothering to open all the compartments, they turned toward the front of the vessel. The bridge was huge, but the controls were few. None of the three humans could make any sense of the levers and their strange markings.

Norden opened a hatch to the compartment next to the control room. She gave a choked cry.

Blaster in his hand again, Conek ran to see what she'd discovered.

Inside, an alien corpse lay on what Conek thought to be a bed, but he knew he was fitting what he saw to his own reference.

And the dead creature didn't fit his experiences. Nearly three meters across and four high, it had a pearlike shape with more than a dozen long, apparently boneless appendages. Somehow the atmosphere in the compartment had preserved it, but by the time Conek reached the doorway, it had disintegrated until nothing but the basic shape and size was still discernible.

Cge had followed Conek. The little droid pressed close to Conek's leg. Cge gave a series of strange whistles, moving up and down the musical scale on discordant notes.

The stench from the compartment invaded their filters, and Norden slammed the hatch, bolting it again. Andro put both hands on his stomach and rushed down the passage. With a gulp Norden ran in his wake.

Conek, disgusted by the smell but not made sick by it, squatted down in the passage and braced his back against a bulkhead. Cge tried to imitate him; Conek considered the droid.

"What did you say to your dead master?"

"I have a new master now, one that will not leave me alone. I will stay with ConekHayden."

"On Skooler, were you allowed to tell your master what you'd do?" Conek regretted the question, afraid the reference would throw Cge into another short circuit. But the droid seemed calm as he gave the three rapid blinks. Conek had learned to expect trouble following those three flashes.

"A droid should always obey his master, but I malfunction."

"Don't carry that trick too far!" Conek shifted, his mind

returning to his budding idea. "You may be able to help me. If I activated those big droids, could you handle them?"

"Handle?"

"Command."

Cge had to stand to nod in rapid bows. "If you command me, I can"—his panel whirled thoughtfully—"translate."

"We'll get one aboard *Bucephalus* and recharge it. I'll go for a re-grav truck."

"Unnecessary. I can recharge him and he can walk aboard," Cge answered, patting his front panel.

In a forward compartment they found a droid lying on the floor, but otherwise he seemed undamaged. Cge rolled up to it, opened the front panels on both it and himself, and fastened its charger cable into his own.

"Now don't give him too much," Conek instructed Cge. He suddenly lost enthusiasm for what had seemed like a good idea. The monster would be on its feet and moving. That big machine could turn mean—he pulled his gun and aimed at the sensor panels feeling a little foolish in the face of Cgc's calm.

"Just enough to get him going a bit," Conek said, repeating his warning.

The big panel lit slowly. The head turned toward Cge, who whistled to it as he removed the giant's cable from his battery. Rolling back out of the way, the little droid whistled as the huge arms moved. The hulking robot got slowly to his feet.

Unlike Cge, the labor droid could move his head up and down as well as from side to side. He turned his sensor panel on Cge and whistled. Cge gave an answering bleep, and the robot turned toward Conek, who stepped back, raising his blaster.

"Tell him to keep away from me."

"He knows you are the master. He will keep the information in his memory banks."

"Well, uh—you keep reminding him in case he forgets." Conek moved closer to the door, wondering what he had done. The black metallic head swiveled slowly; the length of time between flashes of the sensor panel were entirely different from Cge's speedy little flickers.

"He cannot forget," Cge assured Conek. "He is not like me. He will not malfunction."

"By the speed of his blinks, he's going to sleep any minute," Conek observed. "Are you sure you gave him enough power to get aboard *Bucephalus*?"

Cge nearly lost his balance, tilting back to gaze up at the labor droid. "He has sufficient for a Beldorph day if he does no hard labor. Do we activate more now?" Cge followed his question with several rapid little bows as he nodded. He wanted them activated again.

Conek considered the idea. It made him a bit nervous for the big powerful robot to stand staring at him, but he knew the Vladmn droids did the same while awaiting orders. The big robot wasn't a threat—at least no more than Norden.

Since she had seen the vessel and they opened a few transport crates, Norden insisted all the cargo must be taken to the scientific laboratories on Radach-I. If he refused, she'd call in government cargo ships and have them haul it.

Sticky fingers might grab the valuable stuff. And he wanted to check the cargo for any more weapons. To keep her satisfied, he had to fill the holds on *Bucephalus* as soon as possible and get off Beldorph when Dursig arrived. He decided to risk the robots. If they were operable, he could load in a few units what would take cycles otherwise.

"How many jolts can you hand out before going dry?" he asked Cge.

"Jolts?"

Conek took a deep breath and repeated his request without the slang. Cge took time to consider, and Conek watched with fascination. So droids counted on their fingers too.

"Fifteen, and I would still have ten cycles of power," Cge answered.

"Oh, no!" Conek said. "Nine and you recharge immediately. Don't you dare go limp on me with these things walking around."

* * *

Conek strode into the forward hold of the *Bucephalus*, followed by Cge and ten blue-black steel robots. The labor droids recognized the recharging sockets on the wall. The first three pulled out their cables and forced the single pronged ends into the smaller, two-holed sockets. Two socket housings cracked under the force, but the slight hum of transferring power was even with no sound of broken circuits. Conek would have to make new fittings.

"I will wait here and recharge also," Cge said.

"There's a separate mess for the skipper. Come on, it's the captain's table for you. Tell your buddies to take a nap after dinner."

Cge's flicker slowed. Conek mentally rephrased his order, but Cge turned, whistled a command, and led the way to the air lock.

"So you're catching on to my lingo," Conek said as he followed.

Cge gave him three rapid blinks. "I'm making tracks in that direction."

To Conek's amusement, Norden lost her cool demeanor and showed a very human anger over his activation of the droids and his announced intention of keeping them as his labor force. Cge accidentally played peacemaker by telling Andro there were three whose energy storages had lost power to accept a charge. Norden overheard. When Conek agreed to allow her to take them to the Institute, she calmed down, but Cge panicked.

"I'm not paying for the investigation," Conek informed her. "And when the big brains finish poking around, I want them back." The last he said to calm Cge, then regretted it. *You idiot!* he thought, *You're supposed to be finding a buyer for him, not giving him a family!*

Norden pushed her superiority button. "I can assure you, Captain, you will have them back!" With a snap she fastened her face mask and pushed through the air lock. In seconds she rushed back into the lounge, her face as pale as a white dwarf. Her voice trembled. "They're so *big*!"

The sun had set on Beldorph when Conek, Norden, and Andro returned to the ghoster. Behind Andro came the hum of wheels as Cge and his crew of big droids arrived, ready to work. Before they left *Bucephalus,* Conek had opened the hatches to the rear holds and explained to Cge how he wanted the crates placed. Later he would correct the little droid's ideas of shipping, but he wanted to use the maximum space in the minimum time. If Cge could follow his directions, they'd be on their way at dawn.

He opened crate after crate, but if other alien weapons were aboard, he didn't find them. Several holds had gaping tears in their outer walls. Some of the cargo had been lost in space, and the gun he'd found was in one of the smaller cartons. Any others were probably floating in the vastness of space. If they were, the chances of them being found was so negligible as to be almost nonexistent.

Dursig, hurry up. He sent his thought out on the winds, wanting the big Gordotl to show up before Norden discovered more than he wanted her to.

While they loaded the Osalt freighter, Dursig landed. Conek left the droids under Cge's supervision and went to meet his client and friend.

He was curious about how Norden would react. Only a privileged few in Vladmn had ever seen the Gordotl, since they kept to themselves. Because they were so reclusive, wild stories had circulated from time to time, including the most prevalent when a species stayed completely to themselves: that they were so repugnant, the other peoples couldn't stand to look at them.

Norden had heard the stories and had steeled herself so strongly, her eyes widened when the tratha entered the lounge. He stood a head taller than Conek, who was tall by human standards. From a strictly frontal view he could have been a large human. But as he turned slightly, the thickness of his body and the second muscular set of arms and legs showed he wasn't.

Like all the Gordotl, Dursig's face, when he removed his

helmet, was gravely handsome. His even features could have been carved at the time the Alexander, for whom Conek was named, rode the first *Bucephalus* into Persia.

The Gordotl were intimidating in size and strength, full of slow ceremony and gentle, formal speech.

Using all four hands, Dursig unhurriedly removed his helmet and crossed to Conek. He gave the human the honor of greeting him in the Gordotl custom of friendship, by clasping him on the shoulders. Conek felt as if he'd been grabbed by a crowd.

"How is my friend, Captain Hayden," he asked in Vladmn Standard.

"Couldn't be better..." Conek mouthed all the proper words the tratha expected to hear and then introduced Norden. To give her deserved credit, she didn't lose a millimeter of Vladmn authority, though she had to tilt her head back to look up at Dursig.

As soon as Andro was introduced, Conek left them to their discussion. She wouldn't have much luck in changing the stoic mind of thc Gordotl. Knowing Norden, if her plans didn't come off, he'd be the one she'd accuse if she could lay the blame on him.

No matter what happened, that woman seemed out to get him.

# CHAPTER TEN

Weeks later, with Cge in tow, Conek made a special trip to the institute on Radach-I. He disembarked from a public lighter when it landed to disgorge a load of passengers. Conek worked his way through the crowds at the public spaceport, bypassing the queues gathering by sight-seeing guides. The scientific planet was famous for its futuristic exhibits and artificial gardens. The amusement parks drew visitors from all over the three galaxies.

Conek hated traveling by public transport, but ever since boarding the ghoster, he had been constantly on the go, carrying arms to the cave and bringing out loads of alien cargo.

Conek regretted Gella's one-tracked ambition to take revenge on Slug. If she had listened to reason, he could have put her to work hauling freight on the legitimate side of his business. Carrying arms for the Vladmn government hadn't prevented the need for a legal cover.

*Bucephalus* was docked on Agnar-Alpha, awaiting a thorough maintenance check. Conek preferred to stay with his ship, but the demands on his time were too urgent. With every shipment the Institute became more anxious for the next. Four pieces of medical equipment brought off the Skooler ship would advance the constant battle against disease and pestilence on overcrowded worlds. He'd collect a bundle, but the what and why was a lot of scientific jargon he didn't understand.

At the moment he had no interest in his royalties. Cge's malfunctions were more frequent. Conek caught him standing as if in a stupor, his panel lights nearly out. A little shake brought a hum from his circuits, and he picked up his chatter in mid-sentence. When it happened for the fifth time on Agnar-Alpha, Conek decided to bring him to the Institute without waiting for a scheduled trip.

Once there, he decided he should have waited. Once the chief security agent at the laboratory learned Cge originally came from the ghoster, the agent tried to declare Cge a part of the salvage. They were engaged in a yelling match when Norden walked in, followed by Bentian.

"Tell him Cge is not a part of the salvage contract!" Conek shouted as soon as he saw the female Quinta.

"How about 'hello' first?" Norden asked.

"Hello, Quinta! Now tell this idiot about Cge!"

The red-faced agent stood up behind his desk. "That android is salvage!"

"Hello, Chief Sornick." Norden ignored the anger on both sides.

"Good day, Quinta. Quinta, this pirate—pilot—"

"Sorry, Chief Sornick," Bentian interrupted. He had been standing behind Norden but stepped forward and patted Cge on the shoulder. "The captain keeps *all* the robots, especially this little one. That's our agreement. Even the three here for study are only loaned to us temporarily."

"But—"

Norden waved away the chief agent's objections, leaving the man red-faced and angry. She chose a small chair, one that suited her diminutive size, and gave her attention to Conek, measuring his possible motives.

"Why are you here?"

Conek was still irritated with Chief Sornick and wanted to

tell the Quinta to mind her own damn business. Why wasn't she running the territory instead of constantly harassing him? He pushed the temptation aside. He just wanted Cge repaired so he could get back to his shipping on schedule. He explained why he'd come.

Quinta Bentian had been the first to offer to buy Cge, and he still seemed to be interested. He had called the droid over to a chair and was teaching him the old custom of shaking hands. He listened to Conek and glanced at Chief Sornick.

"Ask Dr. Sardo to step in here. He can take the droid to his laboratory."

"Cge will stay with ConekHayden," the droid piped up and whipped behind Conek's chair.

Bentian was still trying to coax Cge out into the room again when the door opened and a short, rotund human entered. He looked as if he had arrived by accident, his mind left somewhere in his wanderings. When the doctor's gaze fell on Cge, he snapped alert. Ignoring the rest of the company, he went directly to the droid.

Norden explained the problem, but her urgency put Conek on the alert. ". . . And return him as soon as possible. The captain will be leaving by unit six, and he'll want the droid."

Dr. Sardo coaxed, commanded, and finally had to pull Cge along by the arm before he got the robot into the passage. Conek gave up both reason and orders after the third try and let the doctor manage alone.

Once the door closed, Bentian turned official.

"You led us a merry chase, Captain. We were on our way to Beldorph to see you when we learned you'd come here."

"The way you chase around after me, I wonder who runs the government."

"Unless we do something quickly, there may not be one," Bentian returned.

Conek knew the Institute had found out about the weapons. He'd checked every carton, looking for any other wierd guns. Somehow he'd missed one—two—a dozen. But he couldn't let the Quinta and Chief Sornick know what he was thinking.

Conek raised his eyebrows. "Ouch."

"Apt, under the circumstances," Norden said. "I'm afraid your salvage isn't all blessing."

"I heard we found some great medical devices," Conek replied. "Don't tell me we have a crate of diseases too."

"No, something able to kill a lot faster."

"Go on," he prompted. "Just remember, I didn't manufacture whatever it was, I'm just bringing it in."

"It's a weapon..." Bentian said, explaining the gun. Most of what he said, Conek knew already, but not that they came in different sizes with tremendous differences in power. "And a model the size of a regular gun on a patrol ship—" He clasped his hands tightly.

"Could disintegrate a planet," Norden finished for him.

For the first time since the subject of the weapon had come up, Conek was surprised. Not pleasantly.

"Handy little gadget," Conek observed, still pretending to be ignorant. "I'd like to see that little toy."

"You have, Captain," Norden replied, nearly knocking him out of his chair with surprise. "Or possibly you didn't. Andro and I opened the crates; maybe we closed them again —I don't remember."

"We found two," Andro spoke up. "You've brought in one."

"At least one is still out there," Bentian said. "There could be more, how many we've no idea, but one is enough to put us in peril if it falls in the wrong hands."

"I'll get it right away," Conek said, deciding his best course was the appearance of cooperation, since he already knew there was one they hadn't found, the one he'd left on *Anubis*.

"Captain, we'll want the laboratory people to collect the rest of the cargo."

"Suits me," Conek agreed without hesitation. He hated unloading the ghoster. He'd only taken on the job to keep the weapons a secret, and now that the Quinta knew about them, he was willing to let someone else do the work. If more of those gizmos were around they were likely to go off in somebody's face, and he didn't want it to be his face. Maybe he'd have some time to search for Lesson.

"I'll take a run to Beldorph as soon as I get back to Agnar-Alpha. Damn! *Bucephalus* is down for maintenance!"

"She'll be ready by c-twelve, Captain," Norden replied crisply. "At this moment every inspector, maintenance chief, and mechanic in the Agnar-Alpha port is working on it." Her smile was one of carnivorous anticipation, making her next words a lie. "I hope you've nothing to hide."

Conek smiled back. "Nothing they'll find."

"Andro will be here at c-six to fly you back to Agnar-Alpha. He'll be going with you," Norden said.

"Why?" Conek frowned, wondering if they thought he'd sell the weapon to the highest bidder.

"You need Andro," she explained. "He's seen these things, so there'll be no mistake."

"So why don't you just show me one?" Conek retorted. She gave a poor excuse to explain his being watched.

Bentian shook his head. "Unfortunately we cannot. The Institute is a private enterprise. It refuses to accept or research weaponry. The . . . gadgets, as you called them, have been shipped to the weapons center in Vilastat."

Quintas Bentian and Norden left immediately after their meeting with Conek, who spent nearly two standard hours in the lounge. Then Dr. Sardo reappeared, still pulling a reluctant Cge. Once the droid saw Conek, he sped over to his master.

Conek nodded to the doctor and tapped his fingers on the droid's metallic shoulder.

"All fixed?"

"Negative," Cge replied in perfect robot tonelessness. Since his original language had been almost musical, he had picked up human inflections immediately, and Conek had nearly forgotten how a regular droid sounded.

Conek glared at the doctor. "What's wrong with him? What happened to the way he talked?"

"I am not to say no anymore," Cge said, the humanlike inflections back in his voice again. "I shake my head when I say no."

Conek turned back to the doctor, puzzled. "So it's not the accepted thing—is it illegal or something?"

The little doctor gazed up at Conek with sorrowful eyes. "No, Captain, but he shouldn't do it. It jars his computer. We've done the best we could—tightened some fittings, replaced a clamp or two. We're returning him on Quinta Norden's orders, but we need days, possibly weeks, to fix him properly. We don't know how he operates."

"So he's alien-made. I thought, since you've been studying the other droids, you'd have some idea."

"Captain, we know how he's supposed to work—it's the damage he's sustained. His computer is scrambled. Panels of circuits are fused together in a hodgepodge. Why he doesn't overload and short out completely is a mystery to us." Dr. Sardo pulled Conek to the side, peering around as if he were evading security.

"I'm following Quinta Norden's instructions, but by law I shouldn't give him back to you. His restriction panel is destroyed." The doctor's voice dropped to a whisper. "There are no inner controls on him. He can override any order you give him."

Conek watched the droid, who had lost interest in the conversation and had rolled off to inspect the holo-paintings on the walls. He wondered what the doctor would think if he saw Cge go into his clown act.

"Don't worry, Doc," he said, trying to pacify the little scientist. "If he runs amok, I've still got ten big ones to handle him."

When they left the lounge, Conek hurried to the flight pad, where a slim little ship with the Vladmn government insignia sat waiting.

"Hello, love." Andro reached down to lift Cge into the cabin.

"Cut that out," Conek demanded, "and be careful with him! Don't bump his head!"

"My goodness!" Andro took Cge with exaggerated care, turning to put him in a rear seat which he reclined to accommodate the droid's inability to bend. "Did you sample the rocket fuel and get a hangover, love?"

"My circuits are fragile," Cge announced with pride. "I

must not be jarred, and I'm not to shake my head anymore. . . ."

Conek took his seat. Andro warmed the thrusters and raised the ship. Cge regaled them with a detailed account of his condition. Andro egged him on by offering sympathy and asking questions. He rolled his eyes at Conek as the droid listed his computer damage. When Cge finally wound down, Conek sighed.

"Exactly what I've always wanted—a metallic hypochondriac."

"And me." Andro laughed at the expression in Conek's eyes as the major leveled off the ship.

"And you," Conek agreed. "They can say what they want, but you were sent along to keep an eye on me."

Andro sobered. "I wouldn't waste my time."

Conek grunted, appeased, but not convinced. He kept an eye on Andro as they sped through a heavy traffic pattern. The flight controller was a good pilot, fast and sure, but just short of being a rocket-rider. The slim little craft could comp within the lower atmosphere, but in consideration for Cge's delicacy, Andro took the extra quarter unit to get into thinner air.

The grayness enveloped them. Andro switched on the overhead lights and pushed another button. Two panels recessed and slid aside. A fully stocked bar rolled out onto the carpeted deck behind Conek. Both he and Andro swiveled their seats, and while Conek eyed the choices, Andro took a plastine container of fruit juice.

"Classy," Conek said.

"Oh my, yes, dear. Auntie couldn't be allowed to travel in anything less than the best. This is her personal ship."

Conek chose his drink and settled back.

"Okay, why the games? There's nobody here but us, is there?"

Andro flashed him an arch smile, then subsided with a sigh. "Hayden, this whole thing scares the hell out of me. I'm in over my head when it comes to weird weapons—and all the rest of it. I've decided I should stay a button pusher."

"Buck up, we'll get the thing. They do any damage when they discovered what it was?"

"You didn't see the new wing?"

"They blew up some construction?"

"You know that most of the institute is underground?"

"It's well hidden."

"Protected from meteor storms, their main concern—back to the point. They tested this thing in an isolated wing, thank God! The 'gadget' hollowed out solid stone. A tunnel four kilometers long, and around the edges the rock is fused stronger than steel—all from one short blast of a 'gadget' you can carry easily."

"Damn," Conek breathed. He knew the gadgets could eat up sand dunes, but solid stone?

"That's not the worst of it. Anyone could make it. They said it's just a new application of some very common materials."

"Like what?"

"They didn't *tell* me, and I didn't *ask*. The sooner that thing is under tight security, the better. I'd like to destroy them. Let the secret die a quick death. We can kill ourselves fast enough the old way."

Conek agreed. In spite of the drink, he grew restless, wanting to reach Agnar-Alpha and retrieve *Bucephalus* so he could go to Beldorph and find the rest of those damn things. Now that Vladmn knew about them, he wanted to make sure no one else found one. And he was getting a crawly feeling.

# CHAPTER Eleven

From the surface of the planet, the blazing sun of Beldorph was hidden by the flying sand of a dying windstorm. On the first trip to the ghoster, Conek had rigged and attached a signal beacon only he could activate when he wanted to land. Using it, he brought the ship down in a blinding storm, no mean feat, since he had never used the thrusters either to land or to take off from Beldorph. The heat of the engines fused the silica into telltale discs, dead giveaways if they were seen. The perverse nature of the winds on the planet would uncover them at all the wrong times.

The ship was suspended in the air by a delicate balance of their forward and braking thrusters and actually lowered by powerful gravity-reversal beams.

As Conek waited for the end of the storm, he sat at his small desk in the lounge, finishing a message disk for the Gordotl. Behind him the *kew-w-ws* coming from various places in the compartment warned him of the running mock gun battle between Andro and Cge.

Conek put the account book in its slot and pulled out the worn, hand-drawn plan of the huge ghoster. Andro had picked three possible compartments where he thought the other weapon might be. But because of the sheer bulk of freight on the big ship, he admitted to not being sure.

An "Aughh!" from Andro ended the shoot-out. Getting "killed" was the only graceful way to stop the game with the inexhaustable Cge.

Wheels slowly coming up behind him alerted Conek to his own personal, if pretended danger. He swiveled his chair and pointed.

"Hands up, friend. You're under arrest!"

Cge blinked and raised his metallic arms.

"Glad you got him, Sheriff. He shot me dead." Andro, relaxed in a lounger, feebly raised his hand.

Conek patted Cge on the shoulder. "Okay, General, go do your stuff."

Cge entered the air lock and headed for the forward hold.

Conek released the safety catch and swiveled a lounger around to face Andro. He spread out the hand-drawn map. "Okay, let's go over this one more time."

Andro peered glumly down at the diagram and shook his head. "I don't know. The damn ship is *so* big, and we were going through it so fast in the original exploration. All I can really remember about those 'gadgets' is wanting one."

"Why?"

"I thought they were sculptures." The major's description tallied with the weapon Conek had found. He shrugged. "I collect primitive art."

Conek was sympathetic. "Sounds like just the thing to have. If the neighbors get too loud, you just disintegrate the next ten kilometers of city."

Andro, bent over the plan again, nodded absent assent. He raised his head, eyes alight. "I remember. The third was in a big compartment. A dislodged vent pipe partially blocked the entrance. I bumped my head on it."

"Then let's go get it," Conek put the map in the case at his waist and handed Andro a breather mask. They were new acquisitions, covering just the mouth and chin and allowing communication. Andro refused it.

"I want a full suit when we go out to connect the worm."

"It's been done. Why do you think Cge plays general?"

In the weeks Conek spent carrying arms to the Gordotl and transferring the cargo of the ghoster to the Institute, Conek discovered unsuspected talents in the little droid. In human company Cge might behave like a child, but he turned benevolent dictator with the ten huge worker droids.

With a minimum list of words suitable for loading cargo, Conek, with Cge's help, reprogrammed the workers, but not being accustomed to ordering machinery, Conek could never remember to keep the slang out of his orders. A command to Alpha to "Knock it off" resulted in a broken crate of chemicals. They ate a hole in the steel plating of *Bucephalus*'s storage decking. When "Make tracks" and "Fall to" met with unfortunate incidents, he turned the management back over to Cge.

Conek and Andro entered the forward hold and paused to watch Cge line up his workers. He bustled back and forth and whistled sharp little orders.

Conek led the way down the worm and into the ghoster. "Give Cge enough underlings and we might be slaves," he said with a laugh, "but since I haven't found a buyer—"

"Ha!" Andro interrupted. "Everyone who's seen him is a prospective buyer. What are you asking, five hundred thousand cranas?"

"Seven hundred thousand."

"That's not a price, that's prohibition."

"Larceny," Conek answered.

"No, larceny is possible. Your price prohibits the sale."

"Seven hundred thousand."

They strode down the long corridor. The hatches on both sides were now marked with X's, with a corresponding mark shown on Conek's plan. he stopped before the last X'd door, looking not at it, but at the folded drawing.

"We emptied this one last. If we did—" He threw the bolt and swung the hatch open. "Yeah, we cleaned it out."

"How many did you clear last time?" Andro asked.

Conek consulted his notes. Working for Dursig had made him a careful bookkeeper. "Two. Both large, all heavy stuff."

"It's definitely on this side of the corridor, in the next two or three compartments." Andro threw the bolt on the next storage area. When the hatch swung back, they saw another empty hold. "Your records must be wrong."

Behind them, the robots rolled up with Cge leading. He called a halt and glided over to stand between Conek and Andro, his light flickering in his slow, puzzled speed.

Conek consulted his plan again and looked down at the little droid. "You emptied this one too?"

"No." Cge shook his head but stopped the motion abruptly. "Negative. We did not. Just *that* one." He pointed back to the last marked door.

"He could be confused too," Conek said, excusing the little droid and blaming himself for not keeping a closer eye on the shipments. He strode down the passage and shot the next hatch bolt, standing aside when the door swung open.

Andro followed more slowly and studied the plan. "So you missed X'ing out a room. No great catastrophe. We start here and—oh, my jangled nerves!"

Andro followed Conek into the huge hold, echoing in its emptiness. Just inside the door, they ducked under a large, dislodged vent pipe. Cge rolled behind them.

Conek turned to the small droid. "What about this compartment? Did you unload it?"

"Negative!" Cge squeaked, his panel flashing rapidly.

"He could have forgotten—lost count." Andro's voice was laced with desperate hope.

A crash of metal on metal interrupted Andro. They watched the huge worker droids bump against the sagging vent in an attempt to follow.

"He'd remember that, and so would I." Conek inclined his head toward the droids, who attempted to push the vent aside. They weren't programmed to duck and go under.

"Pirates," Andro surmised, since not only Conek and

Cge, but even the actions of the slow-witted loaders, denied any mistake in their records.

"Well, it wasn't us," Conek said. "You'll have to contact Bentian and Norden, but first let's see how much they took."

A quick survey showed one other compartment looted. Back on *Bucephalus,* Conek did some figuring after carefully checking his records.

"Four class-189 freighters could have managed it. Two Osalt ships, same class as *Anubis*. Little more than one load for *Bucephalus*."

"But it's impossible, Conek. You've got the only two Osalt ships in the federation. If a Vladmn freighter landed, the patrols would have been swarming in before they cut their engines."

"What?"

"Conek, you should have *known* Auntie would arrange security for *this*! She has her heart set on another time-comp or some such, and with the ghoster as a legitimate excuse, she can protect the arms shipments to Dursig with no one, not even the patrols, the wiser. They have orders not to land, to let nothing on Beldorph but Osalt freighters—" Andro frowned. "I forgot all about the Gordotl. Could it have been Dursig?"

"I sure as hell hope so," Conek grunted. He didn't believe it. Dursig was too honest to raid his claim. But for Vladmn's sake he hoped the thief felt a loyalty to the federation. He might not get along with the government of Vladmn, but at the moment it was the best available.

Dursig wasn't guilty. Back on Radach-I, Conek, Andro, Norden, Bentian, and Chief Sornick, the security agent, filled the chief's office with the tension of distrust. Cge hid behind Conek's chair. The droid remembered the chief security officer's efforts to claim him and suddenly turned stubborn. He refused to acknowledge anyone except Conek.

Sornick kept throwing suspicious glances at Conek, who grew more restless and irritated. He disliked the agent anyway.

"Sornick, why don't you say what's on your mind?" he snapped.

"Because I don't have the proof *yet*." The agent snarled, raking Conek with a sharp-edged glare.

"Say it, anyway. It might be good for a laugh."

"All right, Hayden!" The security chief leaned forward, his face flushed with anger and frustration. "As sure as I sit here, *you* took the cargo. Somewhere you found a higher bidder. You would have gotten away with it, except for the weapon."

Conek leaned back in his chair, watching the agent with a calculated, deliberate calm guaranteed to send the chief's blood pressure up ten points. The big man's right eye twitched. He squirmed with resentment at Conek's attitude. Everyone but Conek was on edge as the captain sat gazing at the security officer.

The tension broke when a small metallic voice came from behind Conek's chair. "Chief Sornick malfunctions."

Andro gave a short laugh. Bentian's lips twitched, but Norden's quelling glance stilled Andro, the other Quinta, and the security chief, who jumped to his feet. His red face deepened three shades. The clatter of a decoding machine at the side of his desk interrupted him.

He waited with a triumphant, almost comical impatience for the printout. When he read it, his face fell. He started to crumple the paper, thought better of it, and handed the message to Bentian. Norden angled her head, unable to read it from the position of her chair. Conek could have seen it, but he refused to look over Bentian's shoulder.

"Oh, Quinta, I can't stand it," Andro cried.

"To Chief Security Officer Sornick from General Kalat," Bentian read aloud. "Surveillance reports indicate departures and arrivals on Beldorph, Radach-I, Arrin, and Agnar-Alpha, no possible time allowance for extra shipments by DA-149-SO-53169-02, registered Conek A. Hayden. Ditto three Osalt freighters on Gordotl (all unregistered). Last attempt of Osalt to penetrate airspace during probable time of theft. Advance warning—Osalt turned back. All accounted for. Sector ten patrol reports confirmed. During probable time of theft two Osalt freighters entered Beldorph atmosphere, exited after fourteen hours. End transmission."

For a few minutes no one spoke, Norden and Bentian traded glances, and Security Chief Sornick looked ready to bite the corners off his desk.

Conek offered what hope he could. "Could be we were wrong."

"You didn't find any weapons in the remaining cargo?" Benetian asked. The question had been cleared up earlier, but he grabbed for hope.

Conek and Andro shook their heads in unison.

"Then someone has three of those weapons," Norden said. "God only knows what they'll do with them."

"Three?" Conek's question was sharp, tense.

Norden shifted, coming back out of her visualization of doom as if she were waking up from a short nap.

"Dr. Sardo has your other droids operational again—"

"Deso?" interrupted Cge, who abandoned his hiding place behind Conek's chair and wheeled out to give a few rapid blinks in her direction.

Norden gave an affirmative nod. "Yes, Deso."

"Why didn't they tell me before?" Conek demanded, his attention latching on to a new subject as a release of tension.

"Because, Captain, this particular droid is invaluable to the Institute in identifying the objects making up the cargo. He translated the manifest. We know that five of these particular weapons were being shipped."

Andro shifted as an idea nudged him. "They could have been lost in space when the hull was breached."

"No." Norden was positive. "Remember, I made a map. They were in holds that remained secure. The droid pointed out where they were."

"Either the droid flipped a chip or the manifest was wrong." Conek felt like shooting off his tongue.

Norden caught his slip immediately. Her eyes narrowed.

"You wouldn't know that unless you'd found one or *more* than one. How many, Captain?"

"Just one. And I didn't go looking. It almost *fell* on me."

Well, he had gone looking, but not for that crazy thingamajig.

"You've one in your possession and you haven't *told* us?" She turned to Chief Sornick. "Arrest him."

Bentian was calmer. "Just a moment, Quinta. Where is it, Captain?"

Conek hesitated. If they knew that nothing-maker was aboard *Anubis,* they might go after Lesson, and the result would be unhappy to say the least."

"It's safe."

"Where is it?" Norden demanded.

"I sold it to the Osalt, what do you think?" Conek shouted. "Quinta, the weapon is safe. I'll get it for you, put it in your hot little hands, and you can blow a hole in yourself for all *I* care! I'll get it—that's all I'll say now."

Chief Sornick rose. His expression said there was a God, after all.

"Captain Hayden"—Norden's voice was chilled with the steel of authority—"I should have known better than to trust you. Chief, put this man under arrest—"

"*For what?*" Conek yelled. "For stealing what every universal law of salvage says is already mine? Not good enough, Quinta! First you have to prove I used it for unlawful gain. *Sit down, Sornick!* I plead guilty to blowing the hell out of some sand dunes on Beldorph before I knew what I had! Do what you can with that!"

"Chief, I said arrest this man!" Norden shouted, her face white with anger.

"Remain where you are, Chief." Major Andro Avvin spoke softly, but his countermanding a Quinta's order shocked the rest of the room. Even Cge, who had hidden behind Conek's chair again, rolled forward enough to peer over Conek's shoulder.

"Andro . . ." Norden stared at her nephew as if he'd lost his mind. But Andro, though he sat back in his chair and appeared relaxed, was every inch authority. His glinting eyes warned off her objection.

"Auntie, with all due respect to you and Quinta Bentian,

and to Chief Sornick, it's a military matter. I have some questions to put to the captain if you don't mind."

Norden eyed Andro thoughtfully, then perched on the edge of her chair, giving in but all attention.

Andro steepled his fingers and looked up at the ceiling. "Now, Captain, did you leave that weapon on Beldorph?"

"Hell, no. Do you think I'd leave it where someone could find it? You know how that sand moves."

"It's a shame you didn't," Andro said softly. "If you had, no action could be brought against you. Once you brought it off the planet and into galactic space, you brought it under the jurisdiction of Vladmn. Consider yourself under close arrest. I'll personally return you to Agnar-Alpha."

"Chief, arrange military transport for the major," Norden said crisply.

"Thank you, no. I'll want his ship—and the droid."

"Why?" Norden was suspicious.

The major seemed fatigued with explaining the obvious. "Because, dear heart, smuggling vessels usually have hidden compartments large enough to accommodate—shall we call them sensitive shipments? I've always wanted to tear that Osalt horror down to its framing." His smile was vicious. "And the military security has ways of going into the memory banks of a droid that would turn poor Dr. Sardo's hair white."

For the first time Norden seemed to waver. "Is it necessary to completely destroy the droid?"

Andro looked pained. "Really, Aunt, what is one droid to the safety of Vladmn?"

She nodded reluctantly, then turned to Bentian. "If he takes half your security force and half of mine—"

"Quite so." Andro rose, slowly pulled his blaster, and pointed it at Conek. "I'll need some help."

Conek moved forward in the direction in which the business end of the blaster pointed, while Cge rolled at his side. Why in hell hadn't he kept his mouth shut? he wondered. Too much togetherness, he decided. He had been caught up in all the talk of doom, and the all-of-us-together atmosphere. Cursing himself didn't help. He looked down at Cge and wondered how to prevent the little guy from getting torn apart by a ham-handed bunch of military investigators. He ordered his mind to come up with a plan. His brain wasn't exactly standing up and saluting.

Two of Sornick's men flanked Andro as they left the building and crossed the landing pad. They were joined by eight uniformed Vladmn patrolmen, wearing the special insignia of the Quinta's personal security service.

Andro acknowledged a Lieutenant Marwit, a bright-eyed charmer with a physique straight out of a bodybuilder's course. If Conek hadn't been convinced of Norden's blind dedication to her position as Quinta, he'd wonder about the lieutenant's duties—if he'd had time left over from worrying about himself, that was.

When they reached *Bucephalus*, the major held out his hand. "The hand control, Captain?"

With nine blasters pointed at him, Conek surrendered the sensor that lowered the grav-rev beams and wondered how much inhibiting programming was in the big droids. If he could somehow instruct Cge, who could pass along his instructions . . .

"Cge, you're to go up first," Andro ordered as they stopped just outside, by the lowered repelling disk. "Send those big androids back into the far storage holds."

Too late; Andro had been thinking, too, and forestalled him.

"Now, Captain, if you'll follow Cge—"

"Excuse me, Major," Lieutenant Marwit interrupted. "But shouldn't one of us go up first, so we can keep an eye on the captain until you're aboard?"

Conek thought the day had been too much for Andro. He seemed to have trouble taking in what the lieutenant said. Then he nodded.

"By all means. Lieutenant . . ." He waved his hand, indicating that the young officer was to step into the beam.

Before the legs of the junior officer were out of sight, Andro shoved the pointed barrel of his blaster into Conek's ribs. By reflex, Conek stepped forward and was taken up into the ship. As he rose, his swinging foot contacted with the major's shoulder. Andro gave an angry yelp of pain, and Conek, not wanting to get shot over a misdemeanor, stepped out of the beam too fast, stumbled and fell against the bulkhead.

He was just regaining his balance when the whine of the grav-rev beam suddenly stopped. He heard the thud of bodies on the paracrete, angry shouts and swearing. The hatch slammed closed. Andro's gun was pointed at the astounded lieutenant.

"Captain!" Andro's voice rose an octave higher than his normal affectation. "Get this warehouse off the ground—now!"

Conek stumbled over his own feet as he dashed into the bridge. They had been on Radach-I less than an hour. The temperature on the engines was down, but *Bucephalus* wouldn't tear herself apart getting under way.

"I love you, boo baby, but it's our lives." As her thrusters screamed, he gave her the order to comp under the fastest possible conditions. He'd written the instructions, but whether or not they were correct, or when "soonest possible" would be, he had no idea.

The *swoosh* knocked him out of his seat. *Bucephalus*'s landing gear couldn't have been more than ten feet off the ground. Below him, he heard an explosion and the scream of strained metal. He picked himself up from the floor, wondering if he was still alive, and checked the panel for damage. A seal on the middle cargo hatch had weakened but was holding. Several hunks of paracrete floated in the grayness beyond the viewer panel. *Bucephalus* had brought part of the landing pad with them.

He was alive, intact, and apparently free of arrest.

The question was: Why?

# CHAPTER Twelve

Back in the lounge, the lieutenant lay sprawled on the floor by the bulkhead. The side of his face sported a dark red weal. A cut over his eye seeped blood. Andro had been more fortunate. He had fallen on a lounger. He tried to rise but looked groggy. Conek offered him a hand, taking the blaster from him in the process. The major didn't seem to notice.

The air lock between the lounge and the storage holds hissed, and Cge skated in, his sensor panel afire with rapid blinking. Behind him came two big droids. His agitated whistle demanded an answer from Conek.

"Speak Vladmn," Conek ordered. "Everything kosher in the backcountry?"

"ConekHayden functions according to specifications?"

"Fine here. Any of your boys in trouble?"

"Some fell down. They will operate correctly when they are standing again." Cge turned his attention to Andro, watched him for a moment, and then rolled over to inspect the lieutenant. "It lives." The droid's tone resembled regret.

"Don't be bloodthirsty," Conek ordered. "Have one of the big boys put him back in a stateroom—fragile cargo. And lock him in."

Cge's panel slowed. New slang always threw the droid until he identified it as such. Then, with an imperious whistle, he sent one big droid back to the cargo area while the other lifted the lieutenant.

"Tell him he's got him upside down!" Conek snapped.

Cge corrected the worker droid's error, and they disappeared down the passage in the direction of the staterooms.

Conek turned back to Andro, who sat up, rubbing his shoulder. The grogginess was gone. He looked around, surprised that they were still in one piece and breathing.

"I said get us off the ground, not kill us. Oh, my God, did you kill the others when you took off?"

"I don't think so. We brought part of the landing field, but the sensors don't register any bodies."

"The lieutenant—" Andro turned to stare at the passage where the droid carrying the injured security officer had disappeared. He looked around the lounge as if the large compartment were strange to him. "I don't believe this."

"Neither do I," Conek said. "What's going on?"

Andro sighed. "I couldn't let them lock you up."

"I won't argue, but why?"

As if all his strength had been left on Radach-I, Andro fell back against the seat. He closed his eyes. "Because you're the only one who can get those guns back. I'll be there to accept them for the government."

Conek stared down at the smaller man, not quite ready to believe what he heard. Major Andro Avvin, Administrator of Vladmn's largest port authority, sticking his head in the same noose with a smuggler? It didn't make sense.

But he'd seen Andro's pale face when he turned the blaster on the lieutenant. The look in his eye had been desperate, as if he were fighting for his last breath. Some things couldn't be faked; and the major had been scared white. He was still pale.

"When you gamble, you don't mess around," Conek said.

"If we don't find them, it's your career. You'll never get to be dictator this way."

"That damn lieutenant," Andro growled, looking back toward the passage. "I had it all figured out. I could have said you overpowered me. When I *do* get promoted to dictator, I'll order a lobotomy for every lieutenant in the patrol."

"You know where you slipped up—"

"*I* should have boarded first and dropped him on his ass." Andro sat up. "Now—you owe me—where's that third weapon?"

"In the closet of a stateroom on *Anubis*. Lesson doesn't even know what it is."

"That's a hell of a place to leave it."

Conek almost told the major where he could go, but fair was fair. The major deserved better. Conek admitted to the fight between he and Lesson.

". . . and I was mad enough to forget it. Now, what are we going to do with bright-eyes-and-military back in the stateroom?"

Andro turned indecisive. He bit his lip. "If we turn him loose, I'm ruined—and I don't want to kill him."

"Great, a permanent, nonpaying passenger," Conek grunted. "If you don't want him dead, let's go patch him up."

The lieutenant had regained consciousness. Cge brought the emergency medical kit, and Conek put a plasti-flesh patch on the young officer's forehead. Still too stunned by the fall to think clearly, he offered no resistance. Conek decided he had a concussion and came up with several imaginary complications resulting from not lying perfectly still, most of them centering around sexual prowess.

Lieutenant Marwit's carefully toned physique had convinced Conek the young officer thought himself the epitome of female dreams. The cautious look in the lieutenant's eyes convinced Conek he'd used the right threat.

"We'll head for MD-439," Conek said when they'd locked the lieutenant's door again. "That's one of Lesson's hangouts. Maybe I'll pick up some other news."

"Auntie's not stupid. It won't take her long to wonder about Lesson."

Andro took the copilot's seat, wanting to see the planet as they landed. More afraid of the contrabanders than the galactic government, the locals had banned the Vladmn patrols from their world. For more than a century only the contraband freighters had landed there.

Cge caught Andro's curiosity about the planet and wanted to see the landing. Conek relented and allowed him to come forward.

Conek made a slow descent for fear of throwing Cge through the control panels, incidentally giving them a good view of the planet at the same time.

The snow from the poles covered all but a wide band around the equator. The rest of the planet with the dark reputation was a bright blue-green world of huge lakes, tall, snowcapped mountains, and carefully tended fields. Agriculture and food-processing plants covered most of the useable land. Ripening crops bounded the circular hypercrete landing area surrounding the small, thriving smuggler's town owned and run by Tsaral, the octopoid who ruled the contraband activities of Vladmn.

Scarred areas on the pale gray landing surface showed orderly rings of landing pads. Andro pointed them out.

"They couldn't have a port authority here."

Conek laughed. "If we can avoid patrols, inspectors, and secret agents, you don't think we'd be dumb enough to come in here and set down on top of each other, do you?"

"Well, love, you needn't be so flip about it. After all, it *is* rather a jolt to learn that neither you nor your job is really necessary."

"Cheer up." Conek grinned at Andro. "If the world discovers it doesn't need you, you can always have a job with me—polishing the big droids."

"Oh, thank you—*so* much." The major was still uncomfortable around the Skooler robots.

*Bucephalus* blocked four pads with her bulk. Conek had put her down slightly away from the rest of the clustered freighters.

"If Lesson was here, we would have seen *Anubis*. Maybe I can get a line on him. You wait here."

"I'm coming with you, Captain."

Conek gritted his teeth. "I'll ask you one more time to stay aboard."

"I repeat, I'm coming with you."

"Fine." Conek started the engines and began a lift-off check.

"What are you doing?" Andro demanded.

"I'm going somewhere, so you can come with me. I can't frustrate such devotion."

Andro stared, disbelieving. "Are you refusing to *try* to find your pilot?"

Conek, busy over his checklist, did not look up. "No, Major, but I am refusing to get my throat cut—that won't get the weapons or Lesson."

For a moment Conek thought Andro would draw his blaster and order Conek from the bridge, but the major relaxed back in his seat.

"You're right," Andro agreed reluctantly. "In your position I guess I'd feel the same. If I were recognized, neither of us would get back alive. If I stay aboard, you can't leave without me."

"And someone's got to feed your prisoner. Don't get impatient. Getting information can take awhile."

"I'll have Cge for company," Andro said, consoling himself.

"I need him with me. He'll attract attention." Cge would be more of a hindrance to Conek than a help, but Conek couldn't leave him on board. If the major changed his mind and decided to leave the ship, he could order Cge to open the hatches. Andro couldn't order the big boys around; they weren't programmed with enough Vladmn Standard.

They arrived at midday on MD-439, but most of the stools in the Singing Star were taken. After the brightness outside, the bar seemed black as a cavern.

When he'd adjusted to the dimness, Conek noticed that every eye in the place was on Cge. There was considerable laughter and some good-natured banter about his size before anyone even looked to see who accompanied the little droid.

"Ha! Hayden!" Conek recognized the voice of Skielth, a rocket-riding smuggler from the reptilian world of Shashar, though because of the lizard's dark coloring and the dimness of the bar, he had a hard time locating him.

Then he saw a mug waving in the air in a figure-eight pattern, an old joke between them. Pulling Cge along behind him, he strolled the length of the bar and took the empty seat next to Skielth. They had been close friends for several years, often pooling their efforts when one or the other had more business than he could handle.

Conek had always liked the two-meter-tall Shashar. Except for the sail starting between his eyes and extending down to the base of his neck, the big lizard resembled the large, upright carnivorous reptiles found on many worlds before their prime races developed more than the beginnings of sentience.

Conek ordered a round for himself, Skielth, and the gray, catlike Orealian on the other side of the lizard.

"How's Shashar?" Conek asked, sipping his drink.

"Rushed," Skielth answered. "With the Osalt pushing on the frontier, it seems every Shashar, Osagen, and Urulean wants an arsenal to hide under his bed. I'm down for a few days to reattach. Ister too."

Conek saw the quiver in the reptilian's hand, a symptom of staying in space until the lack of on-world time brought disorientation. Since his first experience with it, Conek was careful to maintain enough ground time. His had been a light case, but scary enough. Severe bouts brought about hallucinations and a loss of reflexes. In the old days the disorientation rendered the pilot incapable of landing, even if he was clearheaded enough to find a planet. The new automatic anti-collision systems prevented crashes, but how many vessels still went down in inhospitable planets was anybody's guess.

"I'll be due for some downtime before long," Conek said. "Sure hope I can finish my contract before then." The last was added to let Skielth know he was not available if the Shashar was looking for someone to take over his deliveries.

"Yeah, everybody is going like crazy, it seems," said Ister. "I just came in from Liston, and the port was nearly deserted. Oh, that reminds me—there were some characters asking questions about you and Lesson. The bartender thought they worked for Slug."

He leaned forward, his head nearly lying on the counter as he looked around Skielth's bulk. His face was purely feline, but his expressions were close to human. Through milliennia of natural and forced evolution, the Orealians had adapted from the animal mind and shape to sentience and walking upright.

He curled his short, stubby fingers around the glass. The voice feeding the translator held all the expression of his thoughts though not actual words, but give the Orealians another few generations and they'd be speaking Vladmn Standard.

"Well, if they were looking for Lesson, they probably found him," Conek replied with careful nonchalance. "At least I *think* he said he was stopping off there."

"He hadn't as of six units ago." Ister paused to lap daintily at his drink. "Ofini said he hadn't seen either you or Lesson in so long, he thought maybe the patrols got you."

"Ha!" Skielth laughed, opening his enormous mouth, baring viciously pointed teeth. "That character would think anything to start a rumor."

A beep of panic from Cge alerted Conek, and he whirled, drawing his blaster by reflex. A big simian-type from a world unknown to Conek was holding Cge up over his head, while behind him, three of his fellows were laughing at the droid's efforts to get free. The ape saw Conek's blaster and gave a chattering laugh.

"What is this, human, a portable keg?"

"Put him down."

"Sorry," the simian's translator crackled, a cheap model. "I didn't mean to upset everybody." He knelt, as if to set Cge on the floor. In a lightning move he jerked upright. He threw the android straight at Conek and grabbed his weapon.

Conek had noted the slight shift in the ape's eyes and had anticipated him. Moving slightly to the right to keep the airborne droid from blocking his view, Conek fired. He reached for Cge's arm with his other hand, not really expecting to catch the droid.

Instead of Cge's arm, Conek's fingers closed on another blaster. With reptilian speed Skielth shoved his own gun in Conek's left hand and pulled the android from the air.

Behind the first simian, two of his friends were drawing, but Conek fired before either cleared his holster. Above the bar, the air scrubbers whined as they intensified their filtering, but the bar was heavy with the smell of burned flesh and clothing.

The fourth ape faced the two blasters Conek held. His companions were on the floor, and he lost no time in raising his arms above his head.

"Out!" Conek ordered. The man wore his gun on the same side with a supposedly broken arm. If he thought he might need a weapon, why not put in on the side with the uninjured hand? Either the sling was a hoax, or Conek could shoot a helpless being. Since he wasn't sure, he gave the ape the benefit of the doubt.

The simian had disappeared when Conek turned to thank Skielth.

The big reptile still held Cge. The droid's limbs were thrashing, but his struggles were ineffective since his programming prevented him from harming a life-form.

The Shashar put the droid on the floor and turned one flat, black eye on Conek. "You'll stunt his growth, bringing him in bars." He was doing the polite thing—ignoring the scene once the trouble was over. He tapped Cge on his top module. "He's still a bit small for gunfighting."

"Cge is a *good* gunfighter! Lesson has instructed Cge!" the droid answered indignantly, his irate voice carrying across the room. His panel flashed angrily.

"Well, let's not prove it here," Conek said, reaching for Cge's shoulder. He pulled him close between the bar stools, out of the narrow aisle. He noticed the sudden silence. Quick looks passed between the patrons. Did they believe Cge was armed? he wondered. Programming a droid for firearms would get an offender a twenty-cycle sentence on any planet in Vladmn.

Ister wrinkled his nose at the odor, his whiskers twitching in distaste. "You're a bit hasty, Hayden, else you don't care to know what Slug had in mind."

"Were they the ones?" Conek eyed them thoughtfully. "I guess we found out, but why is he after my skin?"

The Orealian shrugged. "Maybe you've got something he wants?"

"Yeah, he's out to steal my android," Conek replied, and for emphasis he put his drink down on the top of Cge's sensor module.

Both the Orealian and the Shashar laughed. On planets like MD-439, both courtesy and personal safety forbade questions unless they were encouraged.

Conek finished his drink and watched the dozen Chimagens who came in to remove the simian bodies. The other patrons of the bar had turned back to their own conversations. Brawls and shooting were commonplace on MD-439.

Tsaral, the smuggling king who owned the town as well as the settlement on Siddah-II, believed in a strict hands-off policy. He left the contrabanders to settle their disputes themselves.

The Chimagens, the fur-bearing bipedal marsupial natives, were under Tsaral's protection. The smuggler who threatened or hurt one of the timid creatures lost his welcome in Tsaral's towns—if he got out with his life.

When Skielth offered to buy another round of drinks, Conek shook his head. "I think I'll be on my way. It's my sensitive nature, I guess. All this violence upsets me."

"Ha!" The big reptile opened his huge, sharp-toothed mouth, letting the volume of his voice rattle the mugs and bottles on the tables. Through the years Conek and Skielth had shared too many experiences for the Shashar to be fooled. The Shashar might appear to be in a jolly mood, but noise was the ancient challenge of his species. He loudly contradicted Conek.

"You're getting back to your ship where you've a nursery full of these things, I bet." He thumped Cge on the top of the cylinder with the claw of a webbed finger. "Think I'll come along. You should sell me one cheap, they're so small."

Skielth continued to joke with Conek, but the small reptilian eyes glittered; his short dorsal sail stood rigid. His defensive senses were on full alert.

"Think I'll come along too," the Orealian said. "I'll make sure you don't take some baby droid too young to leave the den."

Ister's semblance of a smile was more convincing, but Conek knew the meaning of the twitch at the end of his tail. He, too, was expecting trouble. The cat moved his whiskers as he gazed up at Conek. "Are you sure they're past night feedings?"

Like Conek, Skielth and Ister expected more trouble before Conek could reach his ship. Their jokes camouflaged a solid but quiet attempt to assist him. He appreciated their help, but they added a new complication. Every delay kept him from getting on Lesson's trail.

Conek, pulling Cge, led the way toward the door, followed by Ister with Skielth bringing up the rear of the procession.

Cge came to a halt, tilting and turning his top module to stare at a pair of Cleostars, whose shell-covered bodies were supported by ten stalk legs and whose eyes turned on thin antennae. Knowing Cleostars were bad-tempered, Conek grabbed the droid's arm and pulled him away, talking over his shoulder to Skielth.

"They're a lot of trouble," he said, shaking Cge's arm for emphasis. "But wait until you see how *big* they grow." They stepped out into the bright sunlight, followed by the laughter from the bar.

"What do you feed them?" the Shashars asked while he set a fast pace.

"Fortified rocket fuel and strained computer output," Conek replied, keeping a tight hold on the droid's arm. Cge slowed to peer at a group of timid natives.

"Get a move on," Conek hissed as he saw the citizens of MD-439 slip into an alley.

Farther down the street the fourth simian, his arm still in a sling, stood in close conversation with three ex-patrons of the Singing Star. Skielth hurried on, and Conek pretended not to notice.

They crossed the pavement of the landing pad and moved into the deep shadow cast by the bulk of *Bucephalus*. All three watched carefully to see if anyone lurked around the huge landing gear. Their footsteps echoed off the underbelly of the ship.

Using his pocket activator, Conek opened the hatch and started the grav-rev beam. When the Shashar started forward, Conek seized his scaly arm. "Let me go first. There's a welcoming committee up there."

Knowing he wouldn't step on, even at a command, Conek unceremoniously pushed Cge into the beam and watched as the droid rose, flailing his arms and kicking. Then Conek rode the beam up.

Just before the beam took him into the ship, he spotted the simian. The ape crouched slightly as he raced from the protection of a Vladmn freighter's engine pods toward the nose of another ship. Behind him, the three patrons of the Singing Star followed the ape.

"Ought to go back and burn the hell out of that sneaky character," he muttered, but the ape had been a little too slow in building his courage, and Conek had more important matters to take up his time. He needed to find Lesson and then try to find out what happened to the other weapons.

Then he forgot the simian. *Damn, I wonder if they* do *grow!* he thought as he rose into the hold and came face-to-face with the big Skooler robots again.

He bent sideways to avoid Cge's flailing limbs and stepped onto the deck, pulling the droid with him. One day he'd teach Cge to ride the beam with dignity, but this wasn't the day. Skielth and Ister would be coming up fast to avoid the simian and his bunch.

Before Conek could send the big fellows away, Ister and Skielth appeared one right after the other. Respectively they spat and hissed as they drew back from the giant robots.

"Hold it!" Conek stepped between his guests and the

droids as Cge whistled the giants away. "I told you I had a welcoming committee."

Ister's whiskers were still bristling, moving a bit as if testing the air for danger. "They do get larg-g-ge," he said.

Skielth, his blaster in his hand, stared at the monster workers. They were only slightly taller than himself, but no one doubted they could tear a being of his size apart if they were programmed for it. Conek had decided their menace came from their having nearly human shape in black metal. Their size didn't hurt any.

"Hayden," Skielth hissed, "what have you been at? On second thought I don't want to know." He kept his flat eyes on the robots. "They're not from Vladmn, they're not from Osalta—they are enough to scare a person into a premature shedding!"

"Sorry." Conek grinned. "I did warn you—not much of a welcome or a thanks for helping me dodge Slug's apes."

"Well, you can make up for it by giving us a drink," Skielth announced. "After meeting your assorted friends, I need one."

Conek bit back a frown. If they entered the lounge, they'd learn about the major, and a lack of hospitality could cost him two valuable friendships.

The upcoming meeting should be interesting, he thought, and led the way forward.

"Not much on board," he said, "But we'll make do with something."

They approached the lock when it hissed open, and four more Skooler droids rolled through. The robots stopped, turning their sensors on the Shashar and the Orealian until Conek waved them away.

"Hasn't Cge told you fellows not to stare at guests?" he asked, tentatively making pushing motions to get them out of the passage.

"You terrify your workers," Ister said as they stepped into the lounge.

"Oh, I'm a pu—" Conek stopped just short of saying pussycat. "Pushover. Cge's the dictator around here."

Once they entered the lounge, Conek wasn't long in finding out how his guests would take to each other.

"Are you back already?" Andro called from the galley. "Did you have anything to eat? I'm just fixing for myself and the lieutenant—uh-oh," he said as he stepped into the lounge and saw Conek's guests.

Ister and Skielth recognized Andro—if not his face, at least his voice. The Shashar had learned to pull in his tongue to keep it from showing his emotions, and with a lightning-quick slurp it was in his mouth.

No less telling was Ister's reaction as his whiskers stiffened and the tip of his tail became tense, moving with an unnatural slowness.

Cge alone remained unaffected. He whistled an irritating tune as he considered Skielth and turned his inspection to the Orealian.

Conek ignored the droid, his mind on the reactions of Andro and the smugglers.

# CHAPTER Thirteen

The room appeared to be full of figures from a wax museum until Ister jumped, giving a yowl of surprise and rage. He whirled around, whipping Cge about as the droid kept a tight grip on the cat-man's tail.

"Hey!" Conek made a grab for Cge as he whipped by.

Ister jerked again, and the robot, flashing his panic lights, held on as if to let go meant death. Conek's second grab succeeded. With one hand he stopped the small cat-man, while with the other he caught the droid's arm.

Andro had dashed forward and hurried the droid away, pulling him by the arm until Cge was a safe distance from the Orealian.

"*Don't* pull tails," the major said, admonishing the droid through pursed lips. "People will look at you funny."

The circumstances were too much for the amused Shashar to stand with a straight face. His huge mouth opened in a bellowing laugh, his words hissing in amusement.

"Hayden, was there ever one like you? Osalt ship, big droids, Port men, and little droids with strange tastes? All on

MD-439?" His slight emphasis showed he was mainly interested in why Andro, an officer in the Vladmn military, was in the smugglers' port.

Conek shrugged. "You take work where you can get it."

Cge, fully chastised by Andro, rolled up to Conek. He proudly announced that his programming would not allow him to pull any more tails. His computers had thought the action would have been a good learning experience.

Skielth's second quick laugh was devoid of humor. He turned his head toward Conek, his mouth snapping closed. His silence said, "What in hell is going on?"

Conek was spared having to answer when Andro suddenly took the initiative. "What we need is a drink," he chirped breathlessly, trying to reroute the conversation before it grew dangerous to their purpose.

"Very good idea." Skielth flashed his wicked teeth again, shelving his questions for the moment. "Anyone from Siddah-II to Liston will tell you: Until you've had a Shashar bolt, you've never been in orbit."

"Uh-oh, watch your stomach, Major," Conek said in warning. So far, so good. Both Skielth and Ister did legitimate hauling from time to time, so they could discuss shipping without incriminating themselves. Andro followed the huge lizard toward the liquor cabinet in the corner of the lounge.

"I think we're out of the Alotor blend, but the Camoden luchar is somewhat similar." He held up the bottle for Skielth's inspection. "In the Shashar bolt, the difference is immaterial."

Skielth eyed the major over his scaly shoulder. "You know how to make a Shashar bolt?" he asked with surprise.

"Of course. There are a number of Shashar in the Vladmn patrol."

Conek sighed and wondered if his luck would last. If the major said a wrong word, there could be one less human in the Vladmn patrol, and one less human flying an Osalt ship. But Andro apparently realized the danger and was being careful.

Conek relaxed after the first few minutes. The little major

could turn on the authority when he wanted to, but he was smart enough to skirt any subject liable to put the two smugglers on the defensive. After his years in the port authority, Andro knew how to keep pilots interested.

Across the lounge, Skielth listened to Andro and Ister as they traded adolescent experiences on their "patched" planet-hoppers. Like Conek, Skielth had a smuggling father, and while his peers were gloating over their first old planetery vehicles, the big Shashar was flying interstellar ships. The big lizard hunched over, his neck curving like a snake's to get his head down on a level with theirs.

Conek listened and watched Cge. The droid idly rolled back and forth between two empty loungers. He softly repeated a singsong phrase in the discordant musical whistle of his original language.

Andro and Ister exhausted the subject of planet-hoppers and began a discussion of various makes of thrusters.

Skielth raised his glass and waved it back and forth to get Conek's attention. "Ister wants a ride to Siddah-II. You going there?"

"You mind reading again?"

Skielth took Conek's reply for an affirmative and nodded. "Then I'll go along. I can always hitch a ride back." He stretched his legs and spread his feet, a favorite relaxed pose of the Shashar. The long toes, ending in short claws, spread out like dark, leather fans on the carpet of the lounge. At ease, Skielth took up a considerable amount of space, even though he sat on the coils of his powerful tail.

"Suits me," Conek replied as he stood up. "I'll get us started."

When *Bucephalus* approached the landing field on Siddah-II, Conek knew that Lesson and *Anubis* were not there. The Osalt freighter would have dwarfed everything around it.

"Are you going to shut me in again?" Andro asked as Conek strapped on his belt and holster and instructed Cge to put the big droids at the holds to prevent unwelcome entry.

"You'd better believe it. You set one foot off this ship and it could be not only your neck, but mine, Skielth's, and Ister's as well. Now stay put so I can ask about Lesson."

Once Cge had whistled the giant droids to their positions, he activated the grav-rev beam and they descended to the paracrete surface of the pad. Conek pushed Cge into the beam, and the little android kicked and fought the air until he stood on a firm surface again.

When they were on the ground, the Orealian's whiskers quivered as his expression turned thoughtful.

"Is it wise to bring Cge?"

"I don't have a choice," Conek replied. He explained about the major's inability to command the worker droids, who were ordered to prevent the grav-beams and lounge elevator from being used.

Skielth gave a roaring laugh. "I wondered, when I saw him, how you kept him on board. He's a bad little man to cross from what I've heard.

Conek nodded, no longer concerned about Andro now that Ister and Skielth were off the ship. His mind was on Lesson. He was passing worry and homing in on fear. The old pilot was usually in one of three places when he put down for ground time. Conek had been to two of those, and Ister had said Lesson was not on the third.

He thought back, trying to remember exactly when *Anubis* had been serviced. Recently, and ninety percent of the time Lesson could detect a malfunction before the computerized warning system could alert him. There seemed to be only two plausible explanations: either Slug had caught Lesson unaware; or the old drunk had found a new place to drink.

*If it's a new watering hole, I'll kill him—hell, I'll be so glad to see him, I'll even stand for the drinks!*

The thriving port, like the one they'd just come from, was owned by one individual, an octopoid aquatic from the water planet of Dexin. His history was unknown, like ninety-nine percent of the rogue pilots who frequented the port. For more than a century, Tsaral, for whom the port was named had been the central figure in the illegal trade of Vladmn.

From his aquatic tank he directed an organization that moved most of the contraband in Vladmn. His spy system stretched through the three galaxies; he kept abreast of who needed shipments and what pilots were available. For a fee he put the two together. Conek, like most of the smugglers who used the port, had never seen him, receiving an occasional message by Tsaral's special messengers.

Skielth led the way between two large complexes of repair shops. Ister followed, and Conek, bringing up the rear, noticed a general air of decay, as if the town itself were aging. He was sorry to see it.

"Stop, Conek Hayden." Conek turned slowly and came face-to-face with the business end of a blaster.

# CHAPTER Fourteen

Conek remained perfectly still, knowing the shaking hand holding the weapon was more dangerous than a steady one. The humanoid behind the gun was small and frightened; his eyes kept darting up at the huge form of Skielth lurking close to the wall, waiting. Ister had simply melted away into the darkness. Cge rolled over close to Conek, putting his metal hand on the captain's leg.

The ferret-faced humanoid with the gun twitched his nose and took a step back as Cge moved.

"Be still, Cge," Conek said softly, resting his hand on the droid's top module. He addressed the nervous creature with the gun. "Just keep your finger from shaking while it's on that trigger, buddy. Tell Slug I'm available anytime."

The nose twitched again. "Slug?" The eyes shifted from side to side. "Tell him to keep away from me."

The little character was too frightened to be acting, Conek decided. "If you're not from Slug, then who sent you?"

"Tsaral."

"I don't believe it." Skielth growled from the shadows.

"When Tsaral sends out artillery, he's through talking. He never sends a gunman to carry messages."

"Then he's true to form," Conek replied. "This is no gunman."

While they kept the nose-twitcher occupied, Ister slipped out of the shadows, crept up behind their captor, and lifted the blaster out of his hand.

"Hey!" Little ferret-face squeaked, surprised.

With lightning swiftness Skielth reached out a long arm and grabbed the little man by the scruff of the neck.

From his great height the Shashar coiled his supple neck, bringing his head down directly over the shaking humanoid. Flat, black eyes stared down on the quaking creature, and the big mouth opened threateningly. "Who sent you?"

"Ts-s-sarl s-sent me. He s-said, 'Get m-me C-c-con—Con-ek Ha—' He s-said, 'Thert, g-get m-me—' "

Skielth shook his captive roughly. "Stop that stuttering before we catch it."

Conek checked the shadows. The street was deserted. He put away his blaster. "I think we'll pay Tsaral a visit and find out." He might as well. He could dodge the Vladmn patrol, but no one got away from Tsaral if they made an enemy of him.

Thert pointed anxiously to a building where several windows showed light. "It's th-this way!" In his agitation he tried to run, but Skielth's clawed hand on his shoulder held him back.

The Shashar gave him another small shake. "We know where Tsaral is, but you lead. Make one wrong step and I'll burn a hole through you!"

"I w-wouldn't have d-done anyth-thing. Don't sh-shoot me," the trembling Thert begged.

"Who said anything about shooting? I can *breathe* a hole through you!" Skielth released his hold on Thert's shoulder just as he leaned forward, opening his big mouth.

Thert gave a squeal of terror and dashed off down the street. They exchanged glances after watching him disappear into the doorway of Tsaral's headquarters.

They followed him. Inside, a Mentot, a meter-long caterpillar with a white body and silvery hair covering her back, awaited them. Around her neck hung a translator that converted her clicks into an apology for the way they were greeted. She ushered them through a doorway where four chairs almost completely filled a small space facing a huge aquatic tank.

Conek, first through the doorway, stood close enough to the glass to notice the confined underwater world extended beyond the walls of the small room they occupied. In the murky water he could see aquatic plants, colorful fish, and several life-forms he didn't recognize.

While they watched, Tsaral swam across the expanse of water toward a platform raised a meter off the floor of the aquarium. Conek was surprised by his first view of the octopoid. Spread out in maximum reach, Tsaral would hardly be a meter from tip to tip of his tentacles. Conek's two fists together were larger than the smuggling king's body.

Cge rolled up to the clear plastorial tank and bumped his metallic head against it in his fascination. Conek pulled him back when a voice came out of a speaker in the ceiling.

"Let him look, Captain. I'm as curious about him as he is about me."

Conek pushed the droid up to the tank again, but Cge caught sight of Tsaral and gave a squeal of fright. He whipped around behind Conek and refused to move. Though the octopoid was much smaller, he bore a closer resemblance to the beings from Cge's home world than any other life-form in Vladmn.

"Sorry," Conek said. Nothing would be gained by forcing Cge once he "malfunctioned."

Tsaral waved his tentacles as if it were a matter of no importance and, with a swift, graceful movement, rose in the water to the small platform.

"You wanted to see me?" Conek said, bringing the small talk to a close. "An invitation would have done the job."

Tsaral's tentacles jerked slightly. "Thert is an accounts clerk." The translated tone carried the octopoid's irritation and explanation, and dismissed the fiasco entirely. He shifted on his platform, bracing himself with his tentacles.

"Hayden, take Icor's daughter off Siddah-II." No request—an order. The mechanical voice was as adamant as the braced tentacles.

The suddenness and surprise of Tsaral's order left Conek without any immediate words. He nodded, pushing aside the irritation of Gella in general, his obligation to Icor, and his need to find Lesson.

Beside him, Ister's inquiring purr wasn't translated by the device around his neck, but the sensitive audio sensors in the room allowed Tsaral to hear it.

"She's a danger to herself and to the community." Tsaral's answer was for all of them. "She'll bring trouble between the freighter pilots—more than just the occasional squabbles."

Squabbles hardly described the brawls and killings in the smuggling towns, but Conek knew what Tsaral meant. Gella was enough to affect the blood pressure of the restless human pilots, and many of the humanoids. Her beauty was an explosive ingredient. She was too intent on finding and killing Slug to realize the danger to herself from other less fatal directions.

"Where's Icor?" Skielth demanded, his dorsal sail arching. Taking Gella out of the smuggling town should have been her father's responsibility.

"Slug burned him," Conek said flatly. Wanting to skip a long explanation, he changed the subject. "Tsaral, you hear everything. I'm looking for my other ship and my pilot, Lesson. Have any of your people reported seeing him?"

"I've heard nothing. Good luck with Icor's daughter, Captain."

Tsaral left his platform just as the white Mentot opened the door to the little audience space. The interview was over.

Back on the street again, Conek told Skielth and Ister about Icor's death. They had known the old rocket-rider, and they shared Conek's hatred of Slug.

While they were talking, Cge had stayed close to Conek. After nearly tripping over the droid twice, Conek pushed Cge back half a meter.

"Give me breathing room, will you? Why in the hell didn't I sell you, anyway?"

He frowned down at Cge, wondering what type of droid programming Skooler used. Vladmn robots were machines. Cge qualified as an infantile neurotic.

"I'll turn you into a garbage disposal if you don't behave."

Cge misunderstood the threat. "You won't sell me?"

"Maybe I'll sell you to Tsaral," Conek replied.

Skielth gave Conek a glare and hissed, "Don't tease him!" He patted the top of Cge's module, his claws rattling against the metal. "He's not going to sell you to anybody, unless it's me." Another hard look at Conek told him he was in for trouble if he did.

They strolled down the street. A shadow disengaged itself from the others and hurried toward them. Conek, Skielth, and Ister had their blasters in their hands before they recognized Andro.

"How did you get off the ship?" Conek demanded.

"By whistling."

"What?"

"I whistled until I found the right tune to turn the droids off. Somebody's waiting for you."

"How would you know?" Conek didn't believe it. Sure, he had enemies, but none Andro would know about.

"I was listening to the ship transmissions. Guttural voice, I didn't recognize it. They didn't mention names."

Skielth's long neck arched as he brought his head closer to Andro. Ister blended back into the shadows again.

"Just what did they say?" Skielth asked.

"Hayden's down, but the Shashar and the Orealian are with him. I heard an affirmative—that was all."

Conek absently gazed into the shadows across the street, just parking his focus while he thought over Andro's message.

"It's time you told us who's after you," Skielth said.

Conek shrugged. "I don't know, unless it's Slugarth."

"We should all stick together," Andro advised. "We don't have time for them now."

"We'll take time," Conek said. "Slug doesn't have too many men here, or they wouldn't worry about Skielth and Ister. The more of his crowd I get off my back, the less we'll have to face later."

"You've got a point." Skielth bared his teeth. No attempt at human humor this time.

Conek nodded. "Skielth, you and Ister take that side of the street. Andro, Cge, and I will take this side. Yell if you see Gella. I'll try to talk her out. No point in getting everybody killed."

The three streets in the business section of Tsaral as seen from the air resembled an *H*, all approximately a kilometer in length. The easterly parallel leg was closest to the landing pads and was flanked by repair shops and suppliers of replacement parts. With the exception of completely replacing a hull, almost any ship repair could be made there. In keeping with the policy of Tsaral, repairs were strictly legal. For other, more specialized equipment, there were less public places. Their locations were available for a fee if you were known.

At the eastern intersection, located between the shops and the business section, was Tsaral's aquatic home.

Taking both sides, they started down the connecting leg of the *H*, a street devoted entirely to other types of supplies. The shop windows featured the newest in men's and women's fashions, electronic games, space suits, convenience equipment, and the thousand sundry items of interest to a traveler. There were several souvenir and exotic pet shops, as well as some that catered to the regular inhabitants of Tsaral and the natives of Siddah-II.

Conek glanced in the windows. They could have been in the main shopping area of any small town in Vladmn Territory. Unlike most shops on other, more reputable planets, no special merchandise was kept hidden from the public eye. The main industry of the town was information. The contrabanding was done elsewhere. If the Vladmn patrol ever landed and searched, they'd find the town of Tsaral cleaner than any city in the tri-galactic territory.

Tsaral's aquarium was the brain of the city, but the pulse

was the third street, called the Hollow, because of its lower elevation. Small hotels lined both sides of the street; each had its own restaurant and bar with entertainment.

Most pilots liked to stay off-ship when they were in port. They spent their waking hours in the bars where they caught up on rumors, listened for mention of jobs, and often contracted with Tsaral's minions for new business.

The buildings were owned by the octopoid, but the individual managers vied with each other, changing their decor, and at times their atmosphere, if they decided to cater to a different clientele. Their main points in common were the dim lighting, the lush surroundings, and desultory entertainment. The musicians were not allowed to interfere with the main attraction. The clients were listening for valuable information.

At the intersection, Conek, Cge, and Andro turned to the left. Some entrances had air locks and signs listing the species catered to on the inside. They checked five bars with oxygen-based atmospheres. Several patrons called out to Conek. Twice he stopped for short conversations, but they continued from one dimly lit place to another. Before they reached the entrance of the sixth, he knew they'd found Gella.

"Get out of my way." Conek recognized Gella's voice as they stepped into the open doorway. The bar was ominously silent. Gella kept the timbre of her voice well below a shout, but it carried across the room with obvious menace.

# CHAPTER Fifteen

Conek stepped quietly into the bar. His green eyes located Icor's daughter and took in the general layout in the same split second. The narrow, L-shaped room had a bar running the length of the area leading off to the left, parallel to the street. The lounge, stretching back into the building, was much longer than its width with six rows of tables, three on each side of the center aisle.

Around the walls were maps of ancient worlds and a huge antique mirror, the glass etched with countless solar systems. The round tabletops were finished to resemble parchment with the drawings of legendary explorers.

Halfway down the lounge, backed up against an empty table next to the wall, Gella stood glaring at a barrel-bodied man. He rose, weaving his way around the table. "Girlie, sit down. Be nice to me."

"I'm to haul freight for you. Until the shipment is ready, what I do is my own business."

"Well see about that!" He lurched at her, but Gella

whipped a chair into his path. He tripped, sprawling on the floor.

She grabbed a bottle from the table, grasping it around the neck. The fallen drunk scrambled to his feet as she retreated up the aisle. Staggering, bumping into tables, the drunk lurched after her.

"Hey, Borth," a Xrotha shouted, turning up his translator for effect. "I never thought you'd be dumped on your butt by a female!"

"Don't let him stop you, girlie." Conek couldn't recognize the voice, but it was human.

The other patrons called advice to both Gella and Borth, but no one interfered. Borth careened after her, grabbing at a table for support. His hand closed on a light jacket flung over a chair.

Over the protest of the jacket's owner, Borth lurched forward and threw the cloth over Gella's head. While she grappled with it she swung the bottle. He caught her hand—luck rather than coordination.

Near the entrance a simian shifted in his chair and loosened his blaster in his holster. His eye contact with two humans across the aisle alerted Conek that he'd found his ambush.

Conek hoped Gella could reach the door without his help, but as the drunk gripped her hand, Conek leapt forward. His momentum added force to his fist. Borth went down without a sound.

"Hey, it's none of your business, Hayden!" A four-eyed Jelinian struggled to his feet, his quartet of bleary orbs trying to focus on Conek.

The other drinkers stopped laughing. The custom of non-intervention had been breached. If Gella had made the door on her own, they would have taken it as great sport to see Borth bested by a woman. Conek's entrance into the argument was an intrusion.

"Let's get out of here fast," Conek hissed at Gella. He started backing toward the door. His hand itched to close on his blaster grip, but one shot could bring a hundred in return. Better to leave the gun holstered.

On the periphery of his vision Conek saw two crablike Xrotha rise to block his way. The first, arched up on his rear legs in ancient challenge, toppled backward. Blue-gray metal gleamed as Cge rolled out from under the flailing legs. The droid's round body cylinder acted like a runaway barrel. The other arthropod suddenly found his legs caught up in those of an upturned chair sliding across the floor. Beyond the stumbling insect, Andro grabbed another chair. The major was as white as if he had been bleached.

The clatter brought the bartender charging from the bar, his arms fluttering. "What happened—no! No fighting in here, I warn you—"

"Look out." Gella shouted, and reached up to deflect a flying bottle just before it struck Conek's head. He glowered at the Txorch who threw it. Txorch would do anything to get in a fight.

"No throwing things," the bartender screamed. "This is an establishment for civilized—oh-h!"

The sailing bottle acted as a signal for the rest of the patrons to take action. A Herodontian waiter tried to get to the back entrance and bumped into a table. The three patrons jumped up, roaring at him. Two Herodontian patrons, seeing one of their fellow citizens in trouble, attacked the trio with flying chairs.

"Stop!" the bartender squealed, rushing down the aisle, all four arms waving.

The Txorch threw another bottle at Conek, but a stumbling victim of a swinging fist jostled him from behind, ruining his aim. The bottle hit a Mentot, two tables away. Until the Mentot, meter-long caterpillars with short stubby legs, were proven sentient, the Txorch had hunted them for food. With screams of rage the quintet of furry catyrpels leapt from table to table, bearing two of the three Txorch down with their weight. The fifth jumped on the Txorch left standing. Using his front and rear pairs of feet to attach himself, he pummeled the back of his enemy with his other six legs.

Old animosities from other worlds needed only a spark to set them off. Two Xrotha at the back of the room resembled windmills as they threw bottles using all six arms. Their intended targets were their ancient enemies, the Rosthmn at a table in the middle of the room, but their aim was democratic. Shouts and screeches, roars and barks, echoed off the walls. Bottles and chairs crashed.

A Luvoir, a climbing rodent from Beta Galaxy, scampered up the wall and ran along a ventilation pipe to the center of the room. His fellows, too small to join in the hand-to-hand combat, tossed him bottles. He targeted on the Cynbeth, reptiles who resembled miniature dragons out of Old Earth's mythology.

"No—no! Not the mugs!" screamed the bartender, rushing toward the Luvoir, who was gathering ammunition from several tables. "Use bottles if you have to, but not the mugs!"

A roar from a huge, maned Talovan who hopped around holding his foot signaled the path of a Cynbeth. The reptile, unable to escape under the tables because of the fighters rolling on the floor, took to the tops, jumping from one to the other. Bottles crashed behind him. The Cynbeth neared the wall, and the bartender sprang across the room.

"Not at the antique mirror," he screamed, throwing himself spread-eagle in front of the wavy glass with an old map etched on its surface. He stood, his four arms splayed out, trying to protect his treasure. A bottle crashed two centimeters from the frame.

Conek pushed Gella under a table and fended off one of the Xrotha with a chair. He knocked the attacker over on his shelled back when a native of Colsar lunged at him; a hairy fist sent him sprawling. Flat on his back, Conek raised his head, shook it slightly to see if it was still attached, and reached for a tabletop. He missed and felt teeth close on his arm. He jerked his head around to face a Cynbeth, who curled around the pedestal of a table, his short wings folded tightly, his long, serpentine neck drawn back. His teeth gripped Conek's arm.

Conek doubted the Cynbeth had the strength to bite through the bone, but he could make some nasty punctures. The reptile appeared to be unsure whether to bite or not.

"Try it and I'll wring your scrawny neck," Conek warned.

That decided the Cynbeth, who loosened his grip and coiled up against the table leg again.

"Sorry."

When Conek started to rise, he was bowled over by six Ionians, smaller relatives of the marsupials on MD-439. They scampered from the shelter of the tables, trying to get to the door and safety. Two dashed across him and knocked him backward. The third tripped, tumbled across his chest, and dislodged the infant it carried in its pouch. The pale gray cub dug tiny claws into Conek's sides and took a grip on his shirt with its teeth.

"Ah, for—" Conek disengaged the infant and thrust it at the Cynbeth. "Here. You're not busy, *you* baby-sit."

"Me?" The little dragon recoiled from the struggling ball of fur.

"They'll be back when they notice he's missing." Conek shoved the cub into the stubby arms of the reptile and watched the Cynbeth squirm as the little claws pierced his soft belly scales.

Conek started up again. This time he made it to his knees. Borth was back in the fight again. The drunk took a swing at a Xrotha, missed, and his momentum carried him across the aisle. He fell on Conek.

"Damn-n!" Conek shouted as he tumbled backward. At first he thought he'd been shot from behind. He had landed on something sharp. Rolling out from under the drunk, he came face-to-face with a Mentot, who twisted around to inspect the horn that grew from his rear segment. A quarter of the horn had broken off and dangled by a fiber. He glared at Conek.

"You *broke* it!" he screeched.

Conek rubbed his butt and ignored the catyrpel as he wondered if the sharp horn had pierced to the bone. He could feel the blood.

"You broke it!" the Mentot screamed again.

"So have it resharpened and charge it to me." Conek snarled back, ducking as a chair sailed over his head.

He decided he'd been in one spot long enough. Three tries

at getting to his feet were two too many. He crawled back toward the wall and scrambled to stand. Then he scanned the room.

Close to the door, Cge stood on a waiter's service counter. His panel flashed in anger or panic. His small metallic hands held a fizzer hose for refoaming drinks. He sprayed a wide arc, building a mound of foam around the counter. A Txorth, staggering in Cge's direction after a blow from a simian, got a face full of foam.

Andro backed up against the wall, paler than ever. He fended off an Olynthr with the remains of a chair. Conek couldn't see Gella.

"There he is!" Conek turned to see Unkart and three of Slug's cronies bearing down on him.

"Now wait a minute," he said, backing up. "Let's be reasonable about this. Four is not an even contest—"

Unkart was in no mood for reason, and the others had their orders. He threw a chair in their path and backed away. Two of the Mentot were still pummeling one of the Txorch, and Conek tripped over the trio. He went down on one knee and tried to roll away. Before he could rise, Unkart and his three friends fell on him.

He was lost under the alcoholic breath and sweaty bodies, but except for the weight he was unhurt. Dimly he heard the crackle of a blaster. Then another.

Someone in the heap covering Conek muttered "Shashar," and the weight rapidly shifted off him. He stood and saw Ister and Skielth in the doorway holding their weapons. Nearby the simian cradled his hand. A blaster lay at his feet, part of the grip burned away.

Most of the room's occupants were brought to a standstill by the danger of blasters. By the aisle, Gella crawled out from under a table. The bartender was still spread-eagle against the undamaged mirror. At the back of the room a Xrotha threw a mug of liquid on two combatants still on the floor.

Conek's path between the tables was blocked on one side by the first Txorch, now unconscious, and on the other by the two Mentot, who were still pummeling the second.

Conek reached down and lifted first one Mentot and then the other off the humanoid. "Recess is over, boys. Let's get back to some serious drinking."

The Ionians scampered back in the door, in search of their infant. The Cynbeth freed the baby, leaving the howling mite on the floor. The small dragon climbed a curtain on the wall, staying well out of the way of the now enraged parents.

Then, over the smells of fear and anger, drawn blood and spilled intoxicants of twenty different worlds, came a stronger odor. Backed up in the corner were two small Gulinora, who used scent as their primary defense. They hid their heads in embarrassment while the Talovan who had been bitten by the Cynbeth shook his head, wrinkling his nose, and moaned.

Others in the back of the room were hurrying toward the door. Suddenly, on the air currents caused by the room's ventilators, a forceful blast of the Gulinora weaponry reached Conek. The air seemed robbed of oxygen; the acrid odor burned his nostrils and mouth. His insides heaved in warning. Two Xrotha gave a series of clicks beyond the scope of their translators and bounded up the center aisle. They were blocked by the immediate intention of everyone else in the room to make a quick exit.

Like everyone else, Conek fought to get to the door. Ahead, he could see the broad back of Skielth, who shook his head as he forced his way through the entrance.

A small creature landed on Conek's back; he felt claws gripping him on the shoulders and around the waist. He turned his head and saw the long, reptilian snout as the Cynbeth twisted, shook his head, and buried his nostrils against the flesh of Conek's throat. Conek shivered at the feel of the cool, reptilian flesh against his, but he let the Cynbeth remain. He needed his hands to force a way through the crowd.

Along with several other life-forms, he pushed out into the night air, gasping for breath. Around him arthropods were forcing air in and out of their sides; other beings were gasping. He glanced around, spotted Skielth, Ister, and Andro standing with Gella.

He strode over. "Somebody sure knows how to break up a party."

Skielth opened his mouth to speak, swallowed convulsively, and settled for nodding.

"Where is Cge?" Ister croaked, looking around.

Conek searched the fast-dwindling crowd. "I'm not going back after him," he warned.

Just then the robot came rolling through the door, his metal body shedding bits of foam. He wheeled up to Conek, tilting forward to view his owner's feet. The angle of the droid's body changed as he gave Conek a close inspection from toe to head.

"You function correctly?"

"Yeah, but what about you? Didn't your maker tell you to stay out of barroom brawls?"

The droid's panel slowed. "Cge malfunctioned?"

"I don't know about him, but I thought I would," Andro said weakly. "This is no way to get to be dictator."

Gella pulled at Conek's sleeve. "Thanks."

"I told you you couldn't cut it over here." When he saw her change of expression, Conek had a few choice names for himself. Gella's experience had sobered her, but his remark caused her anger to swing from herself to him. Her eyes held a fighting light.

"So I approached the wrong person! You didn't make any mistakes when you began, I suppose?"

"Lots, and I'm going to tell you all about them," Conek growled. He caught her arm and propelled her down the street. The patrons of the Explorer, who had been ousted by the odor, were entering other places along the street.

Conek hurried Gella along until they came to the intersection and started up the deserted business section. Gella tried to pull away when she saw his direction, but he tightened his grip and towed her despite her objections.

"Where are you going?" she demanded.

"To tell you about my mistakes. I'm going to tell you all

the way to a place where you'll stay out of trouble. And I'll see you stay there!"

"No you're *not*!" Gella fought his grasp. Up the entire length of the street, she struggled. Conek grimly continued on, ignoring the occasional blows on his shoulder. Behind him, Andro volunteered a few words about young girls who took up smuggling.

Cge, bringing up the rear of the column with Ister, alternately whistled and gave the Orealian his views on life-forms who fought with one another. Skielth, once seeing them safely out of the barroom brawl, had headed for another bar, where he would stay until he wanted to return to MD-439 and his ship.

When they reached the landing pad, Conek turned left, heading for *Bucephalus*. Gella, who hadn't succeeded in stopping him any other way, dropped to the pavement.

"You're not taking me on your damn warehouse!" she yelled, kicking at him. "If I leave *Starfire*, in twelve hours there won't be anything left but the paint!"

"You'll be better off without that ship," Conek replied, dodging her feet. He caught her arm and spun her around, then, with one arm circling her waist, jerked her to her feet. But he couldn't take her away from her vessel. His indecision was caused partly by her stricken expression. He remembered his feelings when someone else took his dead father's ship.

Ister understood Gella's feelings and offered his opinion. "You can't leave the ship, Hayden. I'll fly it, but you can't leave it."

"Let's talk it over on Conek's ship," Andro said suddenly. "I've an idea."

Aboard *Bucephalus*, Conek fixed a round of drinks while the others relaxed. When everyone had a glass, the contents deliberately less potent than a Shashar bolt, he eased down onto a lounger, careful of how he sat after his run-in with the horn of the Mentot.

"So what's the bright idea?"

"She's too young to be a smuggler."

"It's none of your business!" Gella snapped.

"But it is—officially," Andro replied tranquilly. "And I've decided you won't continue."

"Who *is* he?" Gella shouted at Conek.

"The only way you can stop her is to take her ship," Conek said. "I can't let you—it's all she's got."

Why in hell didn't he mind his own business? As if he had all the time in the world for juvies who were out to get themselves killed. But he'd fought for *Anubis*, even though he never flew her. *Starfire* was all Gella had left of Icor.

"She can't legally carry a shipment without a pilot's license," Andro argued. "How long before she's old enough for one?"

"Less than a year."

"Who *is* he?" Gella demanded again.

"If we impounded the ship on Agnar-Alpha . . ." Andro was thoughtful.

"Hell, no, she'd never get it back."

"If we had it impounded for suspicion of having been down on Tulafore, it would be sealed for a year."

"Health regulations. No question of it being a smuggler's vessel?" Conek saw Andro's reasoning. "But can you manage it?"

"Who *is* he?"

Andro took a sip of his drink, seemed to give the subject more thought. "No question. I can call in a favor or two."

"Health regulations . . ." Conek considered the idea. "I like it."

"I've got a condition. Lieutenant Marwit goes back to Agnar-Alpha in her ship."

"That's your neck," Conek warned.

But the major turned adamant. Since Lieutenant Marwit was attached to Norden's security guard and reported directly to her, Andro was relatively sure of getting a message through.

When Ister raised *Starfire*, both Gella and the lieutenant were aboard, the lieutenant carrying a voice-disk to be turned over to Norden.

"Will she listen to you?" Conek asked him as they sat in

the bridge, warming the thrusters while they watched the old CD-51 lift off.

"She's had time to calm down. She might. If she does, she'll keep the patrol off our backs. If not, you're no worse off."

"But you are," Conek reminded him. "Until she gets that disk, she could believe I was holding both you and bright-eyes prisoner, but now she'll know the truth."

"It's worth the gamble," Andro said. "If the wrong people get their hands on our gun and start manufacturing it, there'll be nothing left, anyway."

# CHAPTER Sixteen

Lesson was missing, and three alien weapons had to be found or someone could make a lot of nothing out of their world, but Conek temporarily gave up the search. The decision wasn't arbitrary. The jump into time from the planct's surface on Radach-I had jarred more of the giant freighter than just one hatch seal. Several bracings were weakened, and if they weren't reinforced, he could end up flying a bridge with nothing but space between himself and the thrusters.

If he returned to his home port on Agnar-Alpha, he should have plenty of time—probably fifty years, if they put him and the ship in the same cell. His only other choice was Gordotl. Dursig might have been partially reassured by the Quinta, but he wasn't exactly involved in a love affair with the Vladmn government. If Conek could get assistance anywhere, it would be on the planetary home of the big agriculturists.

"The tratha's apparently in residence," Andro said as they circled down from the upper atmosphere.

Conek leaned forward, wondering if he saw reality or a hopeful hallucination. "Maybe, maybe not."

"I meant the ships—you said the Gordotl had three." Andro was referring to the three Osalt freighters sitting together, taking up more space than the small farming community.

"Two are Dursig's," Conek said, his voice hoarse. "That beauty gleaming like a mirror in the sun is *Anubis*!"

"Lesson's here!" Andro leaned forward as if he could see the ship better by being half a meter closer. "Why here?"

"I don't know, but I'll sure as hell find out."

They landed by Conek's second ship. Conek hurried through the air lock and across to the smaller ship with Andro and Cge close behind. On *Anubis*, Lesson was startled as the three walked into the lounge.

"Where have you been?" Conek demanded, half drunk with relief, half angry to find Lesson calmly taking his ease on Gordotl.

"Sounds like you missed me." Lesson chuckled. He laid his book aside and rose, stretching.

"Where is the weapon?" Andro demanded.

"What happened?" Conek overrode the major. "You don't look as if you've been on downtime."

"Where is the *weapon*?" Andro repeated.

"Not guilty," Lesson replied to Conek, though he watched Andro as if the major had sprung up out of the floor. "I ran into Slug and got my tail feathers burned. One of his ships got the worst of it."

"*Where is the weapon*?" Andro shouted.

"Good." Conek had dropped onto a lounger and watched as Andro clenched and unclenched his fists and ran his hand down the side of his leg, apparently wishing he had brought his blaster with him when they rushed aboard *Anubis*. His questions about his pilot and his ship partially satisfied, Conek took pity on the little major.

"What about that box I left on board?" With a gesture he included Andro. "We need it."

"I put it back on Beldorph." Lesson shrugged. "What I want to know is how Slug's boys knew I had it."

"What were you doing on Beldorph?" Conek asked, surprised.

"I want to know about the weapon!" Andro shrilled. He seemed surprised by his own vehemence and lowered his voice. "Pilot Lesson, I am Major Andro Avvin of the Vladmn Patrol Service, and I demand you tell me about that weapon."

Lesson sat down on the end of a lounger and folded his arms across his chest. "Sonny, I *know* who you are, and you could be a piebald mare for all the difference it makes. I left that damn thing on Beldorph."

"We've got to get it and fast," Conek said. "That thing packs a gullywomp of trouble, and we can't risk Slug finding it."

Lesson grinned. "You don't think I left it in the cave, do you? You said it was all-fired important."

"You didn't put it on the ghoster?" He didn't think Lesson could find the ship, but the pirates hadn't had any trouble.

"Nope, under the cave," Lesson answered, his eyes alight with mischief. "I blew the sand away from the rear and put it underneath. Safest place I knew. We may call it a cave, but it ain't nothing but a fused sand building if you think about it."

Lesson watched, satisfied, as Conek shook his head in wonder. Slug would never find it, and neither would anyone else.

"But why there?" Andro asked.

"The captain said it was dangerous. I had to come here for repairs—couldn't go back to Agnar-Alpha with Slug on my tail. Someone's hitting Gordotl from time to time—I didn't want to bring it with me. Hell, what would you do?" He shrugged, letting them infer that he didn't have a lot of choice.

Lesson told them about being followed and the short space battle. ". . . A piece of insulation, blasted loose when the planing linkage went, fell across one of the time-comp's cooling vents. Half a unit in comp and then I had to come out and cool it off. I was twelve cycles getting to Gordotl. Dursig had left to pick up the first shipment of arms and didn't know I had arrived." He couldn't resist needling Conek. "Dursig seemed a lot happier to see me than you are."

"Oh, buddy, he couldn't have been. You've saved my *neck*."

"Not only *your* neck but possibly a great many more." Andro, who'd remained standing, sunk onto a lounger. "My apologies, Pilot Lesson."

Lesson was glad to forgive and forget, and insisted on making drinks and putting prepared meals in to heat. They sat sipping drinks in tall glasses. Andro made conversation with the old pilot.

"The captain tells me those books on *Bucephalus* belong to you—the Westerns."

"Oh, yeah, an interesting time," Lesson said, and then leaned forward, all attention. "Did you read them?" He seemed incredulous.

"I did." Andro nodded. "All four. I'm normally more interested in ancient wars, but I enjoyed them."

"Well, anytime you run out of war, I've plenty of these, and none of them on film or on animated holo-cubes, either. The real thing—books, like the old days." He tapped the cover of the one he had been reading and then sat up abruptly. "And I got something else too. Found a store on Stellar IV specializing in the gear to go with these books—" He stopped, glancing around the lounge, frowning. "Funny, I thought I put my hat down on that lounger."

They turned in the direction in which Lesson pointed. A small metallic hand came into view from behind the lounger, dropped the wide-brimmed felt hat into the seat, and quickly withdrew.

Conek tensed, remembering Lesson's feelings about the droid. His tension was unnecessary. Lesson stepped over to the lounger, picked up the hat, and reached behind the chair. He caught the droid's arm and gently drew Cge out into the open.

"So you like my hat?" Lesson said to the droid. "Well, I guess I owe you something after calling you a spy."

Cge, his panels blinking rapidly, tried to withdraw, but

Lesson kept a tight grasp on the small metal arm as he put the hat over Cge's sensor module.

The old pilot frowned down at the droid, who still exerted pressure to pull away. "I said I'm sorry. I know now you weren't a spy, so let's be friends, okay?"

Cge's panel lights slowed their speed, but his answering "affirmative" had a doubtful tone. Lesson ignored it.

Lesson threw a surreptitious glance his way to see if the captain noticed his peacemaking efforts. Then Lesson turned his attention to the droid.

"Remember what I taught you about shooting?" Lesson pointed his forefinger and his hand gave a slight jerk. "Kew-w-w!"

"It is in my computer," Cge said cautiously. "What is a hat?"

"Here, look at this." Lesson picked up the book and showed Cge the front cover. Cge's panels whirled as he pointed a metallic finger at the picture.

"Cge is not programmed to run that machine," he announced. His quick look at Conek said he had no desire to learn.

"That's a horse," Lesson said with a trace of impatience. "Now, here's what you do. . . ." Taking the hat, he put it on his own head, pulling down on the brim with his left hand while he pointed his right forefinger. "Kew-w-w . . . saw it in a holo-film on Stellar IV." He put the hat back on Cge's module. "Now you try."

Conek sat watching as the droid lost his fear of Lesson and wholeheartedly entered the game. Conek was glad to have Lesson back but didn't want to admit, even to himself, how much he had missed the old pilot and how worried he had been.

If Lesson could accept Cge and the two of them were on friendly terms, it would make life easier—until he sold the droid, he amended hurriedly, a little angry with himself for including Cge in on his long-range plans. He conveniently forgot he'd turned down two more offers to buy the droid.

He remembered the food heating in the galley and went to

check it. Andro followed Conek and helped him remove it from the heating cabinet.

The major divided his time between helping Conek and peering into the lounge. By the sounds, Lesson and Cge had perfected their stand-up gunfight and were working on shooting from cover. From the instructions Lesson seemed to think that the old lead bullets traveled somewhat slower than a man running in triple-g's.

Conek gave a shout as he entered the lounge.

"I'm a'warning you, Pawd-nahs, the first galoot who draws a bead on this here grub gets strung up to the nearest cottonwood."

Cge abandoned the fight and come rolling over. "Cotton . . . wood?" he asked slowly.

Lesson accepted the food from Conek. "You educate him while I hunker down to this grub." Then he frowned and pointed a fork at Cge. "When does he eat?"

"We don't know yet," Conek replied.

Lesson jerked his thumb at the bridge. "Little feller, you go right in and help yourself anytime you want. I know what you're doing, and you're perfectly welcome."

Cge's panel flashed slowly, and he edged toward Conek. He was still wary of the control room on *Anubis*.

Conek remained on Gordotl less than one standard day. Dursig was visiting another village, but the Gordotl pilots knew Conek and were glad to assist him with his repairs.

Since *Anubis* would be staying on the agricultural planet until the Gordotl could make several more parts, Conek headed for Beldorph to pick up the weapon Lesson had hidden.

Now that he could produce the gizmo he found, Conek's thoughts had turned toward the other missing Skooler armament. Several previously unrelated bits of knowledge seemed to fit more closely than he first expected.

While they were in comp, he entered the lounge and, in a surprise move, snatched a book from Andro's hands, startling the major.

"Are you being funny or starting a fight?" Andro demanded.

"I need an ear."

"Permanently or just for listening?"

Conek ignored the flippancy.

"Fact one: Osalt ships pirated my claim. Fact two: Dursig and I own the only known Osalt freighters in Vladmn. Fact three: The Osalt attacks on the perimeter have been driven back—nothing got through. Conclusion: There are two or more Osalt freighters hidden somewhere in Vladmn."

Andro disagreed.

"I think two ships probably got through the line and they now have our weapons."

"Think about that. The Osalt launch a solid attack just to get two ships through. They bypass Gordotl and the thereil, which they need as much as we do, and go straight to Beldorph—"

"Well, but—" Andro tried to interrupt, but Conek overrode him.

"—to raid a ghoster on a gamble that something of value might be aboard?"

"Then you don't think the stolen cargo went to Osalta?"

Conek swiveled his seat. "Probably, but they didn't come here to get it."

"Translation?"

"They *couldn't*. They never would have gotten through our lines."

Andro shook his head. "Then what about the attacks on Gordotl? Are you saying Dursig's people are all hallucinating—or lying to get weapons from the Vladmn stores?" His eyes narrowed.

"Hell, no! Dursig was attacked, and in Osalt ships," Conek replied. "Only they're based somewhere within Vladmn."

"Wait. Go back to the points one, two, and three. You're giving me a prickly feeling at the back of my neck, but I'm not following you yet. Explain it to me."

"Lesson put me on the track in the beginning, but I didn't see it. He said the Osalt couldn't get through, and he was right. There's always been a certain amount of smuggling trade between Osalt and Vladmn. The Osalt have made a deal to get the thereil. And some smuggler raided Gordotl since I've got the exclusive on trade there.

"No Vladmn freighter captain could, or would, attack the Gordotl in his own ships, so they sneaked him two of theirs, probably with uniforms. When the contrabander raids, the Osalt make a feint at the border and draw off our patrols from the center of the galaxy to help cover the perimeter."

Andro wasn't convinced. "That would take a lot of coordination."

"Think about it. Do you really believe our intelligence is suddenly so efficient that we always know in advance when they're going to attack? Once or twice, maybe, but not *every* time. I think raiding the ghoster was just icing on the cake."

"That's a beautiful theory, but one fact is missing. How did they get the stuff into Osalt? The defense line is thick with fighters."

"In Vladmn teacups. We can jump all the way, remember, and pass the defense line undetected. But *I've* got the only Osalt ships with Vladmn time-comps."

"Perfect," Andro breathed. "Look in your crystal ball and tell me who the smuggler is, and we'll have General Kalat after him within the hour."

"We find out who it is by going to Osalta," Conek said quietly.

Andro frowned. "A bit drastic. We'd get blown out of the sky."

"In an Osalt freighter?"

"That *was* stupid. This may be, too, but how could we find him in Osalt if we can't find him here?"

"Andro, will you think? He has to make the jump in a Vladmn ship. How many teacups will be on Osalta? His ship will be obvious."

The major digested Conek's logic and sighed. "When do we leave?"

"You're not going."

"See if you can leave without me." Andro sat back, folding his arms across his chest.

"Look, you don't want to go. This is no sight-seeing—"

"You're damn right I don't want to go, but we've got to get those weapons, so you're stuck with me. Now get going before I lose my nerve."

# CHAPTER Seventeen

On the way to Osalta, Conek made one quick stop. On a deserted rocky planet not much larger than an asteroid, he landed and bolted an Osalt registration plate over the Vladmn designation. Using a codebook he had taken from the last ship he'd stolen for the Gordotl, he made up the plate using the call numbers of a small, but secret, scientific department of the Osalt government.

"I hope they haven't been naughty," Andro said as Conek installed the sheet of flexible metal. "I'd hate to get there and be arrested for being a traitor."

A quarter of a unit later they slid smoothly out of time again and were challenged by the Osalt Air Service.

On the way Conek had practiced his little-used Osalt, managing a dialect from a remote area to cover any mistakes. He rattled off his registration numbers and waited, prepared to follow it up with a common name and cover story. He didn't need it.

After hearing the registration code, the controller took time to check, then came back on the air, oozing respect and cooperation. He waived all customary questions on point of origin and necessity classification, asking simply what berthing Conek required and if he needed security for the ship.

"Guards would cause unnecessary attention," Conek replied crisply. "Berth us back away from the main area. We require time to check out a possible malfunction. We would rather handle it ourselves."

The reply was quick. "Of course." A brief silence followed. Then Conek received directions to a landing pad with immediate clearance to land. "Shall I code you in for radio silence while you are making your repairs?" came the tentative question.

"Just so," Conek answered.

They eased their way through the slow traffic of the busy port. The heavy upper atmosphere protected the planet from bombardment by meteor storms, so hangars were nonexistent. Hundreds of freighters, transports, warships, and sleek government and private vessels sat in tight rows according to their classifications. Conek eyed the rows of fighters and thought one good blast of the new weapon would effectively end the Osalt threat for a generation.

Ground vehicles rushed around carrying passengers and freight to and from the huge transparent domes of the city.

Conek had never understood why the Osalt had settled the inhospitable planet they'd named Osalta. Lifeless and without a breathable atmosphere, it was neither well lit nor warmed by its two distant suns. Little of its surface allowed for building. Vast stretches of the planet were barren. The few overcrowded cities, covered by huge, transparent domes, had degenerated into teeming warrens of misery. The largest, like the planet, was called Osalta.

A standard Vladmn year before, word had reached Vladmn of a catastrophe in the enemy capitol. A freighter had crashed through the central dome and into the city. The death toll, most of it from suffocation, had been in the millions.

High up on the transparent shield, the workers repairing it were almost microscopic by distance. Around the edges of the huge hole, a new, glossier surface showed the slow progress.

Conek eased *Bucephalus* down on the paracrete. Once he shut off the engines, he cut the sending switch on the communicator.

"They'll be another year on those repairs," he said. Andro gazed at the damaged dome.

The major shuddered. "In the meantime they have to live in masks. Give me Agnar-Alpha and dodging meteors—and if it's not a secret, who *are* we supposed to be? My fellows wouldn't spill over like that if the entire council flew in, which it often does."

"I don't know, but I'll use it until I've worn out my welcome." The lowering suns were chasing each other toward the horizon. "There's an Osalt suit on my workbench. Get it on and inspect the underside of the hull. Stay in the shadows and make like a mechanic."

Conek took his distance glasses and scanned the port. Few citizens of Vladmn spoke Osalt. If the smuggler had to speak Vladmn Standard, the communicator would alert him immediately. Conek thought he'd recognize the smuggler if he spoke Osalt badly, but Andro wouldn't know the difference. Either way, watching or listening, they wouldn't get much warning.

Just at dusk, when the port lights were being turned on, Andro scurried back aboard. He grinned as he pulled off his suit.

"I made a lot of nice noises," he said.

Conek nodded and went back to scanning the airspace above the port. He had been listening to Andro's tapping, following the major's progress.

"I take it our malfunction is electrical, since you stayed away from the fuel lines."

"Of course! If a strange ship came into my port and started fiddling with their fuel lines, I'd have the fire boys out in one minute flat."

They took turns watching the port. They were well into the second night when Andro sent Cge with the news. A Vladmn freighter had landed.

Cge came wheeling into Conek's cabin beeping the alarm. Conek had just drifted off to sleep, and he stumbled with grogginess as he entered the bridge. Andro handed him the distance glasses and pointed.

"I didn't have any warning at all. If they had any communication over the regular channel, it must have been in Osalt."

Halfway across the port, close to the main cargo entrance, he could barely make out the Vladmn freighter, and only because of its difference in height from the larger Osalt ships around it. Crowded in with the other vessels, only the featureless amidship section was visible from the view ports of *Bucephalus*. He saw movement as someone disembarked, but it was only a shadow.

"Damn! I can't see who it is! Not even the type of life-form. It would be helpful to know if it had two legs or four."

"Two legs," Cge said softly. "Yet it has the shape of my old masters."

"Two legs and not human," Andro said, musing. "I don't know what it could be."

"My sensors say human. A head, two arms, two legs, but it is round like this . . ." With his utilitarian extremities Cge shaped a graphic description Conek recognized.

"Slug." Conek grunted. "I thought it might be, but I wasn't sure."

Andro picked up the glasses Conek had laid on the control panel top and watched the small freighter. "They've started unloading. He must be in a hurry."

"How long does it take to unload a teacup, saying it was crammed full?"

"If they keep up their speed, he'll be out of here in three units."

"We'll take off just before he does," Conek said. "We'll hang in the upper atmosphere and follow him back."

"That should be quite a trick, since it takes you longer to warm up than it does him," Andro replied.

"I'll think of something!" Conek snapped, giving his words the force of his own doubt. He'd been wondering how to accomplish what he had so glibly announced as his plan.

Andro threw him a glance. "I know you will. You have a talent," he said encouragingly.

"You're calling me devious?" Conek said through gritted teeth. He resented what he considered the condescending support Andro gave him. "Remember, I didn't get into this mess by myself. Until you and your aunt came along, I was a simple hardworking criminal. This is what 'support your local government' gets a person."

"The local government is showing up now." Andro pointed.

Dawn had broken, the lights were winking out over the spaceport, and an official vehicle rolled across the pavement.

Conek dashed back to his cabin and struggled into his Osalt suit. The local representative of law and order was just arriving when he grabbed the tool chest and descended on the passenger elevator.

Some junior-grade official, Conek thought. He was not too familiar with the ranks among the Osalt. The humanoid was tall, a member of the port authority by the badge on his chest, and his nervousness showed. The insignia lacked the horned circle of the higher ranks. Conek decided to take a haughty tack; he'd ignore the official status rather than make a mistake.

"I gave instructions that no one should come near this ship," he growled. He put the toolbox down, glad he had liked the Osalt equipment well enough to keep it. He knelt, searching among his tools as if the official didn't exist.

"Well"—the creature edged back a bit— "we wondered if you needed help."

"Of course we need help," Conek snapped. "If you want to assist, we'll be glad to have you. I doubt your commander will like it much, though. You'll have to spend six months in quarantine if you board."

The controller stepped back another two paces. "No, I don't think he'd be very happy."

"Well, you know our project, don't you?" Sadistically Conek started toward the creature, watching him back up still more. "You know what we keep on board?"

"Oh, uh, of course! I'd be glad to assist you," the Osalt said, backing up again. "But if you can manage without me, we are shorthanded right now. It wouldn't be fair to my commander."

Civil servants were the same everywhere. Self-important in their little jobs, their pettiness did more harm to their governments than declared enemies could ever do.

"A pity," Conek said sadly. "But if I'm right, this adjustment should complete our repairs." He removed a wrench from the box and started loosening the first handy bolt. Then a thought hit him. *Oh, you doll,* he thought complimenting himself on his idea. He met the Osalt official's segmented eyes with a dagger-like stare.

"We don't want any more communications over the air than necessary, so I'll tell *you* what we're doing. In a short while we'll warm up and make some equipment checks. If they prove out, we'll lift off and make others in the upper atmosphere. If everything checks, we won't land again today. But keep this area clear. We'll be needing it again in a few days."

"Oh, I'll be happy to." Anxious to get away, the official almost bowed, ready to agree to anything.

"And by the way, who are you?"

Sergeant Clenishe at your service, sir." The controller grew more nervous.

Conek nodded. "When we come back, I'll ask for you. Saves trouble when I deal with someone with intelligence."

"Oh, thank you, and anytime I can be of service . . ."

Conek didn't turn around, but from the quick footsteps and the receding voice he knew his visitor had left the area with more haste than dignity. Conek replaced the panel and hurried back into the ship.

Andro waited at the top of the elevator, his face drained of color, his blaster in his hand.

"Oh, put it down," Conek said with a grin. "You can congratulate me. In a quarter of a unit the news will be all over the port. This pad is to be held for this ship. We just acquired another home."

"Marvelous," Andro said, cocking his head. "Why?"

"Was I wrong not to tell him we'd be on our way as soon as we caught our traitor?"

Andro shrugged and changed the subject. "Cge is counting the crates being taken off Slug's ship. He's really pushing."

Conek threw his suit into the shop compartment and went straight to the bridge. He warmed the massive engines while Andro and Cge put away the loose gear. By the time the major strapped Cge into a lounger and took his place in the copilot's seat, Conek was ready to lift off.

As they raised the ship, the first thrusters were fired on the Vladmn freighter. When Slug's ship rose and grayed into invisibility, Conek's giant freighter locked in and followed.

# CHAPTER Eighteen

*Bucephalus* was running dark when they came out of comp-time. Just above and to port, a red planet took up half the sky. The computer kicked out the coordinates of their location. They were entering the upper atmosphere of Weios, the fourth planet in the solar system of Oshiliror, conveniently close to the center of the Vladmn Beta Galaxy.

They watched the small Vladmn freighter enter the atmosphere. Luck was on their side. Slug crossed the terminator and dipped into the darkness of a night without either moon or other planets to brighten the sky. They stayed fifty kilometers behind Slug's ship. When the sensors indicated that Slug had landed, they dropped as close to the planet as they dared. They landed behind a low hill, four kilometers from the smuggler's base.

"The rest of the way is afoot," Conek announced. "You and Cge make yourselves comfortable. I may be gone for a while."

"Oh"—Andro pursed his lips—" "by yourself?"

"I thought you could stand a rest from my company,"

Conek replied. Knowing the major, he could imagine Andro trying to surround and arrest who knew how many smugglers. They'd all be safer if Andro remained aboard.

He went back to his catchall space and dug out a refraction light and the special glasses needed to use it. When he returned, Andro blocked the doorway, stiff with determination.

"Do you have another light, or will I have to stumble after you in the dark?"

"I told you, you're not going. I can search the cargo and get the gadget if it's there."

"Conek, I want more than the weapon. I want all the cargo from the ghoster, and fully as important, Vladmn wants Slug—and not just for treason."

"I know. For smuggling," Conek's eyes narrowed. "When this is over, you'll be after me, too, I guess."

"Don't be ridiculous! Don't you know why Slugarth dropped out of sight?"

"No."

"He caught two Vladmn patrol ships aground on Koona. One vessel had malfunctioned, the other was lending assistance. He burned them where they sat, along with eight helpless men. Murder, Hayden. As an officer of Vladmn, it's my duty to—"

"Oh, get off it!" Conek bent to pick up two extra chargers for his blaster. "Slug's got a small army down there. He likes big operations. You haven't got a chance of bringing him out."

Andro stepped back and grabbed for the door, attempting to slam and lock it, but the movement of his shadow had warned Conek. He grabbed Andro and jerked him into the compartment. No match for the captain's size, Andro put up a futile battle. Conek forced him to the floor and locked a chain around his waist with a code-lock from a handy drawer. Then Conek caught Andro's feet and pulled him into his own compartment where, with another lock, he fastened the major to the strong metal frame of the bed.

While Andro cursed and struggled against the chain, Conek shook his head, wondering why the major was so stubborn. "One thing at a time, friend. Let me get the damn gadget. Then you can bring back the whole Vladmn force, for all I care."

"Captain! I'll remind you one more time! I'm a Vladmn officer. If you continue to interfere with my duty, you're aiding and abetting—"

"Write your Quinta!" Conek laughed, slammed the door, and shot the rough-weather bolt.

He turned to see Cge standing in the passage, his panel lights blinking slowly in his confusion.

"You get in the lounge—no, you get your big buddies out of storage and make sure nobody but me leaves the ship—or comes aboard. Got me?"

"It is recorded."

Conek let himself down on a grav-rev beam and worked his way around the hill. Once his eyes adjusted to the darkness, he worked his way along without the aid of illumination. Two hills in the distance served him as landmarks.

The rotation period on Weios was just a little more than nine standard hours. He had to get back to his ship within three if he hoped to take off before daylight. He wanted to be gone before anyone recognized *Bucephalus*. If he left the planet before dawn, Slug would never know he'd been around.

"Errecth!"

Conek recognized the Chelover word for *halt* and obeyed the command. Hell, he'd never thought about sentries this far from the base.

He could stop thinking of getting away before daylight and concern himself with getting out alive.

After Conek left the ship, Cge remained in the lounge, standing by the seat Conek always used when he was relaxing. The droid rolled back and forth within a short distance and whistled a repetitive phrase in his original language. He wasn't happy with being left alone. He'd wanted to go with ConekHayden.

But his master had given him an order, and his programming would not let him disobey it. No one was to leave the ship, including him. He shook his head, hoping for a malfunction, but he didn't get one.

If he were sentient, he wouldn't have programming, he decided. But only ConekHayden and Andro-the-Major were sentient.

One of his crystals fairly glowed with an idea.

He rolled swiftly down the passage and stopped outside the major's cabin. He whistled softly, but the major heard him.

"Cge!" he heard the major shout. "Open the door!"

The droid shot the bolt back and threw open the door.

"Hand me that gun!" Andro pointed to the blaster Conek had taken from him and kicked to the other side of the compartment.

"You will follow ConekHayden?" Cge asked.

"You're damn right."

"I will go too."

"You'll stay aboard—"

"Cge will go!" He retracted his wheels for emphasis.

The major glared at him for a moment, then nodded. "Okay, you can go—just get that blaster."

Cge whistled happily as he rolled over to pick it up. *I certainly can't disobey Andro-the-Major, who wants to go after ConekHayden.*

Conek knew better than to turn or move. Behind him, he could smell the sickly odor of the Chelover, a wormlike biped known for superior night vision and often hired as night guards. He didn't know there were any in Beta Galaxy.

"Turn to the right," the biped ordered. Conek followed a path that snaked around grotesque tree shapes. The Weios growth was rumored to be carnivorous, feeding on the varied small-animal life.

Under the cover of the larger treelike shapes, he saw several buildings, and behind them, cut into the bluff, was a cave large enough to house a number of ships.

"In here!" the Chelover commanded. He opened a door and pushed Conek into a brilliantly lit room. As he tried to shield his eyes he heard Slug's laugh.

"Captain Hayden! Do come in and join the party. I think we're holding a reunion."

When Conek could open his eyes, he recognized the obese smuggler sitting on a huge divan. Still blinking, Conek was struck by the man's size. His head and ridiculously tiny hands and feet seemed to protrude from a mountain of shining material.

The glare in the room didn't come from the light alone. Around the walls on glass shelves, hundreds of crystals caught the light and threw it back and forth, splitting and magnifying it. Small star bursts of red, green, and yellow flashed out as Conek moved his head and came in line with their refractions. The room was out of place on the stark planet.

Thick carpets in bright Niltean patterns were scattered on the floor, overlaying each other. Heavy drapes covered sections of the walls, though Conek doubted there were windows behind them. In the corner, sitting on his divan like a despotic ruler, Slug wore a silk robe. Where it opened at the neck, his spacer's suit strained to cover the smuggler's obesity.

Conek kept his eyes on the pirate and the part of the room directly in front of him. The remark about a reunion put him on his guard. He knew Slug meant Lesson, so when he turned his head to follow the motion of the small, fat hand, his face was a careful blank.

In the corner he saw Gella, guarded by the simian survivor of the fight on MD-439.

Slug's disappointment in Conek's lack of visible surprise was comical. Then the little eyes, nearly closed by the fat of his face, narrowed still more.

"I've been wondering how she got here. So you brought her—" A sly grin widened the grossly full lips. "I never thought of you. To let a woman come forward alone isn't your style, Hayden."

Conek wondered, too, but instead of voicing his question, he shrugged.

"She's got a mind of her own. Who am I to stop her? Live and let live." *And you keep on believing I came after her, you pile of vermin,* he thought. The fewer questions he answered, the better. Possibly Andro could get *Bucephalus* up and bring help. He swore under his breath as he remembered chaining the major to his bunk.

Slug relaxed against the pile of cushions, his flab spreading out like solidified grease as he chuckled softly. "The avengers," he muttered. "You went after Gerdozd when he bested Tobard in a disagreement, and now she thinks she can do the same. If you start a trend, the entire contrabanding business could be seriously damaged. Not very thoughtful of you, children."

"But enterprising, you'll have to admit."

"True, quite true." Slug shook with gentle mirth, though his eyes weren't enjoying the joke. "But since both of you have exhibited your desire to make me the prime target, I'm afraid I'll have to veto the idea."

Conek didn't argue. Across the room a curtain moved, and two apes slouched into the room. The numbers were up to five, including Slug, against two.

"You can have your share," Conek said with a shrug. "I've got all I can handle."

Slug leaned forward, all pretense at good humor gone. "What you've got you took partly from me. The Gordotl trade was both simple and lucrative. I didn't like losing it."

"Then speak to the Gordotl. They hired me. If they want a change, they can say so."

"I intend to." Slug smiled without mirth. "But when I do, they'll need another supplier."

Suddenly his Chelover guard pushed Conek aside. Cge and Andro stumbled into the room, followed by another of the stinking, wormlike creatures. The major stood blinking in the bright light.

"What *is* this?" Slug pounded his pudgy hand on a cushion. "Am I to be accosted by every fool in Vladmn?" He drew up his rounded shoulders, giving the impression of an outraged ruler. Conek thought he did a pretty good job.

"Major Avvin, Chief of Port on Agnar-Alpha," Andro said crisply.

Slug's mouth dropped open. He stared at Andro, who still

wore the remnants of the chain fastened around his waist. With one bloated hand Slug waved in the direction of the chain. The last link had been melted by a blaster.

In answer to Slug's unspoken question, Andro picked up the end and held the last links in his hand, displaying it with limp affectation. He turned to glare at Conek before speaking to Slug.

"I thank you for your rescue. We suffered a slight difference of opinion. I assume I was to be deep-spaced on the return flight."

"Sweethearts do fall out." Slug gave Conek a scornful look.

"Don't insult my taste," Andro said, turning haughty. "Simply an unsuccessful business deal. I should have known better then to bother with small-timers—" He broke off in mid-sentence, his attention drawn to one of the glass shelves. He appeared awed. "Do I really see a truc Eithoral crystal?" The major took one tentative step toward one of the shelves. "It's from the Herondic Era too. I've never seen one so large."

Slug's tiny eyes widened. "You're familiar with Eithoral crystal?"

"Oh, but certainly. I have two smaller ones, and nothing as lovely, certainly nothing from the Herondic Era, but I have hopes."

"Step closer." Slug magnanimously waved Andro toward the shelves, though he gave the Chelover the sign to stay close to the major.

"Certainly not!" Andro refused the invitation and with an airy wave indicated the two small tables in his path. "With this chain I might knock over your shopping list. So clever of you to keep those copies of Samolian stoneware. A physical reminder of your next acquisition, perhaps?"

"Huh? Uh, yes." Slug eyed the highly lustered crockery as if it were suddenly offensive to him. He recovered quickly. "Perceptive of you to understand. Are they paying Vladmn officers well enough for indulgence in galactic rarities?"

"Oh, Vladmn," Andro said, dismissing the territorial government with a knowing smile just for Slug. "*You* know there are ways if you're in the right position. That is, if you have contacts. And you're removing the only one I've acquired so far—but no great loss." Andro flicked a cold glance at Conek.

Slug turned his attention to Conek, who stood throughout the entire exchange without a word. The pirate's face widened again in a grim smile.

"You could do better, Hayden. Your little sweetheart hasn't fooled me. Now the plan is for him to agree to give me advance information on shipping if I let all of you leave —correct?"

"On the contrary." Andro's voice turned venomous. "I don't know what your plans are, but if Hayden reaches Agnar-Alpha alive, I won't be in the position to give anyone anything." He raised the end of his chain and offered it as proof.

"You filthy little—" Gella made a lunge at Andro. The simian who guarded her caught her arm and roughly pulled her back.

"Be still, Gella," Conek warned her. "Someone will get the little bastard."

Gella's outburst seemed to be the last step in convincing Slug of Andro's sincerity. He addressed one of his men. "Get something and cut his chain."

Andro gave Slug a beatific smile and turned toward Conek. He blew him a kiss, gave a sneer, and then froze where he stood. With one hand halfway up, he slowly raised the other. Conek could have sworn he turned pale.

Slug's eyes followed Andro's gaze. Cge crouched behind an ornately carved old stone table. Only his blinking sensor panel and his right hand showed. His metallic finger pointed straight at Slug.

# CHAPTER Nineteen

"It's just a droid!" Slug sneered at Conek, his lips causing one fat cheek to distort. His attitude wasn't completely successful; his tiny pig eyes kept sliding back to Cge, who hadn't moved, his finger still pointed at their captor.

Andro stared at Cge as if he'd forgotten anyone else was in the room. He backed up slightly: the breath passing between his half-open lips sounded ragged in the silence.

Conek remained silent, assuming a confident pose. If Andro's plan was to convince Slug that Cge was armed, the major had slipped a cog. Not that Conek had a better idea at the moment. The situation called for some dering-do, and he was fresh out.

"You can't arm droids," Slug argued in the stillness. "Their computers are made so they won't activate weapons." He refused to look straight at the little robot, but he kept sliding his eyes toward Cge.

"That one is," said the simian who had been on MD-439. "I heard 'em talking about it."

Cge kept his finger pointed, remaining so still, only his slowly blinking sensor panel showed he was in active mode.

Stay where you are, baby, Conek prayed. Slug had started to sweat.

"But you *can't* arm them," Slug insisted, his voice low, as if talking to himself.

"Not Vladmn androids," Andro said hoarsely as he edged away. "This one's off the ghoster on Beldorph. If you don't mind, dearie, I'll just get back out of the line of fire."

"I don't believe it, it's a trick," Slug announced. He shifted, his fright over. The ploy had failed.

"Have it your way," the major murmured, as if nothing either of them said could change the circumstances.

Suddenly he ape who had been guarding Gella jerked her in front of him and fired at Cge. A streak of energy flashed red as it streaked across the room, targeted on Cge's right hand. The apeman's jaw dropped as part of the table disintegrated, but the droid was unaffected.

Cge's servos whined softly as he pivoted slowly on his wheels, turning toward the source of the shot. The simian's translator jabbered unintelligibly as he shoved Gella forward and leapt behind the drapes. His receding footsteps echoed back into the room.

"Idiot!" Slug shouted after him.

The panic of the ape affected the other hired minions. The two Chelover who'd brought in the prisoners had forgotten Conek and Andro. They moved together, turning their weapons on Cge.

Taking advantage of the moment, Conek tensed, kicked the one on his left, and with his right fist he smashed the back of the other's neck. Falling with them, he grabbed the blaster from the one on the left, firing into the soft, segmented body as he wrestled the gun away. He rolled over the other, whose weapon had been trapped under him when he fell. As he tried to move, Conek's second burst of fire cut him in half.

While Conek scuffled with the Chevoler, Andro had stepped back behind the two simians, who still stood by

Slug. The major lifted the blasters from the holsters of the one nearest him. The apes stood unmoving, watching Cge.

"Hold it," Andro ordered as Slug fumbled for a weapon, his holster shrouded beneath his robe.

Andro relieved the other ape of his weapon and gestured for them to move closer to Slug.

"Call him off." The ape nearest Slug still eyed Cge.

"I tell you, he's not armed," Slug said, snarling at his minions, but they weren't listening.

Conek wondered how a droid could cause more worry than a living adversary, but he was afraid to risk letting Cge continue. If the droid gave out with one of his "Kew-ws," they'd lose the advantage of fear. Slug might know the truth, but the others were still unconvinced.

"That's enough, Cge, we've got them now. See if there's a door behind the curtain." He pointed to where the ape had disappeared.

Gella, who had fallen, sprawling, when the ape shoved her, now crouched, waiting. When Conek turned to Cge, she sprang across the floor and grabbed the unconscious Che-lover's blaster. Still crouching, she turned it on Andro.

"Now, you slimy little toad," she said, rising, "we'll see who won't make it back to Agnar-Alpha alive."

"Conek, *do* something," Andro demanded, eyeing Gella in a half panic while he kept his captured guns turned on Slug and his men.

"Stop squabbling in the ranks!" Conek snapped, without turning.

Since Andro was covering the three captives, Conek trained his weapon on the concealed entrance. He flattened himself against the wall, waiting as Cge pulled the curtain back, peering around it. A passage led into the darkness.

"Scuttle along here and check it out," he told Cge. "Don't go far, and no gunplay."

He returned to the brightly lit room where Andro still guarded Slug and his minions. Gella had stepped back to keep Andro and the others in her sights.

"He was selling us out for a profit!" Gella argued.

"Just a good con act," Conek retorted. Why didn't she

shut up? They didn't have time for long explanations if they were to get off the planet alive. There were three of them, with three prisoners and who knew how many other enemies to deal with. The situation wasn't exactly a thrill ride on Radach-I.

"Too good," Andro muttered, part of his confidence gone as he divided his attention between his captives and the smuggler's daughter.

"But—"

"If you've *got* to shoot somebody, shoot Slug!" He snarled at her, reasonably confident she wouldn't. As she started toward Slug, he shifted; his hand bumped a small bag lying on the edge of the divan and knocked it to the floor.

Gella picked it up and opened it. She poured out a number of verdirl disks stamped with the four spirals of the Osalt Federation.

"Evidence," Andro said, holding out his hand for the bag. "Additional proof Slug was on Osalta."

"Is this all they paid you?" Gella asked Jon Slugarth.

"Walking-around money," Slug said with a sneer, but Conek laughed, knowing Gella had wounded his pride. Conek wondered what Slug had been paid but figured he'd never know.

Cge bleeped softly from behind the curtain, rolled back into the room and over to Conek.

"Where does that passage lead?"

"Steps, and another passage below. My sensors indicate the vapors of thrusters in the air. Can ships be underground?"

Conek remembered the caves he had seen. "The cliff is probably honeycombed," he replied. "What about them?" He pointed to their three captives. The little major would insist on marching them into Agnar-Alpha to the tune of "Onward Glorious Vladmn." Capturing Slug should help get Andro out of trouble. Conek decided he owed the major.

"Slug's going to pay for what he did to my father." Gella leveled her blaster.

"They're my prisoners," Andro objected. "I arrest them." He looked to Conek for support.

"Then tell them, don't tell me," Conek retorted.

Andro bit his lip and eyed the three pirates. "As an officer, duly sworn in and authorized to act in behalf of the government of Vladmn"—he frowned, trying to pull the words from his memory—"for which I am an authorized—"

"You're repeating yourself," Conek snapped.

Andro, thrown off his speech, started again. "As a major in the government of Vladmn peacekeeping forces, and as such, responsible for upholding the laws—"

"You're *upholding* the law, not *writing* it," Conek said with a growl.

"Why don't you just let me shoot Slug and be done with it?" Gella demanded.

"No, you can't shoot him!" Andro glared at the girl. "I'm arresting them."

"Then do it!" Conek lost all patience.

"As a Vladmn officer—"

"You said that three times!" Gella advanced menacingly toward Andro.

He took a step back, threw her a disdainful glance, inhaled as if he were planning to recite the Constitution of Vladmn, and faced the prisoners again.

"Consider yourself arrested."

When Conek swore in disgust, Andro scowled. "All right, so I forgot the speech! I'm not in the law-enforcement side of the military. I'm going back to pushing buttons and loving it."

"You should." Conek transferred his frown from Andro to Gella. "How did *you* get here?"

"I stowed away on one of Slug's ships," she answered as she checked the charge in her blaster. "I went back to your hangar to see if Lesson would help me find Slug. He wasn't there, but I found one of Slug's apes sneaking around. I climbed aboard his ship while he searched the hangar."

"I've never known anyone so determined to get killed," Conek grunted. "How many others might be out there, do you know?"

She shook her head. "They caught me right after I got out of the ship. There's three, I know. More?" She shrugged.

"There's not a lot of ground cover between here and the cave."

"They brought me in by tunnel," Gella said. "The passages go off in every direction."

"Is it all dark?" When Conek checked the tunnel beyond the curtain, he'd seen no lights.

"A regular black hole," Gella answered.

"We'd have a better chance going out that way," Conek said thoughtfully. "We can see in the dark better than they can." He nodded at Cge, whose sensors weren't hampered by the darkness.

"That's where the stuff from the ghoster is stored," Andro surmised. "There or still on the Osalt ships. Which is it, Slug?"

Slug's lips curled into a snarl. "If you want it, find it."

Conek left Cge to watch the opening to the underground tunnel, and strolled across the room, deliberately keeping his movements slow. Threats of menace and force would be lost on Slug, but two of his apes were still standing, their hands at half-mast.

"Where is it?" Conek demanded of the fat smuggler. "Either you talk or I'll put you on Beldorph until you do."

"To hell with you, Hayden."

"Gella," Conek called. "You wanted a chance to get him. Here it is."

"Now, wait a minute—" Andro started forward, but Conek pushed him back.

"Shut up! Vladmn authority ends where atmosphere begins. Gella, do you want him or not?"

"You bet I do. He killed Icor in cold blood—without a chance to defend himself. Why should he have a trial?"

Slug stared at her through little pig eyes. He was wary, but like Conek, he had known Icor and didn't really believe the girl would fire.

Conek swore to himself and decided to change the focus of his threat.

"But you probably didn't kill Icor yourself." Conek spoke slowly, as if he were considering the guilt. "These apes do a lot of your killing, don't they?"

He noticed Gella's eyes as she swung her weapon on the simians. She wasn't emotionally ready to change her target, but the movement of the gun was enough to make the apes shift their small eyes. They raised their hands slightly and slouched as if moving into a tenser, more defensive pose.

"Yeah, these are probably the two that burned Icor," Conek said.

Gella firmed her hold on the blaster. She took a deep breath. Conek hoped she could hold the threat a few seconds longer.

"All the stuff is on the ships," said the taller ape, the one who stood farthest from Slug. When his boss glared at him, he shrugged. "They'll find it with no trouble."

"Where did you deliver the stuff you took to Osalta?" Conek prodded.

The simians exchanged questioning glances, then looked at their boss. They didn't know. Slug had flown the Vladmn freighter into enemy territory. Logical. He'd keep his foreign contacts to himself. Conek didn't waste words on Slug. He pointed his blaster and fired, burning a hole in the divan, just centimeters from the obese hips.

His next shot was closer; when the second hole appeared in the silk cushions, a fold of Slug's ornate robe smoldered too.

"To a research facility," Slug growled as he slapped at the smoldering cloth. He tore away the smoking material and stared at Conek, his expression an orgy of anticipated revenge. "Why don't you go get it back if you want it that bad?"

"I just may do that," Conek replied. "Describe the place."

As Slug answered, Conek went over his memories of the enemy capital. He vaguely remembered the building where Slug said the Skooler cargo was stored.

"On your feet. You're going to be our passport out of here," Conek said. "Cge, you lead us to the ships through the underground passage."

Cge blinked slowly. "I can determine the directions of the vessels from the fumes of the thrusters," he replied.

"I don't care if you do it by Ouija board, just do it—no,

dammit, I'm not going to explain Ouija boards!" he yelled as the droid bent backward to look up at him with slowed panels.

Cge negotiated the steps, and Conek prodded Slug to descend in front of him. "Now you're going to walk slow and easy. I'm right behind you. One wrong move and you won't get a chance to correct it. And don't expect the major to save you. He may have you in custody, but when he thinks about it, he's supposed to save the government money. Trials are expensive."

"They are!" Andro, backing up Conek's threat, appeared struck by the idea. "Then I do my duty, even if we have to shoot them while they escape, don't I?" He pushed the two simians across the room. "You guard one, Gella. If he makes a break, pretend he's Slug."

At the bottom of the stone stair the passage was smooth, the area pitch-black. Conek kept one hand on Slug's shoulder, the blaster pressing against his ribs. Ahead, a small humming sound located Cge. Then he spoke, his small metallic voice muted.

"Vessels. Five. I detect their computers. Two are Osalt, three are teacups."

"Life-forms?" Conek asked.

"No life-forms."

"You're a doll," Conek replied. "Keep your sensors tuned, and if you get us out of this, I'll buy you the best lubricating fluid money can get—or anything else you want, I promise."

"I want my hat," Cge replied. "The life-form who captured us knocked it from my module."

"We'll get you another one," Conek promised, but Cge stopped. Conek heard the clink on stone as the droid retracted his wheels and stood flat-footed.

"Cge wishes to have the one Lesson gave him," the droid said slowly.

"Oh, great!" Conek muttered. "I knew this was too easy. Okay, we'll find your hat."

They were crossing a small cavern when Cge whirled on Conek, beeping an alarm and whistling the discordant notes of his original tongue. Conek gave Slug a shove to the right, feeling for and locating some boulders and the wall behind them. Grappling in the dark, he found both apes and pushed them along with Slug. He hissed his orders.

"Gella, you guard them. Andro, move back and find some cover." Conek put his hand on the droid's shoulder, and Cge rolled quietly across the cavern, finding and guiding them to the protection of an outcropping.

Cge gave another soft bleep, and Conek bent close to the droid's speaker.

"Try that last bit in Vladmn Standard. How many, and what are they?"

"My sensors indicate four. Humanoid? Like ConekHayden and yet not."

"That's what I like. An exact description." Conek patted the droid on the shoulder and set his blaster. "Are they all together?"

A creak of metal told him Cge moved.

"Are you nodding or shaking?"

"Nodding."

"How close?"

"Ten meters."

"Tell me when they're at five," Conek said, adjusting his blaster for wide discharge.

Mili-units seemed to drag before Cge announced, "Now."

Conek jumped out from behind his shelter and gave the area of the tunnel a good spray, running first across the cavern and then back again. The clatter of weapons and two thuds said he'd reduced the number they'd face later. He waited. Silence. The odor of seared flesh drifted down the passage and across the cavern.

"Any still alive?" he asked the droid.

Cge's circuits hummed as he rolled out from behind the rock, scanned the area, and scooted quickly back again. "Two life-forms have quit functioning. My probes do not show the location of the others."

"They'll be behind us, following and hoping for a chance to—"

Gella screamed. A blast from her weapon struck the ceiling of the cavern, sending down a shower of dirt and small stones. In the light of the shot, the dim shapes of the two simians and the bulk of Slug were visible as they escaped in the direction of the ships.

Conek fired after them. Both simians fell, but Slug disappeared in the darkness.

"Where's Slug?" Conek hissed at Cge.

The droid's sensors hummed. "My sensors do not find him."

"Damn," Conek breathed. With Cge leading, he loped across the cavern to the boulders and whispered for Gella.

"She's here and okay," Andro answered. "Did Slug get away?"

Silence was Conek's answer.

"No life-forms are in my sensor range," Cge prompted.

"Let's get to the ships," Conek growled. "We can't let Slug get these Osalt freighters out."

With Cge leading, and the others walking in a chain, they hurried along the passage Slug had taken, trusting the droid to find their way in the blackness. After two more turns they saw a gray light outlining the passage as it opened into the large cavern where the freighters were hidden. As faint as the light was, it served to outline the bulky shape of Slug as he waddled in his semblance of running.

"Get him," Andro whispered, raising his weapon. Before he could aim, a blast of lethal energy streaked from the cavern.

"Hold your—" Slug started to shout, but he ended in a scream, cut down by his own men.

"That takes care of your revenge," Conek said to Gella.

"I wanted to do it, but I couldn't," she replied, a trace of sadness in her voice.

"Well, don't consider the inability to kill in cold blood a failing in your character," Andro replied kindly.

"Skip the philosophy until later," Conek hissed.

Conek dispensed with Cge as leader as soon as he could see by the light from the larger cavern. With the robot bringing up the rear, probing the darkness to prevent a rear attack, Conek led the way with Andro creeping behind him.

Conek hugged the right side of the tunnel. He could see the back wall of the big cave and the sterns of the big Osalt freighters. He crouched down, remaining still as the whisper of footsteps warned him that someone was approaching the passage entrance.

"Be ready to cover me," he whispered to Andro, risking a glance over his shoulder. He didn't like what he saw. The major's mouth twitched with nervousness, he bit his lips, his eyes stretched wide. Conek wondered if he might be better off with Gella to back him, but she was behind Andro and he couldn't risk too much shuffling about.

Easing up to the end of the passage and keeping low, Conek peered into the cavern. Close by, an Ortavan kept watch on the passage exit. Conek fired, hitting the long-snouted humanoid in the head just as the Ortavan's return shot tore into the wall just above him. He saw a blur of movement a two more Ortavans rushed to the dead man's aid. They ducked behind a cluster of barrels.

Conek jerked back behind the protection of the tunnel wall and considered the distance to the nearest ship. "When I stop firing, you start," he told Andro.

After two shots at the barrels he made a dash for the Vladmn ship, hoping Andro would do his part. The crackle of fire over the barrels told him the major had risen to the occasion.

He had just reached the starboard leg of the vessel when he swung to see Andro running behind him, while Gella held down the two behind the barrels.

Conek threw out a hand. Andro caught it and skidded to a halt with Conek's help; otherwise, he would have been carried past the shelter by his own momentum.

"Five in here," Andro said, panting as he peered around. "Cge did a fast probe job. Two over there, and one at the back somewhere. Cge said they were moving around."

"That's less than I counted on," Conek muttered.

"And they can account for us, love," Andro replied softly.

The major was still nervous, but he had steadied. If he could still put on his affectations, he wasn't as close to panic as Conek had first thought.

Across the cavern, a flash of light glinted on metal, and while Conek tried to pinpoint it, he noticed a movement closer to the entrance.

"Let's get those two first." Conek pointed his blaster at the barrels. "We should spread out. Give me cover and watch your back."

Snapping off a quick shot at the barrels, he raced toward the front leg of the ship. Both Gella and Andro were dropping shots over the tops of the barrels. A container exploded, followed by the others. Two figures staggered out, burning like torches. Conek whirled behind the shelter of the forward landing legs and took careful aim. The power of his blaster was getting low, but burning seemed to him the worst way to go. Two short flashes and the torturous struggling and screaming stopped.

"Behind you!" Andro yelled. His blaster crackled. Conek spun to see a short, swarthy human fall from the top of the nearest Osalt freighter.

A discordant whistle and the sound of racing wheels warned him that his constant shadow was on his trail.

"I told you to stay in the tunnel," he said.

"ConekHayden is functioning correctly?" Cge's panel whirled in distress.

"In the best of health, but you left Gella alone. She can't see in the dark like you."

"She is no longer in the tunnel." Cge pointed toward the closest leg of the nearer Osalt freighter.

Conek considered their position. *I must be a peaceful person by nature,* he thought. He wished the last two pirates would just slip out of the cavern. Live and let live.

Cge gave a sharp bleep and pointed toward the front landing leg of a Vladmn freighter in the middle of the cavern. A blast of fire came from behind the wheel. Another shot followed from the rear of the huge cave. The rear fire swept across and drove both Andro and Gella to circle their protection, bringing them into the view of Conek and the other pirate. Conek let go a blast as the pirate aimed at the major.

"Only one to go," he shouted as the last Chelover fell. "Right?" he asked Cge.

"There is one left," Cge replied. By the time he finished speaking, his answer was inaccurate. Andro changed his position. As the major ran, the last simian raised his head to take a shot. Conek emptied his charge into the hairy face.

While Andro and Gella watched the entrance to the tunnel and the mouth of the underground hangar, Conek recovered two blasters and several rechargers dropped by the dead and still smoking pirates. Working carefully, he put half a charge into the front wheels of the three Vladmn freighters, fusing them solid. They wouldn't leave the cave without extensive repairs.

"Rest time," he called to the others, glad to be able to relax and crack a joke. He couldn't come up with a joke.

"You think we've got them all?" Andro looked around, not ready to let down his guard.

"We should. We've been burning holes in Slug's crew for weeks," Conek said. "Gella took out a couple on Beldorph. The ship Lesson described isn't here, so he's probably got a notch for his six-shooter he didn't know about . . ." By the time they listed the fights in the smugglers' towns, they could account for seven, and doubtless the Gordotl had made some of their attacks count.

There was no longer any doubt about who had attacked the agricultural planet. Several of the crates sitting at the side of the cavern were supplies Conek had purchased for the big quadruped humanoids. And someone had really fouled up, Conek though as he read a loading manifest stenciled on a box.

What in the hell would Slug want with repair parts for an automatic threshing machine?

Conek checked the Osalt freighters. The first one was fully loaded with cargo from the ghoster. The second also held part of the Skooler shipment. The free space aboard corresponded with the capacity of Slug's Vladmn freighter.

But the Gordotl stuff could stay. They had to get the Osalt freighters away and find those damn weapons.

"Now's your chance, Major. You know you've wanted to fly an Osalt ship."

"One of these?" Andro looked at the big freighter doubtfully.

"They're too dangerous to leave," Conek replied, "We'll take them back to Gordotl and search them there."

"You want each of us to fly one?" Gella's eyes glowed with an anticipation she attempted to hide in her reply. "I wouldn't mind."

Conek knew she was a little shaky, but no worse than Andro. He was glad he wasn't looking in a mirror.

The sun had risen, and Conek could see the details of the cavern, a great hideout, deeper than he'd first supposed. Nature had created the perfect design. The ships sat on a level floor, but beyond them, the stone sloped downward. From the top of the slope he could see less than three meters outside the cave. A searcher would have to be within hand-weapon range to see the vessels at all.

He sighed for the loss of an excellent base of operations. Andro would send the Vladmn patrol to confiscate the three Vladmn freighters. The "hands-off-planet" policy didn't include leaving Vladmn property on uninhabited worlds like Weios.

With Gella in one ship and Andro, Conek, and Cge in the other, Conek gave careful instructions for warming the thrusters and rolling down the ramp. They slowly and majestically lifted off, Gella to wait in the atmosphere and Andro to carry Conek to *Bucephalus*. Or so Conek planned. On the way, Cge's cold little hand kept patting Conek's leg. He looked down at the droid impatiently, seeing the slow, thoughtful blinking of the panels.

"Damn!" he spat out, realizing what bothered the little droid. "Andro! Swing around, drop down to fifty feet and follow your path from the ship to Slug's place."

Andro sounded incredulous. "Why?"

"To find Cge's hat, damm it!"

Conek grabbed the controls as Andro went into a spasm of laughter. Gella's outburst rattled the speaker on the communicator.

"Just shut up, both of you," Conek yelled, "and find that hat!"

# CHAPTER Twenty

Back on the agricultural planet of Gordotl, Conek, Andro, Lesson, Dursig, and Gella searched the Osalt vessels retrieved from Slug's hideout. They found the fourth weapon. No sign of the fifth.

In the lounge on *Anubis,* they sat glumly sipping at semi-lethal concoctions Lesson had created to ease their worries. Dursig had turned glassy-eyed and couldn't decide which of his four hands he should use to pick up his glass.

"That's what comes of being quadridextrous," Conek told him. To Andro: "I knew there was a reason why I wanted a home base on Osalta."

"Now wait up, boy," Lesson spoke up, but having had more to drink than Dursig, when he tried to rise, he tilted, fell back on the seat, and passed out.

Andro nodded, filling in what Conek had left unsaid. One alien weapon was still missing and had to be on Osalta, taken with the first shipment. If they didn't get it back, the enemy would discover a technology that could wipe out Vladmn.

"You know, I liked being a button pusher," Andro said with a moan. "And I remember Slug's expression when he told you where the shipment was. He wanted us to go after it." Andro shuddered.

"Just think about it," Conek retorted, ignoring the shudder just as he had Slug's threat. "If we pull it off, you'll be a step closer to being promoted to dictator."

Andro had lost all interest in his ongoing joke.

Luckily Gella had remained sober enough to assist Conek with his major difficulty before heading for Osalta again. Stealing a ship from the Osalta landing pad was dangerous enough, but going into the enemy's capital city was like playing catch with a blaster beam. He didn't want to take the eleven droids on the trip. If he didn't make it back, he wouldn't reward the Osalt with the Skooler robots.

A few minutes later Gella left *Bucephalus*, reluctantly pulling Cge by the arm and followed by the ten big droids.

"Let's get going before she changes her mind, or we change ours," Conek said.

"Then get us moving in a hurry, before we see how impossible it is." Andro replied.

He was raising the ship when he noticed a warning light indicating that a grav-rev beam was down. Before he could reach for it, the light winked out and the safe-closure indicator lit up.

"Must have been a fluke," he muttered, and made a mental note to check the seal when and if he had an opportunity.

They were in time-comp and heading for Osalta when the air lock leading from the storage holds hissed. They leapt to their feet, blasters in hand. Through the door rolled an agitated Cge.

"Cge will stay with ConekHayden," he announced, his panels flashing.

"How did you get away from Gella?" Conek demanded.

Cge zipped across the lounge to his favorite seat. Instead of answering immediately, he crawled up, scooted himself around, and leaned back. He eyed Conek and Andro complacently.

"Gella is afraid of the worker droids. I commanded one to

advance on her, and she let me go. They know I speak for you."

"They didn't hurt her?" Andro asked.

"Negative!" Cge answered, a touch of superiority showing. "The droids of Skooler are programmed never to harm a life-form." He gave Conek three rapid blinks. "But nothing is my programming says I must tell Gella."

"You—con man!" Conek yelled. "Is there anything in your computer about obeying your owner?"

Cge pushed forward, trying to nod. "Oh, I *must* obey my owner—but I malfunction, you know."

While Conek glared at the robot, Andro laughed.

"Just what every smuggler needs. A droid with a touch of mutiny."

*Bucephalus*, wearing her Osalt designation, sat on the landing pad at the Osalta port. Conek sighed and stared through the sky ports at the lowering sun of Osalta.

"In less than half an hour they'll turn on the port lights. If I leave just before, I'll have a better chance of slipping into the city undetected." Conek left the rest of his thought unsaid. He unfastened the safety belt and hurried through the lounge to his compartment, where he struggled into an Osalt space suit and breathing filter. Back in the lounge, Andro, similarly dressed, waited for him. The major checked the charge in his blaster. Then he noticed Conek.

"Love, there is no *way* you can leave me behind."

Conek eyed him warily. He knew Andro would increase the risks, but if he left him and the major decided to follow, he'd get them both killed. Andro was a good administrator, but when it came to the other side of the law, he didn't know when to leave well enough alone.

"Who's going to let down the elevator if we have to make a run for it?"

Andro gazed down at the droid, who stood leaning back, blinking up at them. "Cge, can't you, dear?"

Cge gave his full-body nod. "I will watch from the view ports and be ready. I will not talk on the radio."

Conek shook his head, disgusted with himself for giving

in. "Something tells me this is one of my idiot days—I should have left you both in Vladmn."

The gray-white of their suits blended with the plasticrete paving. the pale scrub brush covering the half-kilometer of open ground grew just tall enough to hide them if they crouched. Then they reached the opening in the wall surrounding the reclamation area. Inside, they threaded their way through heaps of rubbish, piled and sorted according to composition.

Nearby, and located by the odor, an organic consumption plant turned the wastes into fuel to power the rest of the equipment.

Using the various machinery as landmarks, they wound their way around through heaps of plastic. Crates, barrels, and a multitude of different containers waited for the reclaimer on the right. Ten Osalt were throwing crates on the moving belt while dodging the malfunctioning, air-grasping clamps.

Conek and Andro kept out of sight. They were searching for a way around the Osalt workers when an overseer consulted his wrist chronometer and called a halt. The workers strode away to the open air lock. The reclaimer spat out five more cubes of solid white plastic and shut off.

Conek and Andro waited several moments before continuing their way across the reclamation center. They strolled toward the air lock leading into the main dome of the city. The doors to the lock stood open, the controls inactive. With the gigantic hole still gaping in the central dome, they were useless.

Conek used the back alleys, hoping to stay out of sight, but every street, alley, and even the meter-wide passages between the buildings were crowded with Osalt. Every structure seemed to be pouring out occupants.

Quitting time, Conek thought. On the perimeter of the area within the dome, the buildings rose four to eight stories, though toward the center of the city, others towered up hundreds of levels. The multi-windows had privacy panels and no closures at all. The dome was meant to provide a heated, dust-free atmosphere.

Everyone wore space suits. The Osalt who had survived the disaster adapted to living in protective clothing and masks. Some took full advantage of variations in style and color with garments totally impractical for space.

Many used the old, bulky suits such as Conek and Andro wore, but the close, tightly fitting styles in brilliant colors and patterns were the recent products of some innovative thinkers. Many masks were also streamlined and decorated to make the most of faces nearly hidden. Conek particularly noticed a Seomet, a dainty, catlike cousin of the Orealians; the shape of her helmet made her green eyes appear three times their normal size.

Osalta was cosmopolitan, and Conek saw every type of being he knew, and some he had never dreamed of. A few species scorned suits, and a few even omitted masks, but all the humans and humanoids were well protected from the filthy air.

Conek and Andro ambled along the street, gawking like provincials. When they approached the building Slug had described, they halted, stood on the corner, and shuffled as if they were strangers without a destination in mind.

The Institute conformed to the general working hours of the city, and a cosmopolitan mixture of species poured from the main entrance. The workers hurried off in different directions, their translators working overtime with gossip and griping.

"What now?" Andro whispered.

"We need a vantage point." Conek looked around. "A bar." He felt the tingle of a plan not yet formulated.

"And money. There goes my evidence." Andro reached into one of the many patch pockets in his suit and pulled out Slug's pouch of Osalt credit chips. "There's a place." He pointed across the street.

"No, too high-class."

Several approaching Osalt were too close for him to say more, but he knew by looking at the bar that it catered to the big shots. The present powers-that-be asked about credentials and gave knowing looks to infer inside information they usually didn't have. Conek wanted a dive where the nobodies griped and spilled all the goodies without even realizing they knew anything.

"That's the place," Conek said, pointing down the street. The electronic sign was loose on one side, and the holo-dancer skipped around, out of sync with the music. The traces of black footprints around the door suggested that the patrons came from a scrungy part of the city.

Conek and Andro sidled in. Conek ordered a couple of drinks, and they slouched against the bar.

Behind them, four Osalt were in loud conversation. The bragging was as farfetched as anything heard in any bar in the three galaxies of Vladmn. Conek doubted that the character in the patched suit made a conquest with a member of the Sula, the ruling echelon of Osalta. The Osalt's friends hooted down his boasts. To change the subject, the braggart started griping about his work.

". . . And I don't care what they say, I ain't touching the third level. Me and Loost do five and six like always."

"Well, somebody's got to. Me and Okral have all we can do with one and two. With Canosta and Timek off somewhere, that leaves nobody."

"We ain't doing it. I heard the new stuff came from someplace nobody ever heard of, and they don't even know what it is. Might have some alien diseases on it. Me and Loost is going to do five and six like always."

Until then, Conek hadn't really known what he'd hoped to find. But it had jumped up and hit him right in the ears. Conek knew he often lived by his luck. Was he still doing the same? he wondered. Could he be wrong? He couldn't take the chance and pass up the only opportunity he had.

There's no old-age home for rogue pilots, anyway, he thought, and decided to gamble. He stepped forward quickly and touched the humanoid, Loost, on the shoulder, causing him to jerk around with a yelp. The others eyed Conek and Andro suspiciously.

"I'm sorry," Conek apologized, shuffling his feet and drawing his accent out to a dull slowness. "I heard you fellers and wondered—me and Yosl here is from Limakar, wanting work."

"Then go to the labor pool," Loost said with a growl, angered by the fright Conek had given him. The other three traded sly looks.

"Now wait a bit," said Okral. His smile was nasty. He laid a hand on Loost's arm. "No reason I can see why we shouldn't help these fellers out. We could use them with Canosta and Timek gone. Tomorrow we could notify the labor pool if they're good workers." He turned to Conek. "Of course, if you don't do a good job—"

"We can't just—" Loost started to object again, but his partner, a sly thinker, stopped him with a hand on his arm.

"You want to do the third floor?" Loost's partner asked him significantly. Then he turned to Conek and Andro. "You two come along. We think we can put you on to something."

They left the bar, and Conek suffered a moment's fright when they bypassed the main entrance of the laboratory. He thought he misunderstood the significance of their talk, but a few steps farther on, they turned into a narrow, less pretentious doorway in the same building. The structure was devoid of any protective shielding from the atmosphere. Nor, as they entered, did he see any security. Maybe they didn't usually have anything worth looking after. He grinned, thinking they really didn't know.

Inside, the walls and floor were marked with gray and black smudges of many feet.

The four Osalt led the way to a supply closet without reporting to anybody. Pretty sloppy security, Conek thought. So much for Slug's threats. He and Andro were each given a canister with a long nose and a flat, widemouthed nozzle, along with basic instructions on what to do. Andro's smaller equipage put out a spray of pale, fiery energy, turning the greasy smudges to a gray powder; Conek's vacuum cleaner sucked up the ash.

"Clean the third and fourth levels and dump your ash bags in the waste vents at the back of the building," Okral told them.

On the third level, they stepped off the conveyer lift. In both directions, long passages curved with the shape of the building. Black, greasy tracks indicated a busy day, but their footsteps echoed in the emptiness.

Andro held out the stiffened end of his fire tube and winced. "If Auntie could see me now," he whispered. "Why such a backward method? This equipment is absolutely *primitive*."

Conek shrugged. "Remember, the air is supposed to be clean because of the dome. I guess they had to come up with a solution they could mass-produce fast."

Andro made a wipe at the floor with the fire nozzle and shuddered. "Well, we're here. You did a good job—if *here* is where we're supposed to be."

"Let's find out," Conek replied. "New men on the job would be expected to get their bearings."

Every ten to fifteen meters they paused, peering into large labs. The featureless rooms were deserted, and in most of them, not a scrap of paper disturbed the barren tables. Computers sat covered with protective fabric, and only the black smears on the floor indicated that anyone ever entered.

Conek and Andro retraced their steps, and off the left passage they found the crates from the ghoster in several labs. In the first four areas the contents had been removed from the containers and placed on counters, covered with clear alothene cloths. In the fifth, over at one end, they found a disordered pile of cartons. A few items had been removed and covered, but the general appearance suggested that the workers had dropped everything at quitting time. Several items sat partially exposed, their packing protection half pulled away. A jumble of carton lids and shipping insulation littered the floor. The debris was unique to the Skooler shipment.

On a table, nearly hidden by the confusion caused by the unpacking, Conek saw the weapon. The shape was different from the one he found on Beldorph, but the color caught his eye immediately.

"Here it is," he hissed at Andro.

"Let's get it and get out of here." Andro hurried around a stack of crates.

Conek jerked off the strap holding the canistered cleaner

on his shoulder. A small compartment on the side held folded filter bags for catching the ash. He pulled one out. While he held it open, Andro slid the weapon inside it. The bag, a heavy, fibrous paper, was lipped and sealed at the top with a drawstring that held it in place within the canister and closed it when it was full and removed. Conek knotted the strings and raised the cord loop to hang from his shoulder, leaving his hands free.

"Here!" Conek handed Andro two empty ash bags. "Fill 'em with insulation. We'll leave as if we're taking out a load—"

A snarl from the doorway cut him short. An ilsate crouched, ready to spring. Ilsates were feline, strictly animal, nearly two meters long and half as broad. The irregularly striped coat of black and tan on this one stood straight up on its back, and the yellow, slitted eyes were fixed on the intruders. Ilsates were reputed to be all teeth, claws, and temper, and totally untrainable.

Conek gave the muscles credit too. The cat sprang, its leap an easy six meters. Conek pushed Andro aside as he jumped the other way, grabbing for his blaster, stacked in one of his suit's outer pockets. The toe of his boot caught under the lid of a carton and he fell, sprawled on his right side.

Since Conek was its target, the cat twisted in its leap, attempting a change of direction in midair. Conek tried to roll over, hampered by the cartons at his back and the weapon in the bag slung over his shoulder. The ilsate landed on the insulation, fighting for the balance to make another jump.

Unable to free his gun, Conek fumbled with its shape within the pocket of his suit and squeezed what he hoped was the trigger. The stream of fire burned through the holster in a steady blast, nicking his suit. With a final snarl, the cat landed half across him, one side of its head burned away.

Conek was just pulling himself free when another cat snarled in the doorway. Andro's blaster crackled, dropping the second animal as it raced into the room. Conek scrambled to his feet, finally freed his blaster, and rushed to the door.

Air was seeping from his suit. If they were going to get out of Osalta at all, they had to be quick about it. His air wouldn't last long.

"How did they know about us?" Andro whispered. His voice trembled as he stared down at the monstrous animal.

"Scent," Conek replied. "They like your after-shave."

"Knock it off." Andro glared, brought out of his momentary panic by anger.

"I read somewhere that they hunt by scent. The tags the others wore probably have a repellent."

"And the bastards didn't tell us," Andro said growling.

"Probably didn't know. They weren't the brightest bunch. We gave them a good run for the title of Stupid. A research center with no security? Any idiot would have known better."

Conek led the way down the hall, glancing quickly into the rooms on either side, hoping for an exit. Andro followed, his head turned to watch behind them. When Conek stopped, checking a side corridor, Andro ran into him.

"Sorry."

"Just don't snarl," Conek replied, hurrying on toward the lift.

They reached it just as an alarm sounded and a growl from below alerted them that another ilsate was on the way up. With quarry in sight, the big cat tried to leap up to floor level. As it scratched for a hold on the slick plasti-steel floor, Conek shot. The dead cat slid back into the lift shaft. Moments later the automatic lift rose to floor level, and the body slid out onto the floor. Below, they heard another snarl. The cats seemed to travel in pairs. From behind them, two more charged up the passages in their direction. Conek downed the one in the lead while Andro shot the other.

Back aboard *Bucephalus,* Cge stood in the copilot's seat and probed the area he could see through the view ports. He was alone aboard the ship. Alone. As alone as he had been on the long voyage from Skooler.

Osalta's suns had set just after his master and Andro-the-Major had left the ship. Cge scanned the isolated section of the landing field and the kilometer of earth and scrub brush between the ship and the reclamation area where his master and Andro-the-Major had entered the city. The enemy city.

His information was insufficient to give him a full computation of enemy. Sentient enemies, in their faulty logic, attempted and often succeeded in stopping each other's life functions. That particular trait bothered Cge. If ConekHayden ceased to live, Cge would be alone again.

"Watch and drop that beam right on the button," his master had said just before leaving the ship.

Cge would obey his master—unless he malfunctioned. He shook his top module, tapped it smartly with his right utilitarian, and listened. No crackle, no sizzle. Just like a computer—never a malfunction when he needed one.

"Watch and drop that beam right on the button."

Cge considered ConekHayden's command. Watch. He had watched; his master had not specified a length of time.

He must lower the beam right on the button, but since there was no button on the paracrete surface, the order must have been one of his master's slang expressions.

His master was in the enemy's city, and Cge's computer, the damaged section, said he must go to his master's assistance. His memory banks reminded him that he had helped his master when they had been captured by Slug. He could help again, and he wouldn't be alone.

His decision made, he scrambled down from the seat, rolled from the bridge to the lounge, and stepped on the lounge elevator. He pushed the button, letting the floor down, glad he didn't have to ride a grav-rev beam. A quirk in his logic system refused to accept antigravity.

He left the elevator and stayed in the shadow of the ship as he rolled to the edge of the paracrete landing surface. Beyond the kilometer of scrub brush was rough dirt and rocks. He dropped a decimeter in height as he retracted his wheels.

Putting one foot in front of him, testing his balance, raising the other foot, and repeating the action took most of his computer capacity. How did life-forms walk and talk and laugh and shoot? he wondered. Perhaps the movement became easier with practice.

When he entered the reclamation area, he could roll again. He sped through the piles of waste and reached the open air lock leading into the central dome. He probed the streets where beings and droids hurried through the sparsely lit streets.

Which direction had his master taken? He had no way of knowing. He computed the number of directions, the number of buildings, the odds of finding ConekHayden and Andro-the-Major within the crowded city. He bleeped his frustration.

Conek and Andro looked back and forth, trying to decide on the best direction in which to run.

"We can't go down if they're below," Andro stated unnecessarily.

Conek took aim on the emerging ilsate as its head raised above floor level. From the corridor where they'd found the Skooler cartons, he heard the sound of two-legged footsteps. He shot the big cat and led the way as they raced toward the other end of the corridor. Suddenly he skidded to a halt.

"What is it?" Andro stopped just beyond him.

The sign over the four small doors announced the need for reclaiming resources. On the swinging panels were listed the various items to be put in each. Conek spotted "plastic." If he was right, he'd found a way back to the ship, one that wouldn't have guards at every turn.

With no time to explain, and only a vague idea of what the consequences might be, he grabbed Andro's arm and threw him into the swinging panel. It gave under the major's weight.

Whatever Andro's fate, Conek expected to share it. He wanted to be out of sight before the Osalt rounded the curve in the hall, but he was just a mili-unit too late. He jerked the door open, and a shot from the Osalt guard shattered it. Without hesitation he dived into the shaft.

He was in free-fall for a meter. Then a cushion of hurricane-strength forced air gave him buoyancy as he tumbled in its path. He jumped to his feet, bounding in long strides as the wind pushed him. Over his shoulder he saw a security guard appear at the opening. Conek threw a shot in the guard's general direction. Then the bottom fell out of his steps. The air lost force, and he slid down a steep ramp. The weapon in its sack trailed behind him, still attached by the cord. Small, evenly spaced emergency lights allowed him to see his surroundings.

Vents on the side of the shaft threw out another storm current, and a few meters ahead, the slope leveled gently. He got to his feet and let the air push him along.

A barrel, its ratio of bulk and weight more easily moved by the current, passed him by with a nudge.

"Hey, quit shoving," he said, arguing with a thin, wide carton. Its bulk, across the shaft, bumped him, pushed him forward. Then he noticed the holes in the side.

"Tell you what, let's rephrase that a bit." He caught it by the broken edges and held it tight against his back, tilting it so the air gave it an upward lift. His steps were three-meter leaps.

Up ahead, he could see Andro grasping a huge crate, trying for the same speed. Other air vents added to the force of the current, and now the tunnel angled up. In mili-units they popped out onto the conveyer belt that fed the plastic-reclaiming machine. The belt swung in a slow arc as it dumped the waste plastic in a wide circle.

Andro peered over the top of the big carton to get his bearings. He jumped off the belt, racing in the direction of the ship.

In the semicircle around the conveyer belt, a ridge of discarded plastic rose three meters high. They scrambled up the inner side and were just going over the top when blasters crackled. Well, what did he expect? The guards in the Institute had known where the tunnel would come out and had called in reinforcements. Did he think they'd give up and go home?

Conek and Andro scrambled down the other side of the plastic ridge. At the bottom, they raced across an open area and ducked into a maze of huge shipping containers without being spotted again.

A low, sharp sound, like an animal in pain, caused Conek to look back. Andro ran into a carton and Conek saw why. Blood streamed down from just under his left arm. The major staggered. Conek grabbed his arm, propelling him along. Andro's face was pinched with pain.

A barrage of fire came from behind them. Conek jumped for cover, pulling Andro behind a stack of cartons. His shoulder bumped a ragged edge of plastic; the string of the sack caught and severed. Conek grabbed for the bag, but it rolled aside by a pile of miscellaneous rubbish.

He was reaching for it when he sighted a guard peering around a carton. One flash of his blaster and both the carton corner and the guard disappeared. He had three more clear targets in rapid succession before the Osalt became more cautious. But he needed to get the major into a better shelter before he went back for the weapon.

"Come on!" Conek pulled Andro over his shoulder, and weaving in and out between the piles of refuse, he found a place near the gate and put Andro down, setting him behind a carton.

"You stay under cover until I get what we came for. Don't try for the gate alone."

Andro tried to move and gasped. "Don't come back for me. Get the damn thing and go!"

Conek, watching for movement, moved his head slightly, giving Andro a side glance. "Have you suddenly found someone you like better?"

Andro blinked, laughed, and caught at his side. "Don't be a fool. Get that thing and get back to Vladmn."

Conek could still hear the major whispering orders as he made a dash across a cleared area and worked his way around more of the big shipping cartons. If the Osalt were following him, they were staying well hidden. He watched his surroundings, but the shadows of the ill-lit dump were still. The bag was in clear sight, blending with the other trash around it. He picked it up and knotted the severed cord so he could sling it back over his shoulder.

An Osalt stepped from behind a box, his blaster ready. Conek had laid aside his own weapon while he secured the bag. He knew he'd never get to it in time.

From behind him came a "Kew-w!" The Osalt fired past him. The energy bolt had hardly left the gun when Conek let go with his own weapon and dropped the Osalt. Behind him, the clank of metal rang loudly in the stillness. Knowing what he'd see, he flipped an emotional switch inside as he turned. Cge sprawled on the ground, sensor panel down.

Conek grabbed the droid and raced back the way he had come, around the various heaps of debris. In front of him a blaster went off, and behind him came a rattle of dropped equipment and a thud. He whirled around the stack of crates to see Andro leaning over one, holding his side with one hand, his blaster in the other.

"I told you not to come back—oh, God, not Cge!"

"He went into his act once too often," Conek said quietly, forcing a steadiness into his voice.

He stared down at the small robot in his arms. He doubted it could be repaired. The sensor panels had been shot out, and inside the top module, the computer still smoked.

He stood holding the droid, considering what he faced. If he could get Cge back to Vladmn, Dr. Sardo just might be able to fix him. He had to take the weapon; it hung over his shoulder, no trouble to carry. But the major could hardly stand: he'd never be able to run the kilometer back to the ship. Only a Gordotl, with four arms, could carry both of them. There was no way Conek could leave a wounded human behind.

He shut his eyes against the memories of the little droid playing games in the lounge on *Bucephalus*. Instead, like a holo-cube, he saw the little character holding Slug's smuggling crew at bay with one pointed finger.

It's a machine! he told himself. They don't die because they never live! He gritted his teeth and laid Cge gently on a plastic carton.

# CHAPTER Twenty-one

"Get going," Andro urged. "You've still got a chance to make it."

"Shut up and do as I say," Conek grunted as he pulled Andro around and hefted him onto the crate beside Cge. "We'll make this a partnership. I'll run for both of us. You play rear guard."

He locked his grip around Andro just under the major's buttocks, hoisting him up. Staggering on the uneven ground, he turned, leaning against the carton until he got his balance. Then he started to run, racing for the gate in the wall. He jumped, startled as something bumped his back, thumping against his legs. The cord holding the bag had slipped off his shoulder and fallen halfway down his arm, he noticed. The banging must be made by the weapon, he decided.

The major weighed more than he expected, and he wondered if he could make it. *This is no time to wonder,* he thought, arguing with himself. *You can run as fast as you're scared, and when you pass an express lighter, that's panic.*

"Here they come," Andro shouted.

"They're all yours!" Conek picked up speed.

To the right and ahead, a blaster bolt fused a misshapen shrub into a petrified stump. Something slammed him in the back, pushing him forward for three long impossible steps. He staggered to keep his balance when he outran whatever force shoved him.

"Cge just saved our lives again," Andro breathed.

"What?" Conek panted, but before Andro could answer, the air was full of roaring, as if every ship in port had suddenly taken off.

"What is it?" he shouted over the noise.

"My God! They're blasting their own people!"

"Who?"

"The Osalt ships! I guess they took them for us! Drop me and run! You'll never make it!" Andro struggled, nearly throwing Conek off-balance.

Conek tried to increase his pace, but his strength was wearing out. His suit was low on air; maybe that was why the major seemed so heavy.

Then his path grew darker as a gigantic shadow fell over them. The roaring grew louder. He glanced up and saw the freighters, hanging over him like a giant roof. They were so close to the ground, he could almost count the stud bolts.

The two ships stayed close together. Their shadows surrounded him with near darkness. They crept across the sky, moving so slowly, he wondered how they stayed aloft. The gun ports were open, energy nozzles still smoking from their recent firing.

Every minute he expected a concentrated attack. The firepower above could turn him, Andro, and the gadget into nothing. Then the two freighters were past. For a moment he could see the ground clearly before another shadow overtook him. A colossus the size of *Anubis* seemed to smother light, air, and his ability to breathe.

The roar of the engines numbed his thought. The possibility of death turned into a certainty once more as gun after gun baited him. Hold hatch after hold hatch came into view as the freighter seemed to be practically sitting in the sky.

Then he ran under *Bucephalus*. He'd run from the uneven

ground onto the paved landing pad without realizing it. The front elevator was down, as Cge had left it when he left the ship, he guessed.

Andro gave a shout, and Conek heard the repeated crackle of his blaster. Just as he reached the elevator, Conek's left leg gave out under him and he fell, dropping the major.

He scrambled to hit the lift button, punching the emergency switch. As they zipped up into the ship, he hastily grabbed Andro's legs and pulled them onto the lift just before it clanged into the lounge.

Conek allowed himself one long sigh of relief, then almost choked in the middle of it. Andro lay unconscious, knocked out when Conek dropped him on the steel platform. In the major's right hand was his blaster, but his left still clutched the arm of the droid. While Conek carried him, Andro had brought Cge along.

When Conek scrambled to his feet, he wondered if he pulled a muscle in his leg, but he couldn't stop to worry about it. He forced it to move him into the bridge. Omitting the pre-flight check, he hit all the starters at once. He had just released them when the communicator crackled.

"Boy, get that cayuse up! This calvary ain't got no whoa!"

"Lesson?" At first Conek thought his ears were playing tricks. The voice came again.

"Dursig, watch the bunch over there. They're fighters, ready to move."

Conek slammed the control panel with his open hand and shook his head, trying to rid himself of the emotions welling up. *The damn fools came after us!*

"Lift, baby," he murmured to the cold engines. "It's all up to Lex's girl now."

He increased the power to the thrusters. They roared and shuddered their protest. Waves of vibration swept through the half-square-kilometer of ship behind him. Over his head, a long-range sensor alarm chattered as it shook within its clamps.

The protesting motion moved the levers of the engine controls as if the vessel itself were trying to alleviate the strain. Then, still screaming their fury, the twelve powerful thrusters raised the ship.

The sky above Conek's view ports was blotted out by the bulk of three freighters. In the center and a little ahead, he recognized the familiar lines of *Anubis*. To port he saw Dursig's ship. In the darkness he couldn't recognize the one to starboard. His rear screen showed a twin formation not a hundred meters off his tail.

With a grunt Andro lurched into the copilot's seat. He hunched forward, his face pale gray with pain and loss of blood.

"Give me the ship, love. You make nasty noises with the blasters."

Andro was on the verge of passing out again. Conek shook his head.

"You can't handle it. You look like hell."

"And you're ready to run another footrace?" Andro pointed. Conek glanced down at his leg. He stared disbelievingly at the puddle of blood forming beneath his feet. He immediately turned his eyes away, willing himself to ignore it. The shock overrode all sense of pain. He hadn't felt it and didn't want to.

Ahead, Osalt fighters were lifting off in squadrons. Andro turned back to the controls, bumping his left arm in his haste.

"For God's sake, fire!" Andro gave a half sob of pain and frustration. He jerked at the controls, sending *Bucephalus* surging ahead. "These old tubs will never make it."

Lesson's voice cut in. "Watch what you say, dolly boy. Just think of them Osalt as Indians and this as a shoot-out. We're the ones wearing the white hats."

"Yeah, they're the Indians and we're stuck in forts," Conek muttered to himself, watching the fast Y-tailed fighters maneuver. "Here they come. Troopers, fire at will."

His moment of panic over, Andro settled down to steady flying, and Conek flipped the switches to open the gun ports. The computers would have done it automatically when they were ready to fire, but Conek needed something to occupy his hands. When the first fighters were close enough for him to set the sensors on target, he gave the order to commence firing.

"Okay, boo baby, do your stuff!" He patted the control panel.

ERROR IN TARGETING flashed across the computer screen. With an oath he cleared the computer input before the message finished. He resighted and gave his command again.

"Ister, you forgot something!" Gella shouted. The volume of her voice vibrated the speaker over Conek's head.

Gella? Her presence was so unexpected, he had trouble recognizing her voice. But Lesson had formed his fleet of six ships with every Osalt vessel in Vladmn and had probably grabbed anyone who could fly them. She'd be in one of the ships captured from Slug. Who would be in the other one? Only one other person knew anything about them. Norden. He'd taught her to fly an Osalt ship on Beldorph when they were searching for the ghoster. Sure enough, he heard her voice.

"Try again," she urged. She was really single-minded in the pursuit of her duty if she'd come that far to arrest him.

Lesson called *Anubis* a swaybacked jackass.

ERROR IN TAR— Conek cleared the computer again and tried to resight. The fighters drew closer, moving so fast that sighting was impossible.

"Will you *do* something!" Andro shouted.

"Shut up!" Conek yelled back. He wasn't able to get a sighting at such close range. Desperately he threw the concentric circles of the target back and forth across the area of sky dotted with fighters, but when he pushed the firing command, he achieved the same result.

ERROR IN TAR— he cleared the computer, his mind racing, trying to find the reason. The Y-tails dived, their oncoming silhouettes so small that they were hardly visible. Conek watched, all hope evaporating. Only his will kept him struggling with the computer.

"Come on, baby, *fire*," he begged. "Come on, baby!"

There wasn't a sound from the other ships. Andro threw one arm up over his face, lowered it to make a slight adjustment in his direction, and raised it again. To Conek, both the protective arm and the adjustment in course were useless. He fought with the computer, but will, not logic, kept him going. those fighters could never miss the big freighters.

Then the Y-tails were on them and past. They swooped in so close, their wind streams rocked the larger, slower ships. Not a shot was fired.

"What's going on?" Gella sounded incredulous. "They didn't even try for us!""

Norden gave her opinion in a voice shaky with relief. "Maybe they couldn't risk a miss. They'd be shooting down on the city."

Conek felt a little giddy. "I've never been invited to a war where nobody shoots," he said.

Andro laughed weakly. His exertion caused him to clutch at his side.

Conek, relieved with the result of the first Osalt pass, forgot to clear the computer. His hand was resting on the button when he read the completed message.

ERROR IN TARGETING. SENSORS IDENTIFY ALLIED CRAFT.

"*Bucephalus*, you idiot!" he yelled. "Didn't anyone tell you you'd changed sides?" He stared through the view ports at the three huge ships in front of him. They were lumbering along majestically, droning up into the upper atmosphere at the command of their pilots. But they were built in Osalt territory, their computers programmed to recognize the Osalt fighters as friendly craft. He hadn't allowed the computer to finish its message, and neither had Lesson. His pilot was as impatient as he was. The other ships still gave their output in the language of Osalt. Not even Dursig's ships were reprogrammed to Vladmn Standard, since the Gordotl traveled by coordinates, taking off and landing manually.

"I *always* think computers are stupid!" one of the taciturn Gordotl announced. "Hayden, will you say how it is I work the guns myself?"

"You can't," Conek replied curtly. "The computer won't let you fire on friendly craft. The only chance is to shut it down, and then we can't comp. How close to time-comp, Lesson?"

"Just waiting on you, boy."

"Then let's skip now," Conek said. "That bunch is coming up too fast. They haven't figured it out yet. Let's get out of here before they do."

"Home in on the Quinta," Lesson replied.

Conek checked his scanners. In the darkness he couldn't tell the Gordotl ships from the ones they had taken from Slug's cave and didn't know which vessel the Quinta was flying. Then the freighter to starboard grayed as it started into time-comp.

"I hope that's her," he muttered as he locked on. Just as the Quinta disappeared from view, a streak of fire from a fighter passed close to *Bucephalus*.

"Somebody's caught on," Conek said to Andro just as they started to gray.

# CHAPTER Twenty-two

Conek had set his finder on Norden's ship as he went into time-comp. He waited breathlessly. While a ship was in grayness, before she disappeared, she was vulnerable. But in comp they were safe.

The major had leaned back in the copilot's seat, his eyes closed. Conek thought he was only semiconscious. The bridge stank of sweat, fear, and blood. He could taste the salt on his lips from the perspiration trickling down his face and feel the clinging wet clothes inside his suit. Then he pulled himself forward to check the oxygen mixture. He felt a little drunk.

As Conek moved, pain swept up his leg. He blinked, trying to focus his eyes. He decided his problems came from a loss of blood and reached for the emergency medical kit on the left panel. He'd been laughed at for keeping it up-to-date with fresh supplies, but after this *he'd* do the laughing. He was just glad he had them.

One by one he spread out the items in the kit. First he tore open an insulated package, and leaning over, he popped a theocine tablet into the major's mouth. Andro, in a half stupor, swallowed before he knew what had happened.

"What was that?" He turned glazed eyes on Conek.

"Theocine."

"Love, you are a bastard," Andro said. He knew he was fired from the job of copilot. Already the fast-acting medication was pulling him under. Conek took two cans of emergency stimulating fluid and wrung the tops on both, putting one in Andro's hand.

"Here, have a nightcap—come on, hurry up." He drank one himself, pushing Andro to finish his and take another. In less pain, Andro downed the second quicker than the first. By the time Conek retrieved the container, Andro was in a deep sleep.

Conek took his knife and slit both the leg of the space suit and his pants. Gasping with pain and sweating profusely, he managed to clean and bandage his own wound, winding the strip of cloth tightly to hold back the bleeding.

Through the years he had cursed the smallness of the bridge, but now he made a note to apologize to the designers if he ever met them. By lowering the back of Andro's seat and swiveling his own, he was able to reach the unconscious major without having to put a strain on his own wound.

Knowing Andro was now oblivious to pain, he cleaned the wound and bandaged it tightly. Lastly he wrapped a restraining bandage around the outside of Andro's suit and over the wound. He hoped the pressure would prevent more bleeding. He knew better than to take the suit off. If Andro went into shock, he would need the warmth, and the blankets back in the passenger cabins were out of reach.

Conek's own pain eased, and he felt stronger after the liquid. The major's color deepened slightly, so Conek swiveled around again and made another check of the medical supplies. Some he packed into the kit. Several he kept close at hand, knowing he would need them later. Among them were the four pressurized local anesthetics, as well as more medication for Andro.

Conek should rely on the locals, but when to use them

would be the next consideration. He needed to be free of pain when they came out of comp and landed. Then he remembered that the flight was locked in on Norden's ship, not a planet.

With stiff fingers he rubbed his temples, trying to get his equally stiff mind to function. Why were they following Norden? Of course! Only *Bucephalus* and *Anubis* were registered in Vladmn, so only they were equipped with Vladmn time-comps. The other five vessels still used Osalt systems and could only jump for four c-units before they came out of comp.

They needed a quarter of a unit to recharge their systems. The Osalt had stolen a Vladmn ship to get the secret, but either that ship's mechanism was defective or they misunderstood it, because the range of their jump was less than a fraction of what the Vladmn ships were capable of.

The Osalt hadn't perfected homing devices, either, but the Y-tails could jump through time as fast and as far as the freighters, and Conek knew they would.

He checked the gauge and decided they had been timing for one and a half c-units. Two and a half and they would break time, become visible and vulnerable again. He'd wait half the period so one local anesthetic would serve for two breakouts.

The gray faded right on schedule. Conek dropped the shields over the sky ports just as the blackness of space and the lights of the stars became visible. Off in the distance to starboard, a freighter stood out in the surrealistic clarity common to deep space. Nearer and to port he saw another.

He looked up and whistled. Over his head, so close it could have been sliding off the top of *Bucephalus*, was a third.

"Any closer and you would have been sitting in my lap," he muttered.

"Sorry, Captain," Norden said as the ship raised, "but I was here first."

A laugh came over the communicator, and Conek recognized it as Lesson's. "Boy, with all the parsecs of space, you hunker down with a pretty woman."

"Where else?" Conek said as he glanced to starboard to see Lesson a good distance below him. *Anubis* was turning to rejoin the loose formation.

"Are we all here?" he asked, checking his screens. He counted five ships. He should see six. "Who's missing? Speak up!"

"Norden."

"Lesson."

"Dursig. Cornata? Hamesh?" The Gordotl leader called the short roll of his pilots. Two affirmatives answered.

"That leaves Gella. Where is she?" Norden asked. "She wasn't hit back on Osalta, was she?"

"I thought I was the last one out," Conek answered, checking the sensor screens. "I thought she left just ahead of me—"

"To your port," one of the Gordotl said, interrupting. "I see her on my sensor screen."

Conek spotted the blip. "Okay!" Everybody waltz! Lesson, keep yor speed down—no point in outrunning the brakes out here. She's moving this way."

"Quiet," Norden called. "Listen."

". . . *is* everybody?" Between the bursts of static they heard Gella's voice faintly.

"How did she get so far off?" Conek demanded as the six ships droned in her direction.

"Because there's no homing apparatus on her ship," Lesson answered.

"When we came across, she and I used the same coordinates," Norden explained. "I didn't have time to give her any when we left Osalta. It was my fault."

"And if you had, we'd have a thousand Osalt fighters down on us," Conek said. "They'd know exactly where we are. It was suicide to let her come without a homer. We can't jump; if we go into hyperspeeds, we'll overshoot her; and we'll never reach her in time at the rate we're going."

"Why can't we speed up some?" one of the Gordotl asked.

"We'll have trouble staying close enough to protect each other at this speed. Remember, we can't use the computers."

"But do we have to worry?" Bentian asked. "The Osalt didn't follow."

"They will," Conek replied grimly.

"You can bet your bandanna," Lesson volunteered. "And they're getting better at it all the time. We've been giving them some practice. It's getting downright dangerous to steal ships from over there."

Confirmation of Conek's prediction showed up on their sensors. At first one, and then two, three, eight, and dozens of blips made a pattern on the screens. Soon there were hundreds of Y-tailed Osalt fighters that jumped the limit of their capacity, throwing a net of pursuers across the path from Osalta to the Alpha Galaxy of Vladmn.

"We shut off the computers now?" one of the Gordotl asked.

"Wait!" Conek shouted as a thought struck him. "Quinta, you can't shut off yours! If we lose our position, we could come out of time in the middle of a planet. One computer has to keep functioning. It's got to be yours, because you don't have a homer, right?"

"Right," Norden answered slowly. "Captain, I hope you're a good shot. You're leaving us helpless, you know."

Conek gritted his teeth. "I know."

He was leaving Gella helpless until the slower ships could reach her. He hoped to increase his own speed, leaving the five others to fend for themselves while he went to her aid, but the two Quinta had to be protected. He seemed to see Icor's face in the configuration of the stars in the distance. Would his eyes be accusing or forgiving? Conek shook his head and concentrated on the Osalt fighters.

Off to port, a squadron formed and bore down on the freighters. Conek watched the erratic streams of fire from their guns. They were too far out of range to be effective and seemed to be testing their weapons.

Ahead, another group of more than twenty Y-tails started toward them.

"Don't come after me!" They heard Gella's voice over the communicator.

"Just keep flying, sweetie, we'll get there!" Conek shouted back as he shut down his computer and tested his manual targeting sights.

"I mean it! Don't come after me! I won't be here!" Gella pitched her voice high, trying to make it carry over the static. Unable to see the ship with his naked eye, Conek glared down at the sensor screen. While he was frowning at it, the blip that was Gella disappeared.

"The bastards! She was just a kid!" Lesson cried, and opened up with all his guns. Even with the strictly illegal boosters on their weapons, the range was still too far to be effective for either Lesson or Conek, but the old pirate made a lucky shot, and a Y-tail exploded in midair. The small squadron coming in from the port side veered sharply away.

"Here they come," Bentian said over the communicator.

Conek watched the larger group coming in to make a pass.

"Everybody ready?" The answers came back, accompanied by streams of fire from the freighters, crisscrossing the blackness. Both Conek and Lesson concentrated on the cluster in the center of the formation; between them they exploded four ships, but the shots were too fast and erratic to know who had scored the hits.

"The others are coming back!" Norden warned.

The smaller squadron came in for a pass. Dursig and one of his men turned their guns on the leaders. The Gundotl were hunters by nature and preference. Their aim was deadly.

From his position at the rear of the formation of freighters, Conek looked out over the other ships. In the blackness of the vacuum the light from far-off stars struck the gigantic vessels; they stood out in their grayish whiteness as if they glowed. Conek flew just above the level of the

others. He could see the rotating sensors, the open gun ports, and the smoking tips of the mounted blasters.

In the distance the small Y-tail fighters diminished in size as they zeroed in again on the big freighters.

"Here they come," Norden murmured softly, her voice showing nothing of her feelings as the deadly warships came on.

"Don't worry, Quinta," Lesson assured her. "They've got to get by us first."

Conek's hands were busy at the guns, but he felt disorientated. He experienced a lack of reality as he watched the small, startlingly white Y-tails coming out of the blackness. Brilliant orange streaks sprang out from the massive freighters. The fighters slashed across his vision.

Dursig, in the lead, directly ahead of the helpless Quinta, put out a steady stream of fire, arrowed straight for the oncoming attackers. His two other ships were concentrating on the center of the squadron, and three Y-tails burst like small stars. Conek and Lesson accounted for two fighters each before the Osalt were too close for manual targeting.

The fighters, as well as the freighters, were moving more slowly. They, too, had to sight by eye. Unlike the fleeing Vladmn, they weren't hampered by having small targets.

Conek gritted his teeth and kept firing as a black void appeared in the side of Dursig's ship. A shot struck the Gordotl to Conek's right. The shot took off half a wing, but the freighter steadied after its lurch. *Bucephalus* shuddered twice from hits, and Conek grabbed for the switches, ready to tell the computer to locate the damage. Then he remembered he had shut it off.

"Blasted rustler, singed my tail feathers good," Lesson said with a grunt.

Looking in Lesson's direction, Conek swore as he saw a group of more than fifty Osalt drawing nearer. In centi-units they would be coming in for the kill.

"Let's get out of here!" he shouted. "We just got outnumbered."

"But we're not fully charged," Norden objected.

"Then shorten the jump, but go *now*!" Conek ordered. "Computers on! Home in!"

In the few seconds it took to go into the comp, the freighters were defenseless, and the Osalt bore down on the ship in front of Conek. Just as he grayed and lost sight of his surroundings, an explosion rocked *Bucephalus* as if she were a toy. She steadied in the oblivion of time-comp, but when they came out again, Conek knew that the Gordotl would be short one ship and a couple of citizens.

# CHAPTER Twenty-three

As soon as he settled into comp, Conek checked on Andro. The medication kept him deeply asleep. Conek swiveled in his chair. He could just see the edge of the elevator platform. On it he saw the outstretched hand of Cge, the little metal fingers splayed out and still.

*Should have sold him when I had a chance,* he thought, knowing that if he had, Cge would now be safe somewhere in Vladmn, playing his silly little games. At least he wouldn't be lying back in the lounge, his panel shot out.

Conek swiveled around abruptly, bumping his injured leg in his haste. The local anesthetic kept the pain away only when he was still, so he forced himself to remain immobile, willing the throbbing pain to subside. He closed his eyes, gathering strength.

The next thing he knew, urgent voices were rattling the speaker on the communicator.

"Conek! Conek! Come on, wake *up*, boy!" Lesson shouted.

"Stop rattling my eardrums," Conek answered, rubbing

his face, trying to push away the dead sleep threatening to overcome him again.

"Come out of it, boy. Push your buttons and home in on the Quinta again. We've hung around overtime, trying to get you awake."

"Captain, can you hear us?" Norden's voice was a knife of irritation, cutting through his grogginess.

"Never give up, do you, Quinta?" he mumbled. "Is getting me behind bars worth it?"

"No, Captain, but getting you out of Osalta is." Her voice was as crisp as it had been when she'd ordered his arrest. His head was just clear enough to know he should understand more from her remark than he did.

"Can you comp it?" Lesson demanded.

"Sure, I can make it," Conek replied thickly. "Let's go." He couldn't believe it. He had slept through the warning bells as they'd come out of time, and only the absence of any object in front of him prevented fatal results. If the Osalt had attacked, he might have slept through that too.

"This will be a full jump," Norden replied. "A full four hours, so next time . . ." Her voice faded away as the freighter disappeared, followed by three of the others.

"Hit the button, boy. I'm not going until you do."

Conek punched himself into time-comp and watched the grayness envelop the ship.

The pain seared up his leg, but for the moment he ignored the locals still spread out on the control panel. The major's medication was wearing off, and he struggled with the safety harness. Conek forced another tablet down Andro's throat and followed it with most of a can of emergency fluid. He held the major down until he quieted.

Conek's own wound opened up again. The pain was so intense, he hardly noticed the fiery stab of the pressure punch as the local pierced his thigh. He worked to stop the oozing blood and leaned back, exhausted.

Drink something, you fool, or neither of you will get back, he told himself, but even as he reached for a can of fluid, he fell asleep.

The alarm announcing the exit from time-comp woke him. He seemed to be swimming out of some dark hole, struggling for moments before he knew where he was. Seeing Andro, he jerked back to reality, both mentally and physically, sending a stab of fire up his leg.

He threw a longing look toward the pressurized locals but turned away resolutely. Then he told himself not to be a fool. If they encountered the Osalt again, he must be ready to fight. It took him longer to administer the local. His head seemed detached from his body, floating in midair. The blood on the bandage showed why.

"Wake up, boy," Lesson demanded, and he could hear other voices. Through his view ports he could see four freighters and knew the other two wouldn't be coming.

"I'm here," Conek replied, opening a can of emergency fluid and draining it in two gulps.

They exited from time on the edge of the Alpha Galaxy of Vladmn, close to a small solar system he recognized as Teolos. Kylar-X, the outermost of the four planets, hung close off his starboard bow, and tearing out from behind it came a squadron of Osalt fighters.

"How did they know we came out here?" Gordotl asked.

"Because we're on a direct route to Radach-I," Norden replied. "I should have had better sense. How could I have been so stupid?"

Conek's head swam. He felt as if he were weaving all over the bridge though he was strapped in his seat. The chatter irritated him irrationally.

"Skip it, Quinta," he snapped. "Concentrate on your flying."

His hand shook. He zeroed in on a ship and nearly fired before he realized his guns were aimed at Dursig.

Fire seemed to be coming from all around him. An Osalt fighter blew up, blotting the rest from his sight in its brilliance. Another glaring flash of light lit the blackness. Streaks of orange and pale yellow crisscrossed like a pattern on a bedspread. He thought he must be well above the others, because below him, the world seemed crowded with

freighters, their massive expanse of tops all around him, blotting the sky below. From above, what appeared to be fast white birds were swooping down.

He shook his head, trying to clear it. They weren't birds, they were Osalt. He kept reminding himself. He wanted to sleep. He felt as if he hadn't closed his eyes in days. The fighters resembled birds. Where were all those orange streaks coming from? Out of the freighters? Out of the birds?

What was that? One of the streaks connected with a bird, and it lit up like a ball of fire. He watched his hands. They worked by themselves, pushing buttons, pulling levers, and all the while the yellow streaks flashed out around him.

Below, one of the freighters jarred and bucked. On the port side a black hole appeared, nearly amidships. The yellow light came from around him and caught a bird dropping down toward the stricken freighter, and the explosion rocked the rest of them.

How long had they been fighting? He felt so tired. Why was he here? What were they doing?

Another freighter took a hit. It went yawing off to starboard. With a lurch Conek's mind cleared.

"Lesson!" he shouted.

*Anubis* arched away from the others, and Conek turned to follow her. Directly in his path, the planet of Kylar-X took up most of the view. *Anubis,* faster and more maneuverable than *Bucephalus,* dived into the atmosphere, followed by three Osalt freighters. Conek eased his course to take the entry at the maximum speed the ship could stand, but before he hit the lurch of entry, he saw the blast of an explosion from the planet's surface.

*Lesson*! His anguish was silent.

"Time to comp it!" someone shouted. He thought it was Norden. He had flown into the upper atmosphere of Kylar-X. He had dived, he realized, and was just where he did not want to be. With a foggy apology to *Bucephalus,* he hit the comp. He heard the scream of straining metal, the ship lurched to the side, and he grabbed at the control panel with

both hands, grasping levers without considering the consequences. He fought to save himself from falling.

*You idiot, you can't fall. You're strapped in,* he thought. He reached out to make sure Andro was still safe, but before he touched the major, he fainted.

# CHAPTER Twenty-four

Conek regained consciousness reaching for Andro's hand.

He was holding on to a bony skeleton.

He gave a bloodcurdling yell and sat up.

Directly in front of him, an arthropod with a triangular head on a thin, sticklike body was drawing back, hampered by Conek's hold on her exoskeletal appendage.

"Captain, you scared me nearly to death," she said breathlessly. The clicks and clacks of her own language came through her translator in a soothing slur, meant to reassure the patient.

Conek blinked and looked around him. He was in a small room, institutional in color and furnishings. The apparatus at the head of his bed indicated a hospital.

"Where . . . how . . . ?" Conek wanted to ask questions, but the sudden movement made him dizzy, and he lay back as the arthropod gently pushed him down onto the pillows.

"You are in the hospital on Radach-I. Now, you mustn't talk. Rest."

But his memories came back; the last thing Conek wanted

was rest. He remembered *Anubis* going into the dense atmosphere of Kylar-X; and Andro, as white as if the last drop of his blood had seeped out on the floor of *Bucephalus*'s bridge. He remembered Cge's blasted panel, and lastly his own wound. He ran his hand down the leg, but the arthropod stopped him.

She must have read his expression, because her voice, rattling through the translator, softened as she reassured him.

"Now, don't disturb the bandage. You can't feel it, but the leg is still there. One standard month and you won't even have a scar to show off." She picked up an anesthesizer. "You must rest."

Conek tried to push her away, but in his weakened condition, she held him down with ease. He remembered nothing after the sting of the gun.

When he awoke the second time, Ister stood by his bed.

"Ister?" He couldn't resist touching the Orealian. "You and Gella made it?"

The cat-man laughed and nodded. "That's some girl. She has her father's brains, as well as his skill. We couldn't fight. We were a danger to ourselves and to you. She took us in the one direction the Osalt wouldn't expect. Back towards Osalta. By getting out of the action, we could free you to fight. We came in roundabout."

"You're right." Conek smiled. "She's some girl." Then he remembered his feelings when he'd thought the Osalt had killed her and Ister. "And when I get my hands on her, I'll break her damn neck."

"I hear you did a good job," Ister said, changing the subject. "They said you were out of your head in the last fight, but Dursig says you hold the record for the number of Y-tails shot down."

"I don't remember anything after Lesson got it,"Conek said. "I don't even know if Andro made it."

"Dursig said you landed on automatic pilot—you still had your hand on the lever when they found you. The major was pretty far gone, but you got him here in time. He'll make it, they say. All the ships took hits. I'm here to patch up that flying warehouse of yours."

"Was she badly damaged?" Conek had a sudden desire to return to Osalta and shoot the tops off every dome on the planet.

"Not so much that I can't fix her," the Orealian's whiskers twitched with humor. "I think Vladmn would appreciate it if you did the flying from now on. On automatic, she's as much of a rocket-rider as old Icor was."

Ister had disobeyed hospital orders and slipped into Conek's room when the nurse was busy elsewhere. But the arthropod came and ordered the Orealian out, complaining that he'd tire her patient.

A week later Conek graduated from the bed to a chair. Dr. Sardo came into the room, his gait ambling, as if he were lost, afraid to go farther and not knowing how to retreat.

"I'm glad to see you so improved, Captain."

"Thanks," Conek replied, wondering why the droid expert was visiting him. His question must have showed in his face, because the little man smiled brightly.

"I came to tell you that we will have your little android repaired in another few hours. We are nearly ready to reprogram him, and we would be delighted to incorporate anything you feel would be helpful."

Conek dropped his gaze before his expression betrayed him. "You'll have to reprogram him completely?"

"We think so. We were forced to keep some of his original computer panels. We haven't been able to connect ours directly to his motor system—it's the difference in types of metals—but we've corrected most of the damage. Do you want him to be a general utilitarian, or have you some specific job for him? Our system is the most advanced in Vladmn. When we finish coding him in on our computers, you'll find nothing but perfection in his skills. None of the erratic behavior you've seen since the shipwreck."

"Just make him general for now," Conek said. "I'll add anything I want later. I might sell him."

"Very well," the doctor replied with some hesitation. "We could do a fine job of making him a—"

"Just leave him general!" Conek snapped, starting up out of the chair. The sudden pressure on his left leg nearly threw

him. In the throes of stabbing pain, he leaned forward, and when he straightened, the doctor was gone.

Alone, he sat back in his chair, thinking about Cge. He tried to imagine a perfect little android, shut down and standing in the corner until needed.

*I'll sell him. I'll leave him here and let them sell him for me. They'd probaby make a better deal than I could. I don't have to see him again. I don't need a droid—I never needed one.*

He kept saying the words over and over to himself. He even said them aloud, but they were just noise. He was saying good-bye to Cge and making quite a job of it. The perfectly programmed metallic shell in the computer center would be a ghost, a reminder of the little clown destroyed on Osalta. He'd let them sell it for him. He could face death, but he couldn't handle a ghost. He wouldn't try.

Three days later they let him out of his room, to walk in the hall, strengthening his leg. Four doors down the hall he heard Andro's voice.

"Hello, love," the major called as Conek passed the door. Conek hobbled in, leaning on his cane. The major sounded weak, but his color and spirits were good.

"You enjoying yourself?" Conek asked.

"Oh, just taking a rest on government time. Incidentally, thanks for getting me out."

"Oh, anytime," Conek said airily. "Getting things out of Osalta is my special talent."

"A skill you won't use again, I hope." Norden spoke from the doorway.

Conek turned to see the Quinta strolling in. After she greeted Andro, she gave her attention to Conek. Her eyes were calm, lacking the suspicion they usually held when they were turned on him.

"Captain, I wanted to bring you up-to-date myself. The ghoster has been emptied, and we've inventoried the cargo. You'll be getting a full list in a few days. Vladmn will purchase most of it. You'll be able to buy the ships you want, so you won't need to pirate anymore."

Conek gave a slight smile. "Quinta, you've flown 'em. You should know—those big old crates become a habit."

"I thought you'd say that. You can claim the two you took from Slugarth. At least if you want to, Vladmn will recognize your right. The three Vladmn ships will be given to Dursig, Gella, and Ister. It's all we can do to reward you. You see, we aren't officially admitting that the weapons exist." She smiled. "We hope you'll use those ships for legal trade."

"Now, *Auntie*, love," Andro chided. "You're not suggesting the captain would do anything illegal?"

"Would I do such a thing?" Her expression was innocent enough, but her eyes twinkled and softened as she glanced at Conek again. He knew he was receiving the only apology she'd give. He was satisfied.

"I'll be strictly legal for a while," Conek replied. Maybe for good, with the two extra ships and the money coming in from the Skooler cargo. He'd have three of the four ships he needed, and the money to buy the fourth. But without *Anubis* and Lesson to fly her, nothing seemed very important. Buying another vessel to replace the missing freighter seemed to Conek a desertion of hope for Lesson, though he couldn't admit it, even to himself.

"You know my interest in the big ships," he told Norden, unconsciously compromising between his hope for Lesson and his need for another ship. "Most of the labor droids off the Skooler ship are programmed for repair work—"

"Oh, my nerves." Andro sighed. "My men aren't used to *Bucephalus*. If you try to land that ghoster on Agnar-Alpha, they'll go nuts."

"I *like* the idea," Norden said firmly. "It's good for Vladmn to see these alien vessels. We're growing too complacent, and they shake up people. Oh, speaking of things alien, I heard the good news, Captain. You can't know how happy I am to hear that Cge is repaired."

"So I'm told," Conek replied in a carefully even voice. For something to occupy him, he stepped up to Andro's bed and handed the major a glass of water he didn't want.

"What is it, Captain?" Norden caught his hesitation. "Can't they fix him?"

In answer to her question he shrugged, turning to look out the window. He couldn't trust his expression. For two days he wrestled with the problem and made thirty decisions.

All afternoon he'd known he would take Cge back no matter how he was programmed.

"They say he'll be fine. Dr. Sardo tells me he'll be completely reprogrammed. A perfect little servant."

"I'm sure you'll be glad to have the malfunctions corrected." The Quinta's voice held a hollow sound of disbelief.

"Of course," Conek answered woodenly. Andro's hand closed compassionately over his. Conek read in the major's eyes the pain he tried to hide. Without a word Conek turned and hurried back to his own room.

A few minutes later he was drinking a glass of revitalizer when Norden entered.

"Captain, I hear you're leaving tomorrow."

"They say I can go if I take it easy. Ister's fixed up *Bucephalus* so I can fly her. In the morning I'll pick up Cge and be on my way."

"To where?"

"Why?"

"No reason, Captain, except you're in no condition to go running around Kylar-X, especially since there's no reason for it."

"That's where Lesson went down."

"No. He didn't. We've searched every inch of the surface. Lesson didn't crash there."

"Look, Quinta, I was in bad shape, but I know he went down—I *saw* the crash."

"We all saw it. Later we found the debris. The remains of the three Osalt fighters. Not a scrap or a chip of paint from *Anubis*."

Conek gripped the end of the bed as he stared at the little woman. "Then where is he?"

"We have no idea—"

Norden was interrupted by the arrival of Dr. Sardo. The

small, rotund doctor was uncomfortable, unusual for someone normally so detached from his surroundings.

"I hoped I could find you, Captain. I wanted to stop you from making an unnecessary trip to our wing tomorrow. When I said the android was repaired, I spoke prematurely."

"What is it?" Conek leaned against the bed, staring down at the doctor.

"Captain, I don't know how to explain it—well, I can't, because I've never seen anything like it. We repaired and reprogrammed the android, checked it over thoroughly, and everything functioned perfectly. Twice we checked it—today we were going to do the finals. One of my assistants activated it. A slight emergency called him away—"

"Get to the point, Doctor," Conek said, interrupting him. His leg throbbed. He wanted to lie down and ease the pain.

"I don't *know* the point, Captain! After its crystals warmed up, possibly they overheated and caused a short, we aren't sure—"

Conek grew more frustrated by the moment. A sick feeling hovered over him. "Well? What happened! What's the matter with him?"

"I don't know what it is—how to explain it—"

"Then don't explain it!" Norden squealed, her eyes alight with excitement. "Just tell us what he's *doing*!"

"It's so illogical—"

"Doctor, I'm warning you—" Norden started forward.

The doctor paled and stepped back. "Two things—two strange things. When his right utilitarian comes up, he points his digit and makes a sound: 'Kew-w-w.' Then his legs lock in a crouch and he rolls around. His audio seems stuck on 'Clow-w, clown.' My technicians are getting ready to take him apart again to locate the trouble. . . . Captain! Come back! There's nothing you can do, and you shouldn't be running on that leg! Quinta Norden! I resent your laughing. In our department we do not consider malfunctions a *joke*."